PAMELA PALMER

RAPTURE UNTAMED

A FERAL WARRIORS NOVEL

AVON
An Imprint of HarperCollins*Publishers*

This is a work of fiction. Names, characters, places, and incidents are products of the author's imagination or are used fictitiously and are not to be construed as real. Any resemblance to actual events, locales, organizations, or persons, living or dead, is entirely coincidental.

AVON BOOKS
An Imprint of HarperCollins*Publishers*
10 East 53rd Street
New York, New York 10022-5299

Copyright © 2010 by Pamela Poulsen
ISBN 978-0-06-179470-4
www.avonromance.com

First Avon Books paperback printing: July 2010

Avon Trademark Reg. U.S. Pat. Off. and in Other Countries, Marca Registrada, Hecho en U.S.A.
HarperCollins® is a registered trademark of HarperCollins Publishers.

Printed in the U.S.A.

10 9 8 7 6 5 4 3 2 1

To Kelly

Acknowledgments

Thanks to all the wonderful and talented people at Avon Books for their effort and support, especially May Chen, Amanda Bergeron, Pamela Spengler-Jaffee, and Wendy Ho. Working with you ladies is a delight. And a special thanks to Thomas Egner and his team for my amazing covers.

As always, thanks to Laurin and Annie, the god-mothers to all my books. This journey would be so much more difficult and so much less fun without your keen eyes, incredible instincts, humor, and friendship. Sisters forever!

Thanks to Kim, Emily, and Misono for all your hard work on my behalf.

And a huge, warm thanks to my readers for your incredible enthusiasm, and for falling in love with these dark, dangerous shifters as much as I have. You make the long hours in front of the computer a joy. A special shout-out to the gang on the pamelapalmer.net BB. You guys rock!

To Keith, my real-life hero, and to my friends and family, my love and deepest gratitude. For everything.

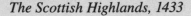

Prologue

The Scottish Highlands, 1433

"The wards, Mystic! Set the protective wards!" The leader of the Therian enclave's voice rang through the firelit cave, his tone at once hard and desperate as he stabbed at the first of the deadly draden to find them. "Ye must set the wards!"

Smoke from the cooking fire spiraled up and out, ghostly fingers reaching for the roof and walls, twisting and twirling from the movements of the agitated Therians.

"I'm trying!" the mystic Isobel cried. "I canna remember the chant. The Mage have stolen the chant." Her voice cracked, tears rolling down her cheeks, though her hands fluttered and swung as they always did when she drew the magic shields to protect them from the draden who fed off Therian life force.

Olivia pressed closer to her mother and felt the strong arm clasped around her shoulders tighten. She looked up to find her mother's lips trembling, her eyes glistening in the firelight.

"Mama?"

"Shh, Olivia." Her mother pulled her hard around, pressing Olivia's face tight against her stomach. "'Twill be all right, my wee girl." But her mother's voice throbbed with a fear Olivia had never heard before, and her own eyes filled with tears, her heart beginning to pound.

"I've lost the chant. I've lost the chant!" Isobel's tearful lament rang through the cave.

"Those few were only the first!" the enclave's leader, Jamie, shouted. "Dinna let down your guard. This close to Feral Castle, the draden will swarm. Goddess help us, if I had known the Mage had cast a spell over Isobel, we'd have fled the other way." His words were filled with an anguish that made Olivia tremble. "There is naught to be done now but fight."

Her mother grabbed her shoulders, wrenching Olivia back as she knelt before her. Tears ran freely down Mama's pretty face as she lifted her hand to stroke Olivia's cheek.

"I love ye, sweet lass. More than any mother ever loved a daughter, I love ye." Raw grief formed dark pools in her mother's eyes.

A sob tore at Olivia's throat. "Mama."

The hands on her shoulders tightened. "The draden will be full upon us soon. I'll fight them and protect ye as long as I can, but if they swarm as Jamie fears, there will be naught I can do but cover you. Ye'll stay there, beneath me, aye?" She shook Olivia gently. "Ye'll stay there beneath me! No matter what."

"Yes, Mama."

Her mother's face dissolved into tears, and she hugged Olivia fiercely against her once more. "Oh, sweet lass."

The Mage had attacked their village just that morn. In Olivia's mind's eye, the fires continued to flame. Jamie had led the Therians into the mountains at a run, toward the protection of the guardians of the race, the Feral Warriors. But the Ferals were more than a day's journey, and the draden hunted them at night. Still, Isobel should have been able to protect the cave with her magic. They should have been safe.

If only her papa were here. Several days ago, he'd gone to meet with the Ferals about some other matter and had not yet returned. If he were here, he would save them.

A scream shattered the heavy silence, then another.

Mama pulled her around, tucking Olivia's back against her front as she hunched over, pulling her knife from her boot. Olivia peered across the cave, her heart seizing with terror at the sight that met her eyes. Draden flew into the cave like a dark cloud, more draden than she knew existed. More than she could count. The little beasties weren't big, not much bigger than Papa's closed hand, their bodies floating and smokelike. But their faces . . .

As two flew right at her, she screamed and pressed back against her mother, squeezing her eyes closed against the sight of the ugly, twisted features and the sharp, horrible teeth. She peeked as Mama stabbed at one, digging out its heart, turning it to smoke. But as that one disappeared, Mama cried out, and Olivia knew the other had bitten her, latching onto her to feed.

More flew at them, and her mother fought them all, but there were too many! One bit Olivia's arm, its sharp little teeth tearing at her tender flesh. As Olivia cried out, her mother stabbed it, destroying it.

The light of the fire flickered on the cave walls, slashed over and over by draden shadows. All around the cave, her people fought the horrid beasties, even as the draden rode them, clamped on to arms and faces and heads. As Olivia watched, Isobel fell to her knees, then Angus, and Barbara. Jeaniene fell all the way down, asleep.

Why would she sleep when she needed to fight?

Behind her, Mama stumbled. "Olivia. Now," she gasped. "On the floor, lie flat."

Olivia had barely sunk to her knees when her mother pushed her down, falling on top of her roughly.

"Mama, you're too heavy."

"Shh, lassie." Her mama's voice was low and soft against her ear. Sleepy-sounding. "I love ye, Olivia. I'll always love ye."

Mama's head dropped heavily beside her own as a

draden bit Olivia on her cheek with a bolt of fiery pain, blocking her sight. She screamed and struggled to free her arm to swat it away, but another caught in her hair and sank razor-sharp teeth into her scalp.

"Mama!"

Terror beat at her chest, tears running down her cheeks, as she freed her hand and pulled at the draden on her cheek, sinking her hand into the globby mass. Her small fingers came in contact with the pulsing, beating heart, and she grabbed it and pulled. The draden disappeared in a puff of smoke, but seconds later, another took its place. They were flying at her from all sides, sinking their teeth into her face and head, hands and legs, wherever her mother hadn't covered her.

Choking on her tears, she fought and screamed until her throat was raw and her voice hoarse. But no one came, no one helped her. And soon she, too, started to feel sleepy. She stopped fighting. Little by little, the world began to slip away.

Then everything tilted. Dizziness ripped through her head, spinning behind her eyes, waking her up. A draden bit her foot and she cried out, but an odd warmth began to flow up through the bite, a warmth that filled her leg and flowed into her body, making her feel strong and good again.

"Mama?"

But her mama still slept.

Slowly, everything grew quiet. Even the draden had

gone to sleep or flown away. Only the sound of the wood crackling in the dying fire and the chirping of the night insects reached her ears.

Olivia lay there for a long time, as she'd promised her mama, but she grew too restless and finally struggled out from beneath her mother's still form. All around the cave, her people, her family, lay still and unmoving. Asleep.

She sat beside Mama and stroked her hair as tears clouded her eyes all over again.

They were asleep. They had to be! Therians didn't die.

Except by draden.

Her tears began to choke her again. If *she* hadn't died, how could the others have? They hadn't. They weren't dead!

But her heart told her otherwise. As she sat in the stillness, she sensed the dead all around her, their spirits whispering over her flesh, bidding her good-bye as they fled the world of the living.

Leaving her all alone.

Her tears turned to great gulping sobs as she buried her face in her mother's hair, clinging to her still form, until finally she fell asleep.

She awoke to the sound of a distant shout. Daylight filled the cave, and she lifted her head slowly.

"Mama?"

The shout came again. "Olivia!" *Her father's voice.*

Her heart soared, and she scrambled to her feet and ran, flying over the still forms of the people she'd loved.

"Da!"

He met her in the mouth of the cave, his orange hair, the same shade as her own, gleaming in the sunshine as he swept her into his arms and held her so tightly he nearly crushed her. She threw her arms around his neck, burying her face against the warmth of his throat.

"What happened, lassie? I felt your mother . . . go." His voice held all the horror of the night as he carried her into the cave.

"The Mage burned the village with fires we couldna put out, so we ran. Jamie said the Ferals would protect us."

"But ye didna make it to the Ferals' castle."

"Nay. Isobel tried to set the wards, but she couldna remember how, Da. And the draden . . ." The night's terror engulfed her, and her voice caught on a sob.

Her papa began to shake as he held her, anger lacing his words. "Isobel has been the enclave's mystic for more than five hundred years. She dinna forget the bloody chant. 'Twas the Mages' doing." He stumbled back but held her tight. "Where's your mother?" His voice broke on the last.

Olivia lifted her head from his shoulder and pointed, but he was already walking in that direction. He already knew.

"Ah, sweet goddess, Alexandra. Sweet, sweet goddess."

Tears slipped down his cheeks as he stared at his mate.

"She's asleep, Da."

"Aye, lassie. Forevermore." His voice cracked. "How did ye survive, my wee girl?"

"Mama covered me."

"Ye didna get bit?" He stumbled again, then sank to his knees, pulling her onto his lap with one hand as his other reached for her mother, stroking her hair much as Olivia had during the night.

She looked up at him, saw that his face was too white. But as she lifted her small hand to his cheek, he grabbed her chin and stared at her, turning her face this way and that.

His expression tightened. "Ye've draden welts all o'er ye, lass. How did ye survive when the others . . . ?"

His eyes widened, his head jerking back as if he'd been struck.

"Da?" The word trembled from her throat.

He shoved her away, and she tumbled onto the cave floor, a rock biting into her hip. Tears welled in her eyes.

"Livvie, lass." His voice sounded choked. "Get ye away from me, Livvie. Back away before ye've neither mum nor da, aye?"

She didn't understand. All she knew was her world had broken, and he was the only thing she had. She reached for him.

His eyes took on a terrible light. "Olivia, get back! Get away from me before ye kill me."

On a heartbroken cry, Olivia leaped to her feet and ran, the tears blinding her as she stumbled through the cave and into the sunshine.

"Livvie, 'tis far enough! Stay there."

Shaking from head to foot, she sank to her knees in the dirt, sobbing. What had she done?

It seemed forever before her father finally came out of the cave and sank down onto a big rock a short distance away.

She started to rise, to go to him, but his hand shot out, and he shook his head.

"Sit ye there, lassie, and listen, aye?" Though his face was stern, his voice was soft with love. "Just listen, Olivia. Ye've been draden-kissed, lass. Do ye ken what that means?"

She shook her head. She'd heard the words and knew them to be bad. Very bad.

"It means the draden changed ye instead of killing ye. 'Twasna something they meant to do, it just happens sometimes."

Her brows pulled together as she stared at him. "I'm a draden?"

A strangled sound escaped his throat, a sound that might have been a laugh had the circumstances not been so awful. "Nay. But ye suck the life from others as a draden does. Ye were sucking it from me, just now."

"I didn't mean to."

"I know it, lass. 'Tisna something ye've any control

over, yet. Whene'er yer feeding, as yer doing now, ye'll suck the life from anyone near ye whether ye be touching them or not."

She didn't understand. All she knew was she was bad now, and her da didn't want her anymore. Her crying grew into uncontrollable sobs.

"Lass . . ." Her father's hands gripped one another hard in his lap. " 'Twill be all right. I've heard stories of draden-kissed who walked among us for years without anyone knowing. They'd not only learned how to turn the feeding on and off, but to control the strength of it so they could feed without harming us, for the draden-kissed must feed on life energy to survive. But they did so without us even being aware. Ye'll learn, too, my wee lass. And quickly, before others discover what you are." He watched her with broken eyes. "They'll kill you if they find out."

"The draden?"

"Nay. The Therians. They'll see ye as a danger they'll not tolerate."

"But . . ." She stared at him. "You?"

"Nay." Tears gathered in his eyes. "Not me. Never me. I've lost everything, my wee girl. I'll not lose you, too."

He swiped his hand across his face. "We'll have to live away from others for now. The draden can no longer hurt you, but you'll have to learn to fight them all the same. And the Therians, too. If your gift is ever discovered, ye'll have to fight and escape. You can do this, lassie. I've seen the strength in ye since the day ye were born."

She watched him, trying to understand. "Did I kill Mama?"

"Nay! Nay, lassie," he said more softly. "The draden did that."

"But I could kill you?" She blinked hard against the hot tears, needing to see his face.

"Aye, ye could, and ye probably will. But ye'll feel no guilt for it, Livvie. If it happens, you'll go on and not look back. I wish ye to live. Even if it means my own life, I will have you live, daughter mine."

He opened his arms to her and it was all the invitation she needed. She flew at him, flinging her arms around his neck as he crushed her to him.

"I love ye fiercely, Livvie, and never shall ye forget it. My life for yours is a price I gladly pay."

"I don't want to hurt you, Da."

He stroked her hair, then gently pushed her away, and she moved back to where she'd sat moments before.

Though his arms no longer held her, his eyes snared her in a fine mesh of love. "Livvie?"

"Yes, Da?"

He smiled at her through the sadness in his eyes. "Ye were meant to live, my little lass. Never forget that. Ye were meant to live."

Olivia perched on the edge of the leather chair, her back straight, her legs crossed, one high-heeled foot swaying with carefully controlled excitement as Lyon, the powerful chief of the Feral Warriors, paced at the front of the wood-paneled war room in Feral House. Outside, the sky had grown dark, but inside, the room blazed with light and energy.

Her gaze skimmed along the edges of the large conference table, staring at the Ferals with barely concealed awe. Only five were in attendance today—Lyon, the leader of the group, Tighe, Paenther, Wulfe, and the pain-in-the-ass Jag—but they radiated such force, such raw, untamed power, their numbers felt much larger.

Each of the Ferals was exceedingly tall, thickly muscled,

and the object of lust of many a Therian woman. Of many a woman, period. They were the guardians of the Therian race, the only remaining shape-shifters on the planet. And they were, quite possibly, all that stood between the world and true destruction.

Amazingly, they'd asked for her help.

Well, not hers specifically. Several weeks ago, Lyon had called the British Guard—the most elite of the highly trained Therian fighting units, and requested a small team of warriors be sent to assist his own. With the Ferals' numbers down to eight, and the battle heating up on numerous fronts, the Ferals were fast becoming spread too thin, and no one knew it better than their leader.

Olivia had been given the assignment to lead the team of three Therian guards to Feral House. The assignment of an immortal lifetime.

Only one thing, one person, dampened the perfection of this moment.

The Feral Warrior, Jag.

From across the huge conference table, Olivia could feel him watching her as keenly as any predator. Though she tried to ignore him, she kept finding herself glancing his way, spearing him with an icy look that only made his eyes crinkle with amusement.

Goddess, but he annoyed her. Yet he intrigued her beyond all comprehension. He was a first-rate jerk. She knew it. Everyone she talked to knew it. Jag had quite a reputation in the Bethesda Therian enclave where she, Niall, and Ewan had been staying.

And yet every time she saw him, her legs turned weak, her body warm. Every time their gazes locked, her pulse took off, lifting and whirring like chopper blades. She was utterly attracted to him and couldn't figure out why. Certainly, he was handsome enough, with his strong jaw, cleft chin, and oh-so-intriguing mouth. But more often than not, the handsome lines of that face were marred by a scowl, or that delicious mouth was twisted into a sneer.

None of the Ferals was entirely tame, but there was something significantly less tame about Jag. His hair hung shaggy around his face as if he'd hacked it off with his knife, and he dressed in camouflage pants and T-shirts, as if he were heading into the jungle—and not as a cat.

She had to admit, though, those close-fitting T-shirts set off his impressive musculature to fine advantage, drawing attention to his broad chest. Around his thick upper arm curled the jaguar-head armband that marked him as a Feral.

She'd only met him one other time, just over a week ago, and been thoroughly disgusted with him. And hadn't been able to stop thinking about him since.

"You've secured the FBI link?" Lyon asked, his gaze swinging to Tighe.

The tiger shifter nodded. "Delaney and I met with

one of her old colleagues, but he won't remember a thing. He's our eyes and ears, now, and doesn't even know it."

Of all the Ferals, Tighe was the most charming, in her opinion, his smile framed by dimples, his eyes dancing with laughter, especially when he looked at his wife, Delaney. They made a strikingly attractive pair, his hair as fair as hers was dark, compounded by the strength that seemed to rise from each one individually, yet blended as one powerful force emanating from the two of them together. She'd heard the story, that Delaney used to be a human FBI agent. That she used to be mortal. And was no longer either.

Extraordinary, really. Then again, things had a way of changing.

Long ago, all Therians were capable of accessing their animal natures. All were able to shift. But five thousand years ago, the Therians and their traditional enemies, the Mage, joined forces, each race mortgaging most of its power in a desperate bid for victory over the High Daemon, Satanan, imprisoning him and his Daemon armies once and for all in the enchanted Daemon blade. When the battle was over, only one Therian from each of the ancient animal lines still retained the strength of his animal and the ability to shift. Today, there were only nine—or would be once the new fox showed up.

Nine Feral Warriors.

All that stood between Satanan and his latest, and far most dangerous, bid for freedom from his magical prison.

Somehow, the leader of the Mage had become infected with a bit of powerful dark spirit—what some believed to be a wisp of Satanan's very consciousness. Through that dark spirit, they feared Satanan now controlled the Mage leader, and through him, the Mage. With Satanan's dark knowledge now at his disposal, he'd found a way to steal the souls of his own people, of those who'd sacrificed so much to stop the Daemon threat all those years ago. The soulless Mage sought only one thing—the freedom of Satanan and his evil horde.

If the Mage succeeded, life as the world knew it would end.

Tighe continued. "We've been able to glean enough about the two serial killers haunting the Blue Ridge to be fairly certain they're two of our Daemons."

Daemons. Even the word gave Olivia chills. The draden were nothing more than the remnants of the powerful and terrifying Daemons. The thought of those small, deadly fiends reanimated with Daemon souls and grown to human size sent a cold shaft of horror raking down her spine. Ten days ago, the Mage, determined to free Satanan's Daemon horde from the magical blade that imprisoned them, had succeeded in liberating three. Not the thinking, plotting kind of Daemons—these were only predatory wraith Daemons—but already the death they'd caused was terrible.

"I want you to head up a team to catch them, Tighe," Lyon said. "I don't have to tell anyone here how critical it is that we destroy those things as quickly as possible."

The thought that Olivia was to be one of the ones to stop this threat excited her all over again. She'd been a member of the elite Therian Guard for more than three hundred years, since its inception, but this was the first time she'd ever worked with the Feral Warriors. To her knowledge, this was the first time the Ferals had ever accepted the help of any non-Feral Therians.

Olivia shifted in her chair, uncrossing her legs and recrossing them the other way, studiously ignoring Jag. Yet it didn't seem to matter. Just being in the same room with him made her feel restless. Fidgety. It did today as it had that first day. She and her men had come to Feral House at Lyon's request to discuss the possibility of their working together. As she was talking with Lyon, Jag had walked right up to her, slid his arm around her shoulder, and squeezed her breast, suggesting she accompany him upstairs and spread her legs for him.

In the shape-shifter's defense, he'd been attacked by malicious magic and had genuinely needed a good sexual cleansing to get rid of it. To be honest, had he approached her with a wink and a smile, and a little re-spect, she might well have done as he asked. Therians were nothing if not sexual. And even as rudely as he'd acted, her body had responded, leaping with excitement at his touch, his nearness, his scent.

But he'd shown her no respect, and she'd responded by smiling at him coldly while driving her spiked heel halfway through his instep.

That should have been the end of it, but Ferals were a stubborn lot, and this one, she suspected, was worse than most. As she met his gaze now across the conference table, her mouth lifted in a cold, taunting smile, silently reminding him of that meeting, of her painful retaliation. But instead of earning herself the scowl she'd hoped for, laughter lit his eyes, a devilish gleam that told her the feel of her breast in his hand had been worth the pain. And would be again.

A thrill skittered through her traitorous body, and she turned away. She had far too much pride to be drawn to a male with a lousy attitude and a foul mouth, but her body couldn't have cared less. Jerk or not, the man possessed a raw sexuality that sizzled across her skin, seeping into her pores.

Determined to ignore him, she let her gaze travel. Beside Jag sat Wulfe, his badly scarred face set in lines of concentration. She wasn't sure how a quickly healing immortal could end up with scars like that, but wasn't about to ask. He'd greeted her cordially enough when they were introduced, but his manner was diffident, almost as if he'd expected her to be put off by his scars.

Beside Wulfe, Lyon's mate, Kara, played beneath his protective and loving eye with the kitten perched on Skye's shoulder. Skye was Paenther's mate and a Mage, though one with a soul, and a particularly sweet one at that. Directly behind the two women, Paenther stood with his arms crossed over his chest like a fearsome bodyguard, the impression ruined by the hint of a smile that twitched at the corners of his mouth every time his gaze landed on his mate.

The Ferals were nothing if not protective. An extremely tight, close-knit brotherhood. Except, she sensed, for Jag.

As hard as she tried, she couldn't ignore him a moment longer, and she found his eyes still boring into her with that unnerving stare. If he weren't in human form, she was certain his tail would be swinging slow, snapping back and forth as he watched her like a cat waiting for the right moment to pounce.

Definitely uncivilized. Not that she needed civilized. Not at all. Especially not in bed. But she absolutely demanded respect. And from what she'd seen and heard about this Feral, he respected no one. Her body might be intrigued by the man, but her pride called the shots. Jag was just going to have to find some other woman to stalk. This one wasn't interested.

If only her wayward gaze would stop making a liar out of her.

* * *

Jag couldn't remember the last time he'd been this intrigued with a woman.

Beneath hard brows, he studied Olivia, his gaze taking in the trim pantsuit, this one deep tan with a dark green sweater underneath. Though he couldn't see them beneath the conference table that separated them, he knew that on those slender feet she wore pumps, or whatever the hell women called them—with four-inch heels. He'd noticed them right off when she'd walked into the room, his instep giving a throb of recognition. The memory made him smile. Damn, he liked a tough woman.

He watched her sitting across the table, her gaze toward the front of the room as she pretended to ignore him. Her bright red hair, thick and straight, hung just to her shoulders, making his fingers itch to know if it felt as soft as it looked. Her features were even and pretty, but nevertheless gave off an impression of strength—her chin determined, her mouth firm and haughty, her gray eyes sharp as glass and cool as a winter sky.

Those eyes flickered over him now. Her gaze tried to dismiss him, yet couldn't keep from returning over and over again. Any more than his could stay away from her.

He'd never been partial to redheads, and feature by feature, there was nothing particularly special about this one. But Olivia proved a prime example of the sum of the parts being greater than the whole. The woman was stunning, and she turned him on in a way he couldn't pretend to understand. From the moment he first saw her, she'd lit a fire in his blood that showed no signs of going out.

Not until he got her into bed and slaked this obsession. Which, considering the way he'd first approached her, was going to be a challenge.

Usually, he didn't much care how women took his peculiar brand of charm. Being a Feral Warrior was enough to get him into plenty of beds despite his piss-poor attitude. Once there, he knew what to do to make certain he got invited back . . . if he didn't piss them off too much later. Which happened sometimes. His charm was an underappreciated thing.

The thought made him smile, a small biting twist of his lips.

Olivia had definitely underappreciated the way he'd greeted her last week. Even for him, walking up to a strange woman and squeezing her breast had been going a bit far. But he'd been out of his mind from the magic crawling on him at the time, and there'd been something about her that had pulled him like a magnet. Maybe that hair of hers was the problem, that glorious red beacon and the way it caught the light. Or the hint of a Scottish brogue he sometimes heard in her words.

Maybe it was way she barely reached his shoulder yet filled the room with her presence until he could think of nothing else. *See* nothing else. Or maybe it was the heat in her eyes that had snared him, the temper she kept carefully banked and masked beneath a layer of chilly frost.

He honestly didn't know, but whatever the hell had drawn him to her showed no signs of letting go.

The woman intrigued him, all right. Sooner or later, he'd have her moaning his name, begging him to take her to bed. She wouldn't want to. He had no illusions about that. Pride was written all over her face and woven into every line of her sweet little body.

No, she'd see wanting him as a weakness, begging him to fill her as a self-betrayal. But she'd beg him all the same because few women could resist him once he set his mind to seduction.

Jag smiled. Not even Olivia. Hard as she tried, the cool, sexy little redhead couldn't ignore him. He'd gotten under her skin. Just as she'd gotten under his.

Beside him, Wulfe cracked his knuckles. "Have we learned any more about these Daemons?"

Lyon's mouth tightened. "No. They appear to be little more than soulless feeding machines, but that doesn't mean they're not dangerous. Hawke and Kougar have been trying to re-create one of the ancient Daemon traps, but so far without success. After five millennia, too much of our understanding of the creatures has been lost. Kougar hasn't given up on the traps, but we can't count on them working. We're going to have to hunt down those bastards the old-fashioned way."

Jag knew what was coming next. It hardly took a brain surgeon to understand why the Therian Guard had been invited to this party. Chiefy wanted them to use the buddy system. Wasn't that cute?

His gaze slid to Olivia, daring her to turn her head, but she studiously ignored him. Beneath that trim jacket of hers he could make out the swell of a well-curved breast. His body tightened at the remembered feel of that softness beneath his hand. A softness he longed to feel again.

He wasn't kidding about being obsessed. He could think of little but getting near her again. Waking or sleeping, she filled his thoughts, his mind, as he imagined her naked and writhing, legs parted as she begged him to fill her.

Gray eyes cut to him, narrowing as if she'd heard his thoughts. *No way in hell* sang in the air between them.

He smiled. They'd just have to see about that, wouldn't they?

Lyon's voice pulled his attention back to the meeting. "There's been a rash of human disappearances up near Harpers Ferry. No bodies, but that doesn't mean the third Daemon isn't behind the carnage." Lyon's gaze swung between Jag and Paenther. "The two of you were in that cavern. Can either of you pick up Daemon scent?"

Jag nodded. "Hell, yes. I'm not sure my nose will ever be the same."

Paenther shook his head. "I'm not sure I can, Roar.

With my link to my animal breaking down at the time, my senses were shot."

"Jag, you're on it, then. I want to know if we've got Daemon or Mage involvement in those disappearances. And if it's Daemon, I want it dead."

"Aye, aye, Captain. Do I get to take me a buddy?"

Lyon glanced at him, a wary sharpness in his eyes. As if he didn't quite trust what his jaguar shifter might do or say. Imagine that.

"One of the Guard will accompany you, yes. Which one is up to Olivia." Lyon turned to Tighe. "You'll take the other two members of the Guard and join Kougar and Hawke. You'll be in charge out there. Paenther, I'm sending you in a different direction. The Shaman and Ezekial are putting together a small team of Mage and Therians to hunt the Daemon blade and get a lock on Inir. You're in charge of it."

Jag leaned forward, willing Olivia to meet his gaze. "Whatcha say, Red? Be my buddy? We'll have oh so much fun, Sugar. I'll fuck your brains out when we're not hunting Daemons."

Olivia's eyes flared with shock, and something more, something dark and hot.

Out of the corner of his eye, he saw her two men go tense as iron rods against the back wall, as if ready to leap to her defense. Against a Feral. Idiots.

Olivia's hand shot toward the pair like a traffic cop's, though her gaze held Jag's.

"Jag!" Lyon snapped. "You will show some respect."

Jag leaned back in his chair, his mouth pulling up in a small, satisfied smile. Ah, yes. He did so love to spread good cheer.

Olivia turned her body fully toward him, mirroring his earlier position as she leaned forward, her expression condescending. If his words had offended her, nothing in her face let on. Instead, one flame-colored eyebrow rose imperiously. "I see my first obedience lesson didn't take. Not a quick learner, are you?"

Jag leaned forward again, as if they were nose to nose instead of separated by four feet of table. As if they were alone instead of surrounded by his team and hers. "I'll learn best with you sucking my cock." Deep inside, his animal growled at him.

I don't need you acting like my damned conscience, he muttered to the jaguar spirit.

Not even a hint of a blush stained Olivia's cheeks, but challenge glittered in her eyes. "Next time I'll have to drive my heel through your balls."

Jag grinned. Goddess, but the woman charged his senses like lightning in a storm. "I dare you to try it, Sugar. *Dare* you." *Come with me, Olivia. Be my partner.* He couldn't say the words out loud. She'd get too much pleasure in denying him. No, he had to appeal to her pride. Unless he missed his guess, that pride of hers was going to be his friend.

Jag smiled. *Hot damn, this is going to be fun.*

"Those heading west should be aware that last night Hawke and Kougar came across a draden swarm of nearly forty. They're not just multiplying here, but apparently everywhere." Lyon glanced at Olivia from the front of the war room. "You and your men are going to have to remain behind warding at night unless you're with a group large enough to handle that many."

Olivia nodded even though the warning didn't apply to her at all. The draden were no threat to the draden-kissed. Their life forces were her favorite food. Of course, she couldn't tell Lyon that. She couldn't tell anyone. Not if she wanted to remain alive.

And her life was finally starting to mean something. She'd had some initial discussions with Lyon about potentially setting up a permanent Guard auxiliary nearby, whose sole mission would be to aid the Feral Warriors in this new war against the Mage. Up until now, it had been her life's work to destroy as many draden as possible. But now, with the Mage trying to free Satanan, her mission had changed. Finally, she had a chance to fight on the front lines, to make a difference on a grand scale, fighting Mage and Daemons . . . if Lyon was pleased with her work and the work of her men.

If Jag didn't screw this up for her. She glanced toward the back wall, where her men, Niall and Ewan, stood, still glaring at Jag for his open sex talk and blatant disrespect of their team leader. Which of the three of them would she force to partner the jackass?

Even as she struggled to ignore Jag, the raw sexual nature of their very public discussion had left her throbbing and damp. If only she weren't so bloody attracted to him. Despite his lousy social skills, every time he came near, she felt his hot gaze on her, stripping her of her clothes and heating her body from the inside out.

But she refused to let anyone know he affected her the way he did, especially Jag himself.

"Tighe, are you taking Delaney?" Lyon asked.

"I am. I need her FBI expertise."

"Good enough."

Olivia watched Jag's gaze zero in on Tighe, a gleam of devilment leaping into his eyes. As his mouth opened, she instinctively tensed, knowing he was at it again.

"Sorry I won't be joining you and your FBI mate, Stripes. I've been looking forward to that little three-some. Like I've said before, I'm happy to let you take her from the front while I take her in the rear."

Olivia gave a jerk of disbelief, her gaze swinging between Lyon's hard displeasure and Tighe's raw fury. She was used to ribald male sex talk, but such blatant disrespect for another's mate in front of not only the female herself, but one's own superior, went beyond the pale.

The growl that ripped from Tighe's throat sounded exactly like that of a furious jungle cat.

"Tighe." Delaney grabbed her mate's wrist. "Jag, for God's sake, quit provoking him."

Jag just grinned, as if that was exactly what he'd done.

"I know you want me, too, FBI. I see the way you look at me when I'm naked."

"Jag." Delaney's voice was a deep groan of frustration.

Tighe's fangs dropped, his claws unsheathing as his irises grew to fill his eyes, making them look like true tiger's eyes. Though he hadn't shifted—he'd only *gone feral* as they put it, that halfway place between man and beast—he presented a terrifying visage as he lunged across the table, taking Jag to the floor with a crash.

Olivia rose to her feet, watching in fascinated disbelief. As Tighe went for Jag's throat, Jag's own claws and fangs sprouted on a vicious smile as if the fight was exactly what he'd been gunning for.

What was the matter with the guy? Did he know how many Therians woke each morning racing to the mirror to see if they'd been marked as they slept? Did he have any idea how badly many Therians wanted to be part of this rarefied band that he so clearly took for granted?

The two Ferals fought tooth and fang, drawing blood, ripping one another's flesh and clothes to shreds.

At least now she knew Jag didn't have it in for her specifically. No, he seemed determined to make everyone furious with him.

As if he wanted their fury.

Recognition slammed into her. *Damn.* He acted as if he needed the punishment on some dark level he probably wasn't even aware of. She'd lived with that kind of self-destructive need once. Was that his problem?

Or was he just a sociopathic jerk?

Lyon allowed the fight to continue for nearly three minutes before finally calling a stop to it.

"Enough!" Lyon roared, his voice thundering off the walls.

Instantly, Tighe shoved himself off Jag, his fangs and claws retracting. Blood splatters patterned his ripped clothes.

Jag stumbled back, the blood running freely down his face and neck. His cheek had been ripped open, but his eyes were alight with an unholy fire and keen satisfaction. He'd taken the worst of it by far, even though the two Ferals were, to all appearances, evenly matched.

Instinct told her Jag wasn't any less of a fighter. No, he'd intentionally drawn Tighe's fury, then done little more than defend himself against any real damage.

Which just supported her theory that he'd invited the attack. He'd wanted the beating.

Lyon stepped between the two combatants, his own claws unsheathing as he shoved Jag back against the wall and dug his claws into the shifter's bleeding neck.

A deep growl rumbled from Lyon's throat. "For two and a half centuries, I've put up with your surly attitude because nothing I do makes a difference. Rile the other Ferals and me all you want, but you will *not* disrespect the women in this house. Do you understand?"

Jag just grinned. "Riling away."

And he had, hadn't he? Tighe was furious with him, as was Lyon.

Another deep lion growl rolled through the room. "Back off, Jag, or the instant those Daemons are dust, I'm going to throw you in the prison and leave you there to rot. I need a *team*, dammit. A team I can count on to work together to contain this threat. And I need you on it."

Jag just smiled that small, nasty smile. "You're looking a little tense there, Chief. That little mate of yours finally figure out she's too good for you?"

Lyon yanked his claws from Jag's throat and shoved him away. "Shut up, Jag."

Olivia watched the confrontation with interest. She'd

have been lying if she had said she didn't enjoy watching Jag get his butt kicked. Except for that stab of unwanted empathy caused by the niggling feeling that she understood what drove him and the suspicion that deep inside he was hurting as badly as she once had. And she wouldn't wish that on anyone.

She resumed her seat, crossing her legs. Regardless of what drove him, he was one messed-up male. She'd be out of her mind to agree to partner him. Yet could she really, in good conscience, make one of her own men go with him?

Jag straightened, his T-shirt hanging in shreds on his well-muscled torso, his camouflage pants stained with blood. As he reached for his chair, a flash of pink caught Olivia's eye, and she turned to see the Ferals' housekeeper, a striking, pink-feathered bird-woman, slowly amble into the room with a tray of steaming mugs, her flamingo legs taking long, awkward steps.

Olivia had met Pink briefly on her first visit and found the woman to be retiring in nature, uncomfortable with her odd appearance in the company of strangers.

"What the hell?" Niall muttered against the back wall, loud enough, unfortunately, for all to hear. He hadn't been with her when she'd met Pink.

Olivia cringed.

Jag froze, going feral once more as he leaped at the unsuspecting man, pinning Niall against the wall with one clawed hand.

"Don't disrespect the bird," the Feral growled through wicked fangs.

Niall turned pale, the blood running into his shirt as he stared up at the furious shifter.

"I . . ." Niall's gaze shot past Jag to Pink. "I apologize. I meant no offense."

"Jag," Pink said softly.

Amazingly, the shifter responded to her as he'd responded to no one else, releasing Niall and whirling away with a low growl.

As Jag took his seat, retracting fangs and claws as he swiped away the blood from his already-healing face, his hard gaze slid over Olivia. In his eyes she saw real anger and a flash of true protectiveness.

Interesting. Apparently there were those he wouldn't torment.

Pink moved away, offering mugs around the room.

Jag's gaze locked on Olivia, his lip curling, his look turning insolent as his gaze dropped to her breast. Coming to Pink's defense had cracked his hard-ass façade and he knew it, which was why he was doubling up on the insolence. Transparent as glass.

Yet knowing why he stared at her breast did nothing to protect her from her body's untoward reaction. Though she fought to ignore his laser stare, she felt her breasts tightening beneath his fierce regard, her nipples turning to small, hard buds. Heat burst inside her, raising her temperature in a telltale flush that warmed her skin and charged her blood. Goddess, what he did to her.

The more time she spent around him, the less control she had over her body's reaction to him. And she needed that control, badly. Part of her trouble was that she was getting hungry. Not for food, but for the life energy all draden-kissed needed to survive. Little pinpricks danced over her skin, telling her it was time to feed.

Slowly, carefully, she drew energy out of the air, as she often did. She drank a mere sip of the raw, testosterone-laden strength that filled the room, skimming a fine layer of life force that none would feel. That none would miss.

Jag snarled, a low, dangerous, animalistic sound, drawing Olivia's startled gaze. And everyone else's.

Jag rose to his feet, his own gaze whipping across the table to spear Paenther. "That witch of yours is doing something again. I can feel the energy rippling over my skin."

Skye's head snapped up with surprise.

Olivia ceased feeding abruptly. *He'd felt her.* No way. *Impossible.*

Paenther uncrossed his arms, one hand clasping Skye's shoulder protectively as the other hovered over his knife. "Skye is as loyal to the Ferals as anyone here."

Tighe shook his head. "I don't feel anything."

"Me either," Wulfe said.

Lyon's gaze zeroed in on Jag, his expression revealing wariness and concern, but no doubt. "What exactly are you feeling?" Jag might be a jerk, but clearly the Chief of the Ferals knew him well enough to know he wasn't making this up.

"Something . . ." Jag shook his head. "It's gone."

Olivia flushed hot, then cold. No one had *ever* sensed her feeding before.

"It felt like magic?"

"I don't know. Not like Skye's. At least not like what I felt with her before."

Lyon turned to the scarred warrior. "Wulfe, get the Shaman over here. B.P. and Skye, make sure there's no damned Mage in this house." He cringed. "Forgive me, Skye. I meant, no *unwanted* Mage in this house."

Skye nodded, a small, wry smile on her mouth. Paenther squeezed her shoulder, then held out his hand to her, and the pair followed Wulfe out the door.

Lyon's gaze swung back to Jag. "If you feel it again, I want to know."

Jag gave Lyon a cocky salute. "Aye, aye, Captain."

Olivia swallowed hard, willing her pulse to slow before she gave herself away. Ferals were reputed to be able to hear even a racing heart. Whether their hearing was really that acute, she didn't know, but now wasn't the time to test it.

Dammit, how was she supposed to feed if Jag could feel her doing it? She couldn't. Not with him anywhere close.

Which made her decision about partnering him easy and critical.

She most certainly could not.

She'd long ago learned to control her feeding so that she stole only low levels of energy, not enough to harm anyone. But she wasn't sure she could shut it off completely for any length of time. She'd never had to try. What if she forgot? What if, in her sleep, she started to suck energy? With Jag close enough to feel her, sooner or later he'd figure it out. Sooner or later the game would be up.

Her life would be over—the life her father had sacrificed his own for. Although Therian law no longer demanded death to the draden-kissed, those revealed had a habit of swiftly disappearing. At the very least, she'd be kicked out of the Guard and ostracized by the entire race. The only ones who would let her live among them were the humans, who didn't know what she was in the first place.

No, this was not a risk she could afford to take. Her heart sank as her grand hopes crashed around her feet. There would be no living near Feral House, not for her. Someone else would have to lead the Feral's Guard auxiliary.

She'd help them find the Daemons because she'd committed to doing so and because it was too late to fly in a replacement. But once this assignment was done, she'd return to Scotland, far, far away from the only man to pose a real threat to her life since she was draden-kissed all those centuries ago.

The first man to get under her skin in too many years to count.

Jag.

Chapter Three

Kougar sliced the knife across his wrist, murmuring the words of the ancient chant as he slowly followed Hawke around the small pond deep in the Blue Ridge Mountains of Virginia. The night was clear but for a thin fog that had formed after midnight. The breeze toyed with Kougar's short hair, but it barely registered any more than the sting of the blade or the blood running across his wrist. He'd long ago lost any ability to feel deeply.

His mind was focused on the task at hand, setting the trap to catch one of the three wraith Daemons the Mage had set loose on the world. For once, everything had come together.

This time, it was going to work.

Wraith Daemons required a certain kind of trap—a small body of water. In the old days, when Daemons were everywhere, the Therians had created their own by digging holes and letting the rains fill them before binding them with blood. But such traps were of limited use when hunting a single moving target. So far, of *no* use.

While Hawke sprinkled the concoction of binding herbs, Kougar added the key ingredient.

Blood.

"If my calculations are right, we should be directly in his path," Hawke said over his shoulder, his voice even and low. "Finally."

For a week, they'd been tracking one particular Daemon; the three appeared to have taken off in different directions after the destruction of the cave where they'd been freed. This one headed northeast, traveling at a fast clip, though Kougar doubted he had a specific destination. Wraith Daemons had always been nonthinking predators of the worst kind.

Hawke's calculations said the Daemon would pass close to this spot tonight. For once, they'd found a small pond right where they needed it to be.

Tonight, they had to catch him.

When they'd finished the circle, Hawke turned to him, one wing-shaped brow lifting. "Another round, just to be sure?" In the shadows of night, Hawke reminded him fiercely of the hawk shifter who'd come before him, the one the Ferals had called the Wind. An old, old Feral, and old friend, who had been killed in a Mage ambush a century and a half ago. The Wind had been Hawke's father, and Kougar often saw the father in the son.

Kougar nodded. "Another round."

As they once more walked the pond's damp perimeter, he felt the silent communion of the two animals, cougar and hawk, creatures who'd known one another for eons. In both the hawk spirit and the feral in which he resided, Kougar had always found wisdom and a fierce, yet quiet strength. When the Wind died, Kougar had lost his last link to the old times, his last link to the man he'd been *before*. He'd feared that the coldness that had long ago encased his heart and stolen his ability to feel might finally destroy the last of his humanity. But the son and the hawk spirit itself had both reached out, filling the void left by the Wind's passing, tethering Kougar to the world of flesh and blood. Of duty and honor.

Kougar's heart might be gone, but thanks to Hawke, he still felt glimmers of emotion. Friendship. Loyalty. Though Hawke knew little about Kougar or his past, he knew something, which was more than anyone else. Of all the Ferals, Hawke was the only one he ever found himself opening up to. Despite Hawke's keen and innate curiosity, he never pressed for answers. Which was why Kougar sometimes gave them to him.

When they'd gone around the pond a second time, binding tight the net of magic, the two shape-shifters moved back into the shadows of the trees to wait.

"It's said the Ilinas used to help the Therians set these traps," Hawke murmured.

A shard of ice contracted inside Kougar's chest. "They did. Ilina blood and magic was mixed with Therian."

"But you believe the traps will work with Therian alone?"

"They'd better."

Hawke's body went still as it often did when his mind was in full swing. "It's said the Ilinas were mist creatures, spiritlike in their natural state."

"That's true."

"Yet they bled?"

"They could turn to flesh and blood at will, and remain that way. In that state, their bodies were much like any Therian's."

"You knew Ilinas, of course."

Hawke alone knew how old he was. "Of course."

The hawk shifter glanced at him, curiosity a living thing in his eyes. "Do you know how they came to be extinct?"

The muscles in Kougar's face clenched. He knew, but he couldn't have told Hawke if his life depended on it. He said nothing, and Hawke didn't press.

"Were they as beautiful as stories claim?"

"They were as varied in looks as Therian women, petite in build, with eyes . . ." He glanced at his companion. "They possessed the brightest blue, green, or aqua eyes of any women I've ever seen."

Hawke's brow lifted, a glimmer of humor easing his expression. "If anyone else had said that, I might accuse him of waxing poetic."

"It's just a fact."

"I believe you." And his voice said he did. "I've never understood how an entire race of women can exist. They couldn't have procreated the way we're used to."

"Only by accident. Their usual method consisted of magic."

"One would think they could have kept the race alive, had they wanted to." Hawke's tone was contemplative, as if he spoke to himself. "Then again, it's said their queen, Ariana, destroyed them herself."

Kougar said nothing. There was nothing he *could* say because the truth was something he could never share. The truth was, the Ilinas weren't extinct at all.

"Kougar." Hawke's voice turned low and sharp. *"Daemon."*

The gnawing hunger drove Olivia from her bed about an hour before daybreak. She'd slept little, and when she had slept, she'd kept dreaming she'd started feeding in her sleep, and the Ferals were barging into her room, knives drawn, ready to carve her up.

Kara had given her an upstairs room, third floor, but she wasn't sure where Jag's room was, or even if he was in it, and she had been afraid to take any chances. If he sensed her feeding again, it would no doubt spark a full-out witch hunt.

But she needed to feed. Usually, she spent her nights draden-hunting, sucking the little buggers dry of life, feeding on them before digging out their hearts with her knife. It drove her nuts to think there were swarms of them just outside Feral House, and she couldn't touch them. Not just because she was hungry, but because her drive to destroy draden was nearly as strong as her drive to live.

If only she could sneak out and find them on her own. But feeding off draden anywhere close to the Ferals was too dangerous. Even if she didn't have to worry about Jag feeling her feed, the others might see her. The moment they did, they'd know something was wrong. No normal Therian could survive a swarm the size of the ones near Feral House.

Her skin felt prickly and uncomfortable as it always did when she began to get energy-deprived. How sad was it that in a house filled with energy, she couldn't feed. In the land of a thousand draden, she didn't dare go outside for fear of revealing her secret.

Which left her with one option, and not a good one. She was going to have to eat food. Tons of food. Even that wouldn't satisfy her forever, but it might tide her over until she could get away from Jag.

Olivia groaned as she pulled on a dark green tank and her black fighting pants, the pockets loaded and ready with knives. She never went anywhere without her knives. She'd learned early and bitterly that safety from draden was never complete. And while they could no longer hurt her, the very fact that they couldn't made it all the more critical that she be able to fight them. In case of draden attack, anyone looking would merely think she was quicker than the beasties. They'd never know she killed them by sucking the life out of them.

Except Jag. *Dammit, this is going to get complicated if I don't get away from him soon.*

As she started toward the stairs, she heard the front door burst open. Her fighter instincts kicked in, and she edged to the corner of the upstairs stairwell, where she could see who invaded Feral House, only to watch as four sweaty Ferals poured inside—Paenther, Tighe, the bald one she thought was Vhyper. And Jag.

They'd been slaying draden, no doubt. Even Jag looked exhausted. His hair hung damp and unkempt around his strong face, as if he'd run his fingers through it a dozen times. His bare chest glistened beneath the glow of the chandelier, the play of muscles breathtaking even from two stories up, his armband gleaming around one massive biceps.

Her wayward body flushed, her pulse tripping, and she cursed and retraced her steps to her room. The last thing she needed right now was another run-in with Jag. She was too hungry. On too many levels.

Closing the door, she pressed her ear against it, listening to the soft pad of multiple footsteps on the stairs. She couldn't imagine fighting so many draden at once. In Britain, the largest swarms these days were usually no more than a dozen. The Guard roamed at night, in groups of four, and easily dispatched them.

But this close to Feral House, and the Radiant, she knew they could top a hundred. Apparently, the scourge was multiplying faster than the Ferals could kill them, a problem that had grown all the more serious in recent months.

She waited silently, listening as three doors opened and clicked shut somewhere in the house. Three, not four. Far below, she heard the sound of the television. Not perfect, but good enough. All four would be sleeping or distracted while she proceeded to eat them out of house and home. Not literally. Hopefully. It had been a long time since she'd tried to live on nothing but food.

Taking a deep breath, Olivia eased out of the room a second time and made her way down one of the twin staircases that framed the elaborate three-story foyer. Feral House was a mansion decorated in an old-world style with lots of floral and gilt. As she descended the curving stair, she found her gaze drawn to the huge and vibrant painting on the floor—a scene of lush foliage, sprightly wood nymphs, and rugged centaurs.

The sound of rugby on the television carried down the hall, accompanied by a puppy's yips and the rumble of deep male laughter. The laugh rolled through her, stroking her with a bold, sensuous pleasure, and she found herself moving toward it on silent feet, drawn against her will.

As she neared the wide-open doorway of a well-tricked-out media room—a huge flat-screen television hanging on the wall before a bevy of large, leather recliners and sofas—the puppy's sounds of happiness rose. The man's laughter rolled through Olivia, lifting the corners of her mouth.

She eased to the edge of the doorway and peeked around, not intending to intrude, merely curious. But the sight of the man holding the puppy brought her up short.

Jag.

He lounged on one of the recliners in nothing but his camo pants, a tiny black schnauzer puppy cradled in his large hand, inches from his face. As she watched, the huge Feral shook his head, a wry look on his face. "I'm a cat, goofus. If you're going to escape the witch's lair, at least go make eyes at Wulfe."

But the pup was clearly exactly where she wanted to be, her body a wiggling mass of joy, her stub of a tail wagging like a windshield wiper in a downpour.

As her tongue leaped out to catch Jag's chin, he chuckled again, then lifted the pup until the two were eye to eye. "You're making a mistake, Toto. Trust me, I'm the *last* one you should be wasting your kisses on."

Something inside Olivia contracted at his words, at the sharp kernel of bitterness she detected beneath the soft, rich layers of gentleness he showered on the pup.

An old truth. An old pain. Neither of which was any of her concern.

With a grunt, the Feral lowered the wiggling pup to his lap, stroking her head and back with a big, gentle hand as she plopped her little black rump on his thigh.

"If you're going to watch the game with me, you have to root for the good guys."

The pup gave a high, happy yip, then hopped down off the chair and ran to greet Olivia.

She grimaced, caught.

"Fickle female," Jag muttered, then stilled as his gaze followed the pup and found Olivia instead, his eyes flaring ever so slightly with surprise. Those dark eyes studied her face, then moved slowly, leisurely, as his gaze slid down over her shoulders, bared by the tank top, to snag on her breasts.

Her breath caught. She bent down to pet the puppy with suddenly unsteady hands, trying to pretend she didn't feel as if the man had just used his own hands to stroke her instead of his gaze.

As she rose again, the puppy took off down the hall

with a happy yip. Olivia looked at Jag, her heart sinking as she saw the devilment leaping in his eyes. Only her pride prevented her from turning tail and following the pup down the hall.

"You here to do a little tail-wagging for me, too, Sugar? Want to crawl up on my lap and lick me all over?"

Even as her temper sparked at his refusal to show her the slightest respect, her nipples hardened, a rush of heat welling inside her.

"I'd love to, Jag," she said silkily. "But I forgot my heels."

To her surprise, he laughed, a soft roll of masculine amusement that lacked the gentle pleasure of the one he'd given the puppy but still set things to fluttering in her stomach and forced up the corners of her mouth.

His own mouth lifted in a smile that was at once lazy and knowing, and yet free of the bitterness and harshness that usually lined his face. But then something flared in his eyes, something sharp and dangerous. He rose with catlike grace to his bare feet and padded toward her.

She tensed as he closed the distance between them, bracing herself for a fight. Her senses swam. If she'd thought he was appealing from two stories away, up close he was breathtaking. His chest gleamed with hard, sculpted muscle, his abs carved from stone.

Her pulse began to race as he towered over her, but not from fear. Like all Ferals, he was a mountain of a man, but if she wanted to, if she opened herself to feed, she could kill him before he knew what hit him.

"Back off, Jag," she purred.

His mouth merely kicked up in a smile laced with challenge and promise.

"Spread your legs for me, Red."

Heat rushed through her, a furious mix of desire and anger. Within the space of one heartbeat and the next, he caged her, his palms pressing against the doorframe on either side of her head.

Asshole. She pulled one of her knives, moving with a speed few could match, sliding it against his inner thigh.

"Spread yours," she countered.

His grin only broadened. "You want me as badly as I want you. I can feel your desire rising from your hot little body like steam. I can smell your heat and see it in your eyes."

"The only heat you see in my eyes is anger."

He dipped his head, his warm tongue darting out to place a quick lick at her temple. "I can taste the desire on your skin. Sooner or later, you're going to spread your legs for me, and I'm going to push deep inside you, over and over, until we're both screaming for release."

As hard as she tried to steel herself against the erotic power of his words, she felt her body melting, *wanting.*

She pressed the knife tighter against his leg. "How about I cut off that cock of yours and see if it improves your manners any."

He lowered his hands, freeing her from the cage of his arms. At least that was what she thought he was doing until his hands clamped onto her waist, his palms pressing against the undersides of her rib cage. The sudden burst of unnatural warmth startled her, rushing into her like a flow of pure, sexual heat. The lava ran down, flowing into her inner reaches, heating her, setting flame to the sparks he'd ignited with his presence and words.

Moisture gathered between her thighs as her deep inner walls began to pulse and swell. Heat filled her, opening her wide as her body begged for penetration. Deep inside her, a pressure began to build, a roaring, volcanic orgasm.

No, dammit.

She sliced through Jag's pants, sinking her knife deep into his inner thigh.

As warm blood rushed over her hand, he jerked away from her.

"Bitch." The word growled from his throat.

With his hands no longer pressing unnatural heat into her, the building orgasm slowed and stilled, whirling close, *so close,* before dying a throbbing, aching death.

Olivia gave him her frostiest look. "You'll keep your paws to yourself, Feral."

Even as anger flared in the brown depths of Jag's eyes, his mouth kicked up in a dangerous smile. "This isn't over, Red. Not by a long shot. Before we're done, you'll be begging me to fuck you."

"Only in your dreams, Cat. Only in your dreams."

To her surprise, he gripped her jaw, something raw and wild in his eyes. "You don't know anything about my dreams."

She stared at him, glimpsing again the torment she'd recognized in the war room earlier. "You might be surprised, Jag." Jerking her chin out of his grasp, she wiped her knife on her pants but kept it at the ready as she turned and left him there. His gaze bored holes into her back until she rounded the corner.

Damn him. Her body ached, so close to release that all she'd have to do was reach into the front of her pants and brush her finger over herself a couple of times to bring on a screaming orgasm. She was sorely tempted to duck into one of the empty rooms and do just that, except she feared Jag would follow and find her like that, in the throes of the passion he'd driven her to. She didn't even want to think about what would happen next. His prediction could all too well come true. She would spread her legs and absolutely beg him to fill her.

Goddess, but she had to get away from that man.

With a growl of deep sexual frustration, Jag strode through the foyer and out the front door. Lavender and pink streaked the eastern sky, just visible through the branches of the thick trees that surrounded Feral House. The morning air smelled of dew and damp earth, of trees and grass and the small creatures that shared the land with the humans and Ferals.

But it was the sweet scent of Olivia's hair, the heady musk of her arousal, and the metallic smell of his own blood that lingered in his nose.

Damn, but he throbbed. His leg had already healed, thanks to his immortal Therian nature, but his body ached for release. He strode across the wide, circular drive lined with cars—everything from his own yellow Hummer to Kougar's silver Lamborghini and the three nondescript sedans Lyon had purchased during Tighe's recent run-in with the law.

Reaching the woods on the other side, he stripped off his pants, tossing them onto the ground as he pulled on the power inside him, the power of the jaguar that had marked him and claimed him over two and a half centuries ago.

In a rush of raw power, pure pleasure, and a flash of sparkling light, he shifted into his animal. A jaguar.

His line of sight shifted, his senses exploding with his cat's. Without a moment's hesitation, he took off through the woods at a full-out run, desperate to douse the fire that burned inside him. Though the shift into his animal form cooled the raging passion that had claimed his man's body, the fire continued to burn inside, deep in the recesses of his mind. Desire for something he couldn't even name. Obsession with a woman he didn't even want, except in the most carnal sense. A fire that licked at his innermost self with a pain he'd long ago learned to live with, though he found it impossible to ignore.

He ran, uncertain of his destination and not caring, as the damp morning breeze blew through his whiskers. But when he found himself high above the rocky cliffs overlooking the Potomac River, he climbed onto the rocks and stood, his cat's body breathing quickly from the run, his jaguar's face lifted to the wind.

What if he kept running? What if he never looked back? Never *came* back? The thought had entered his mind too many times to count. And he might have done it. A thousand times, he might have run, never to return. Except for two things—being a Feral Warrior was the one thing that made his life worthwhile, and the certainty that running would accomplish nothing. Because the thing he most wanted to be free of, he couldn't outrun.

Himself.

Finally, he turned back for Feral House, his thoughts on the woman who wouldn't leave his mind. Olivia. Dammit, but she intrigued him. He'd never seen her out of her pantsuits until tonight. He'd thought her hot in her trim business persona, but dressed for action, she'd set his blood on fire. He could still see her as she'd stood in the media-room doorway, her thick red hair deliciously sleep-tousled, her feet bare, the pants clinging to her narrow hips, the tank top molding every sweet dip and swell of her breasts.

She put on that ice-princess act, but she was as hot for him as he was for her. And when he'd touched her with his palms, pressing the pleasure into her, he'd nearly melted from the heat that had roared off her.

The odd ability to heat or cool with his hands had seemed useless until he'd long ago learned to use it to excite and pleasure his lovers; but never had a woman risen so fast, so violently, when all he'd done was touch her waist. What would happen if he slid his hand between her legs and palmed her?

The thought of it, of the scream of release that would almost certainly follow, excited the hell out of him.

This thing wasn't over between them, not by a long shot. Somehow he had to make certain she decided to partner him herself. And he knew just how to do it. He had her number. He knew pride when he saw it, and Olivia was made of the stuff.

Yeah, she was going to be his partner. And before this mission ended, that neat little package of a female body would be his.

Olivia sat alone at the huge table in the Feral's dining room, devouring the piles of food on her plate. It was nearly noon, the time they'd agreed to meet to grab lunch and leave for their respective Daemon-tracking assignments. With no true understanding of the wraith Daemons, they weren't certain if they were nocturnal like their draden hosts, or could move freely during the day. Nor had they any idea where they'd hole up during daylight if they *were* nocturnal.

So the teams would head out in broad daylight to begin a hunt that could take days.

She cut another thick bite of ham and shoved it into her mouth, amazed her stomach could hold so much. After her frustrating encounter with Jag just before

dawn, she'd devoured a plateful of food out of a re-
frigerator mostly stocked with meat, then returned to
her room, where she'd given in to the need to relieve
the awful sexual tension Jag had left her with. As she'd
guessed, only a few quick strokes of her finger had
brought on a cataclysmic release.

She'd fallen asleep almost immediately after, sleeping
a solid six hours. And woken starved again. Her body
was burning through the food at an alarming rate.

Pink set a platter of thick-sliced toast on the table,
preparing for the rest of the household, who should be
arriving any minute. With a smile at the pink-feathered
bird-woman, Olivia grabbed a couple slices, eating
them quickly. The others better get down soon, or there
wasn't going to be anything left.

What she craved and needed was life energy. She
couldn't get away from Jag soon enough.

She'd decided Niall would be the one to partner
him. Niall was by far the more even-tempered of her
two men and far less likely to let Jag's antagonistic
remarks draw him into a fight. And while her instincts
told her Jag would never intentionally kill one of their
own, a Feral with his claws and fangs drawn could be
deadly to mortals and immortals alike. No Therian
would ever win against a Feral. Not unless the Feral
let him.

Or, in her case, unless she had an unfair advantage.

She had confidence that Niall would be able to handle

Jag for a few days, and that should be all they needed to find and kill the Daemons.

The sound of male footsteps and the low sound of voices beyond the dining-room door warned her she was about to get company. A moment later, Ewan and Niall walked into the room in uniform, dressed in black pants and boots much like hers, and dark red T-shirts.

A bear of a man, Ewan possessed fair coloring and a neck as thick as her upper thigh. Niall, on the other hand, stood lean and wiry, as dark as Ewan was fair. Of the two, Niall's eyes were by far the softer. At least when they looked at her.

Both men followed her without question, or they wouldn't be under her command. But she and Niall had known one another for more than three hundred years and had been intimate on and off during most of that time. And while that wasn't unusual, she knew Niall wanted more from her. A relationship. Commitment. Neither of which she would ever give him.

To his credit, he didn't push. She'd have him reassigned if he did, and he knew it.

She didn't hear Jag enter, but knew the instant he did. The Feral, even in his human form, walked as silently as his animal counterpart. Jag wore a black T-shirt over a different pair of army green cargo pants. As Niall and Ewan took the seats on either side of her, Jag claimed the chair directly across from her. Naturally.

She braced for more carnal remarks, longing to ignore

him, but if she'd learned anything by now, it was that he'd only take her feigned indifference as more of a challenge. As if she hadn't presented him with enough of one already.

She met his gaze with a simple nod, but the flash of devilish fire that lit his eyes had her groaning silently.

Here we go again.

Jag served himself from the platter piled high with thick slices of rare roast beef, a smile playing at his mouth as he considered the best way to force Olivia's hand, to make her partner with him instead of tossing him one of her men, as she wanted to. And he had no doubt she wanted to.

His sex talk in the war room yesterday had clearly riled her pair of bodyguards, though they'd been good little soldiers and stood down when Olivia's slender hand shot out to stop them. What would it take to push them too far?

Ah, wouldn't it be fun to find out.

His gaze skimmed over Olivia's pretty face, dipping to her shoulders and lower, before returning to her eyes. "Did you dream about me, Sugar?"

"And why would I dream about you, Jag? You'd have to cross my mind first."

He smiled with true enjoyment. Matching wits with this one was the most fun he'd had in . . . he couldn't remember how long. "Why, Sugar, I dreamed about you.

The feel of you beneath my hands, your sexy little cries as you rose toward release."

Niall's mouth tightened, but he made no other indication he'd heard. Ewan didn't seem to care at all, but really, why should they? The two men probably just assumed he'd coaxed Olivia into his bed.

Pity that wasn't the truth.

To hell with the truth. He needed something more.

Mouth twisting unpleasantly, he leaned forward. "In my dream it wasn't my fingers I shoved inside your wet heat when I trapped you in the media room early this morning, Red, it was my cock."

Deep inside him, his animal growled with disapproval, the damned beast. Everyone was a critic.

Olivia jerked, staring at him in shock at the blatant lie.

Niall and Ewan lunged to their feet as one, their hunting knives in their hands.

And looky here. His little ploy had worked like a charm.

"He's lying," Olivia snapped.

Jag just grinned at her. "My fingers are still throbbing from the squeeze of your tight, wet little sheath, Red."

Niall started around the table as if he intended to defend her honor. But the daggers in Olivia's eyes had Jag wondering if she wouldn't slice him and dice him herself.

Olivia shot to her feet. "Niall, stand down!"

Lies or not, Jag's words reeked of disrespect, and her men weren't having it. Olivia fisted her hands on the table. She appreciated their loyalty, she really did. But dammit! A fight could only end in disaster. Instigator or not, Jag belonged here, and they didn't. If there was trouble, she had no doubt who'd be out on their asses.

The Therians.

And she was not ready to lose this one chance to work with the Ferals.

Damn Jag!

He rose lazily to his feet, the muscles rippling beneath his T-shirt.

Olivia glared at him. "You are one messed-up fuck."

The jackass winked at her. Winked! But there was nothing lazy about his stance, or his eyes, as he followed Niall's progress around the table. Every line of his body said he was itching for this fight.

"Niall, *stand down.*" When he didn't respond, she slammed her fists onto the table, sending the china hopping. *"Now!"*

The last of Olivia's hopes of escaping Jag sank like a rowboat in a storm.

A deep, rumbling growl came from the doorway, and Olivia turned to find Lyon and Kara walking in, Tighe and Delaney close behind. Lyon's gaze slid from Niall, now standing stock-still three feet from Jag, his knife gripped tight in his hand, to Jag. Lyon's face turned dark as a draden cloud.

Niall sheathed his knife and quickly retreated to his seat, as if that warning had been directed at him. Olivia felt certain it hadn't been. Lyon had no illusions about the troublemaking nature of his jaguar Feral.

The frustration and resignation clouding Lyon's eyes as his gaze met Jag's confirmed it. She commiserated with the Feral leader. How did you manage a man like Jag? A man so adept at antagonizing others. A man you were forced to keep on your team through circumstances far beyond your control. Only eight Feral Warriors currently existed in the world. Eight with the strength and power needed to fight the Mage, who sought to free Satanan and his horde. And if one of those eight happened to be a trouble-causing asshole, what choice had you but to deal with it?

Just as she had no choice but to partner the jackass. Sending either of her men with him would only end in disaster. Niall might be the more even-tempered of the two, but not when it came to her. As he'd gone after Jag, his feelings for her had shone from his face as clearly as a beacon on a clear night. And Jag had seen them. She was sure of it.

If she tried to pair either Niall or Ewan with Jag, he'd goad them into attacking him, she had little doubt. Which could well prove fatal. And not to Jag.

Dammit, I am going to have to partner Jag myself.

Olivia sighed. Such was the price of leadership. Though her situation was considerably more complicated than merely dealing with a surly warrior.

Jag was a danger to her in a way he was to no one

else. Because he could feel her feed. Which meant she was going to have to find a way to escape him on a regular basis. Either that, or they'd end up spending hours a day trying to keep food in her, which would only raise his suspicions as well.

As the others joined them, Tighe met her gaze across the table. "I'd like for you to accompany Delaney and me, Olivia, if that meets with your approval."

Olivia glanced at Jag, unable to help herself. The gleam in his eyes laughed at her. He knew he'd backed her into a corner. That was exactly what he'd meant to do.

"I'll be sending Ewan with you, Tighe. I'll be partnering Jag."

She felt the sharp disapproval of her men, but neither showed disrespect by undermining her position out loud.

Tighe looked at her askance. "Are you sure? He's an ass."

Olivia's surprised gaze slid to Delaney, beside him, and they shared a moment's amusement. Tighe wasn't averse to calling it as he saw it.

"I'm aware of that, Tighe. I can handle him."

She glanced at Jag, daring him to make one more inappropriate comment.

But for once the shifter remained silent, satisfaction written all over his face. He'd gotten just what he wanted.

"Niall will partner with Hawke," Olivia continued, turning her gaze back to Tighe.

The tiger shifter nodded, his eyes holding a mix of concern and respect. And no small amount of speculation. Did he believe her interested in the jaguar? Did any woman have so little self-respect that she willingly sought such crass dominance in a male? It didn't please her that he might think she was such a female.

Then again, what did it matter what anyone thought so long as her reasons were sound? And they were.

Tighe nodded. "All right, then. As soon as we eat, we'll head out."

Jag smiled a thoroughly self-satisfied smile as she took her seat again. "I'll make all your dreams come true, Sugar."

Beside her, Niall growled low in his throat.

"I suspect you're right, Jag," Olivia said coolly. "Since my dreams all involve knives. And blood."

Several of the Ferals snorted, someone chuckled.

"She's got your number, Cat," Wulfe drawled.

Olivia had expected to draw a glimmer of anger from Jag at the reminder of what had really happened early that morning, but he disappointed her. The smile that lifted his mouth was hard-edged, but genuine.

"Bring it on."

Jag glanced over at Olivia, sitting in the front passenger seat of his Hummer as he drove to Harpers Ferry a short while later. She'd donned a leather jacket over the tank and black pants—not a prissy, tailored little jacket, but one that had clearly seen its share of battle. She might still be the haughty ice princess, but she looked the part of a warrior now.

Goddess, she turned him on.

They'd left the crowded D.C. suburbs quickly enough and now drove along the narrow roads winding through tiny towns and across farms and vineyards.

"Why does a pretty little girl like you want to get her hands dirty fighting draden? That's what I can't figure out."

Though she barely moved a muscle, he felt her annoyance at the *little-girl* crack. He enjoyed annoying her, enjoyed watching the anger snap in her eyes.

Unfortunately, the crack failed to get a rise out of her.

"What's with the Scottish accent? Your words and phrasing are all American."

Again, she didn't answer, and he figured she'd decided simply to freeze him out. He wasn't sure why he wanted her talking to him, but he did.

"I'm an ass, Olivia. We both know it. But I'd like to know a little more about you."

She cut him a look, assessing. Contemplative. Then slowly turned to the front again. "I was born in Scotland and lived there for several hundred years. But I spent half the nineteenth century and all of the twentieth in the New England enclaves, mostly Boston and New York. Six years ago I was promoted to the rank of team leader and reassigned to the British Guard."

Her voice had a depth to it, a feminine richness that slid over his skin like satin. The brogue added just the right touch of texture and warmth.

"And now you're back."

"I am."

"Why did you join the Guard?" He found himself genuinely interested in her. Not just her body, even though that interest continued to erupt like fireworks in his blood, but in the person. Olivia. She intrigued him more than any woman had in a long, long time.

But again, she was silent so long he didn't think she intended to answer. When she finally did, her words surprised him.

"My mother was killed by draden when I was seven. You might say I have a score to settle."

"If you've been doing this for centuries, I'm thinking that score's been settled a few hundred times over."

"You're wrong, Feral. That score will never be settled so long as draden continue to exist on this Earth."

He heard the conviction of her words, felt it all the way to his bones, where it resonated deeply.

"I'm good at what I do," she said simply. "And I enjoy it."

"I get that. I feel the same," he added, surprising himself with his honesty.

Surprising them both. Her brows rose as she shot him a curious look. "You *like* being a Feral Warrior? You have an odd way of showing it, Jag."

Wasn't that the truth. But yeah, he liked being a Feral, liked fighting draden and Mage. It was the only thing that gave his life purpose. But he'd never tell her that. Touchy-feely pillow talk sure as hell wasn't his thing.

"It gets me laid, Sugar. All the girls want to fuck a Feral, you know that."

She rolled her eyes. "Everything goes back to sex with you, doesn't it?"

"You ever order your men to go down on you, Red? I can't stop wondering if you have freckles down there, swimming in the cream."

He expected her to turn away in disgust, ignoring him again. Or maybe, if he was lucky, she'd lose her temper and slug him a good one. Instead, she turned toward him, shoulders and all, but remained silent.

He glanced at her, thinking she was giving him the evil eye or something, but she was studying him as if she'd shoved him under a microscope.

"What?" he snapped. He was starting to feel twitchy under that cool, intense regard.

"Do you even know why you do it?"

"Do what?"

"Annoy the hell out of everyone?"

Jag shrugged. "It's just who I am, Sugar. Like I said, I'm not a nice guy."

"See, I don't believe that."

Tearing his gaze from the road, he gave her an incredulous look.

She leaned her shoulder more firmly against the seat as if settling in for a nice long discussion. *Hell.* His gaze returned to the road.

"I saw you with Pink in the war room, Jag. She was by far the most vulnerable person in there, the easiest target, yet you defended her. Violently. And she hadn't even been attacked, not outright. You wouldn't allow anyone to so much as hurt her feelings."

Jag scowled. "Pink's had a rough go of it."

"That's my point. She'd be the easiest of targets if your aim was to hurt, but it's not. And you never aimed your barbs at Kara or Skye, either. Only at Delaney and me, but you can't hurt either of us with them, and I think you know that."

She was starting to piss him off. "I'm not looking to hurt you, Red. Just fuck your brains out."

"You use sex talk as a defense, do you know that?"

"You can shut up now, Sigmund Freud."

Olivia didn't bat an eye. Nor did she shut up, dammit.

"You don't hurt the vulnerable, Jag. What you do is make people mad at you—the other Ferals, my men. *Me.* You want us mad. You *need* us mad at you. Do you know why?"

He gripped the steering wheel hard, throwing her a glower that would have had men three times her size quaking in their boots. And he knew it wouldn't make an ounce of difference. "I'm sure you're going to tell me."

To his surprise, she turned forward again, tilting her head back until it rested against the seat behind her. For several moments, she was silent, and he thought maybe she was through with him after all. But when she began to speak, he felt transported—to a place he didn't want to go.

"Years ago, something happened for which I blamed myself bitterly, Jag. I hated myself and everything about me." Her voice was low, her words devoid of emotion. But the emotion was there, buried so deep he felt it tugging at the hole in his chest where his heart used to be. "I let others hurt me. I practically begged them to hurt me. At the time, I didn't understand why. It wasn't until years later that I finally figured out that my own self-hatred had sought out the punishment. It almost destroyed me. The thing is, after living with that kind of guilt and darkness, after suffering it myself, I've come to recognize it in others."

She turned back to face him. "I see it in you."

Goddess, he didn't need this shit. "I like myself just fine, Olivia."

"Do you?" She let the question hang in the air, her tone telling him clearly she didn't believe him. *Damn little prissy psychoanalyst.*

"The way I see it, you can't stand for *anyone* to like you. You need them to hate you as much as you hate yourself. So you antagonize and annoy them as your own personal form of self-punishment. Deep down, you're a decent guy, Jag. You don't actually hurt anyone—you don't break their things, you don't kill their pets. You don't even punch them in the face. Instead, you heckle them until they're the ones punching you. Until all you see in their eyes is the same deep, raw dislike you feel for yourself."

He scoffed. "You've known me *how* long? How the fuck do you know I don't break the other kids' toys or twist the heads off their hamsters?"

"I know."

Goddess, her know-it-all attitude was pissing him off.

Okay, maybe he didn't do those things, but she was wrong about the rest of it. Totally off. He wasn't a decent guy. And he wasn't some fucked-up self-hating loser. He was just who he was.

"A pretty little theory, Sugar. But I'm tired of hearing you talk."

He snatched her arm, curling his hand around her wrist and pressing his palm hard against her skin, willing his hand to heat, filling her with sensual fire.

Olivia gasped, trying to jerk her arm free even as her breasts rose, her back arching in an intoxicatingly passionate move. Her head tilted back, and he knew she was feeling the pleasure, the warm, throbbing heat all the way down.

"Now I want to hear you scream. Come for me, Red."

Her sexy little gasps tore through his senses, lifting his pulse and his blood pressure, sending that blood spiraling hard and low. Goddess, but he wanted to hear her cry out with that ultimate release. She'd been so close last night he'd almost been able to taste it.

She was so close to it again . . .

He didn't see the knife coming for his hand until it was too late. The steel of her blade sliced right through muscle and tendons, hurting like a son of a bitch.

The moment she pulled the knife free, he jerked his bleeding hand away. "Damn you!"

"You don't learn, do you?" But her rough, sexy voice held a hint of amusement.

He snorted. One point to the redhead. "Where in the hell did you get that kind of speed?"

He didn't expect an answer, so he was surprised when he got one. "Many Therians have gifts left over from the days when we were all shifters."

The defensive note in her tone told him he'd touched a nerve. Which was interesting, now, wasn't it?

The stinging in his hand slowly dulled to nothing as the flesh healed. When he glanced at her, he found her watching him with cool eyes. Cool eyes that throbbed with ill-disguised heat. Goddess, but he wanted her.

Even better, she wanted him.

"You know I'm going to win this game, Red. Sooner or later, you're going to spread your thighs and invite me in. You're wasting your time fighting it."

Olivia let out a long sigh. "We're both wasting our time if we're doing anything other than trying to catch those Daemons, Jag." She raked her hands into her hair, pulling the bright locks back from her face in a move that was decidedly unsettled. "It would be wise for us to remember that."

He turned his concentration back to the road, his lips twitching with satisfaction. Oh yeah, he'd gotten under her skin. As badly as she'd gotten under his.

But she was right. They did have a job to do, and the one thing he never did was shirk his duty.

There was too much at stake.

But that didn't mean this game had come to an end. Hell no. Sooner or later, she'd be begging him to give her exactly what they both wanted.

Hot, sweaty, mind-blowing sex.

Then maybe he'd finally get her out of his system. He was beginning to think that couldn't happen soon enough.

By the time Jag and Olivia reached the dramatic con-
fluence of the Shenandoah and Potomac rivers and
crossed into the small tourist hamlet of Harpers Ferry,
West Virginia, the sun was high in the sky, well past
its zenith.

Olivia watched out the window of Jag's Hummer
as they drove along the river road, enchanted by the
towering cliffs rising above the rivers where Virginia,
Maryland, and West Virginia converged. As many
years as she'd spent in the United States, she'd never
before been to this spot.

Jag pulled up in front of the small, quaint Slumber-
side Motel. "Wait here while I grab the room key."

"Is this place warded?" she asked with surprise.

"No. But we'll need a place to crash come daylight."

He returned a few minutes later and drove past the small town and onto a quiet residential street, where he pulled over, parking the car.

"Now the real fun begins," he murmured, throwing her one of his patent devilish smiles as he opened the driver's door and unfolded his long frame. She was about to reach for her door handle when he opened the back door and climbed into the backseat, closing the door behind him.

"What are you doing?"

He didn't answer, merely pulled off his T-shirt, giving her a first-class view of hard muscle, then began to unbuckle the belt of his camo pants.

"I won't be joining you back there, cat, if that's what you're thinking."

He lifted a single brow, snagging her with his sharp gaze. "I could change your mind."

She whipped out one of her knives and twirled it between her fingers. "You could try."

The grin that lifted his mouth turned bright with challenge and wide with genuine amusement. "I'm going hunting."

Perfect. Finally, the opportunity she'd been waiting for to get away from him to feed.

The full import of his words hit her, and her eyes widened.

"You're shifting?" A small thrill caught her at the

prospect of watching him shift into his animal right in front of her. The first time she saw him shift, the first time she'd ever seen any Feral shift, was that day last week when she, Ewan, and Niall had come to meet with Lyon at Feral House. Jag had shifted unintentionally—the fault of Mage magic, but it had happened quickly, and she'd been trying to ignore him at the time so hadn't been watching. This time she wasn't taking her gaze off him.

"I always used to think Ferals could keep their clothes on during the shift," she murmured. "But you can't, can you?"

"Some can. I can't. The magic steals them away." Jag lifted his knee to remove his boot. "The only way I can catch the scent of that Daemon is in my animal. You're coming with me."

Not a chance. "I thought I'd drive around a bit, see if anything looks suspicious." She sensed no capitulation on his part. "Besides, I need to find a loo."

His gaze flicked to hers, resignation in his eyes, and she knew she had him.

"Don't go far. I can only talk to you within about a half a mile radius. I'll let you know if I pick up anything. You do the same."

"All right." She knew Ferals were capable of telepathic communication in their animal forms. For half a mile he'd be able to communicate with her. Beyond that, the link would be broken. If she had to guess, the same was probably true of his ability to sense her feeding. Which meant the first thing she had to do was get at least half a mile away.

Jag wouldn't be pleased if he found out. She'd come up with some excuse if that happened.

Jag struggled out of his pants in the confines of a vehicle that should have been large, yet felt small and confined when filled with a male his size. She knew watching him undress would only encourage more sex talk but, pride be damned, she didn't want to miss a second of this.

With a final tug, he tossed his clothing aside and sat back, hands on knees with a rough exhalation of air.

Goddess, but he was a fine-looking male. Striping one inner thigh were four long scars, like claw marks. With a thrill, she realized they were his feral marks. Every Feral Warrior received them somewhere on his body when the animal spirit first marked him.

Her intrigued gaze slid from the marks on his thigh to the other part of his anatomy that most fascinated her. Nestled amid the brown thatch of hair in his lap, lay a fine, large penis.

Beneath her admiring stare, the thick length of flesh twitched and began to thicken.

"Like what you see, Sugar?" Jag drawled.

Her gaze rose to his, meeting hard eyes glittering with amusement and growing desire.

"The root has merit. The tree to which it's attached, not so much."

His mouth kicked up into a hard smile, his eyes beginning to glitter. "You're wanting a ride. Don't think I can't tell, Red. I can smell your heat."

She couldn't deny it. Well, she would deny it . . . to him. But to herself, no way. Watching him swell and grow set off a flood of damp warmth between her legs as her breasts tingled and began to ache.

"All you smell is your own conceit, Feral." But her voice sounded tight even to her own ears, and she knew he was all too aware of how much the sight of him moved her.

He watched her a good long time, the promise of challenge . . . and passion . . . thick in the air. Finally, with a snort that somehow told her he thought she was a coward, he nodded toward the steering wheel. "Keys are in the ignition." Without warning, he began to sparkle, a million colors at once, and the man disappeared. Where he'd sat now perched a perfectly shaped jaguar, the size of a house cat. His fur was darker than most jaguars', almost black on his face and legs, but the spots showed clearly through the lighter brown fur of his back and tail.

She struggled not to gasp with the excitement of watching something so rare, so magical.

"You're kind of small, aren't you?"

Bitch. She heard his voice in her head as clearly as if he'd spoken, the word trembling with laughter. As she stared at him, she realized he was growing. And fast. Inch after inch, a foot, two feet, until his length stretched across both seats, from one side of the vehicle to the other. A *large,* full-sized, jaguar.

She suddenly understood why he drove a vehicle with darkly tinted rear windows.

His tail twitched, stirring the air with the rich scent of warm fur, delighting her senses. Her pulse rose, part delight, part ancient, primal fear.

As if hearing her accelerated pulse, he swung his head toward her and gave a low growl, revealing massive jaws and sharp, wicked teeth.

Olivia jerked back toward the dash, unable to stop herself, her hand reaching for her knife.

In her head, she heard his laughter. *Who you calling small, Little Red?*

She stared straight into those jaguar eyes and saw wicked amusement and keen intelligence, reminding her this was no real jaguar but simply another form of her annoying companion. Slowly, her pulse began to calm.

"Point taken, Feral. Why the mini-me?"

I can pass for a house cat when I'm smaller.

"Only to someone who doesn't look at you carefully."

His dark whiskered face bobbed up and down.

I'll attract some attention. I always do. But those who notice me will just think I'm an oddity. They're humans. What else are they going to think?

Slowly, he began to shrink again. When the animal in the back once more fit on one seat, he leaped into the front and onto her lap, his paws pressing into her thighs, his nose making a beeline for her crotch.

Smelling good, Red.

Olivia shoved his face away. "You're rude in any form, aren't you?"

Wouldn't know how to be any other way. Open the door and keep the windows down. The Hummer's warded against draden, which also blocks my communication.

Holding his face at bay with one hand, she opened the front passenger door with her other. With a low growl of approval, the small jaguar leaped out onto the grass.

Stay where you can hear me, Olivia.

Of course, she replied, knowing full well she wouldn't. *Can you hear me?* Only once had she ever communicated telepathically, last week when she'd first met with Lyon at Feral House. Things had gone a little crazy when several of the Ferals had shifted unintentionally, and Lyon had pushed a request for the Therians' help into her head. But she'd never tried to speak to someone telepathically herself.

I hear you loud and clear.

A horrible thought occurred to her. If he could hear her thoughts, *could he read her mind?* Real fear banded around her chest, squeezing her lungs.

Jag?

What is it, Olivia? he demanded, his voice sharp.

She must have communicated her fear, dammit. Calm down, calm down, calm down.

I was just wondering how this works. How many of my thoughts can you hear?

She heard his chuckle in her head. *Worried I'll learn all your secrets, Little Red?* The lazy drawl was back.

Taking deep breaths, she struggled for control. *Just wondering.*

Relax, sweetheart, I only hear the thoughts forcibly directed my way. Usually. Though as tuned to you as I am, who knows. I might hear all the lurid things you want to do with my body.

Olivia pushed the hair back from her face with an unsteady hand. Was he toying with her? Or telling the truth? Shit. Could she take a chance?

With a groan, she started counting backward from a thousand. Anything, *anything,* to keep him from reading her mind. Because if he did, if he learned her secrets, her life was *game over.*

Jag took off on all fours, his cat's senses straining to pick up the foul scent he remembered all too well from the cavern where the Mage had first released the three wraith Daemons from the enchanted Daemon blade. The smell had reminded him of rotting meat, only worse. Much worse. As if evil itself had an odor.

Recognizing that scent should be easy if he came across it again. Unfortunately, that might prove a mighty big "if." Harpers Ferry was a long way from that cavern. In all probability, all they'd stumbled upon was the work of a human serial killer. A problem for the humans to deal with, not the immortal cavalry.

He padded through grassy yards, staying close to the bushes, where he could hide his true appearance as much as possible from prying eyes.

Too bad he hadn't been able to talk Olivia into joining him. He'd have enjoyed her company. The woman had claws, nice sharp little claws that dug into him in all the right places. As hard as she tried to hide her attraction to him, she failed. It flashed in her eyes and rose from her skin in a lush scent that stroked his loins until he turned hard and throbbing and ready.

He loved sex, had loved sex since he first stumbled upon a pair of teenage humans rutting in the woods when he was fourteen. The female had seen him and smiled, watching him as she screamed her release. The next day, she'd come alone and indoctrinated him into the carnal world—a world forbidden young Therians. But he'd never been much for following rules.

That was nearly three and a half centuries ago, hundreds of sexual partners ago, yet never could he remember feeling the blazing-hot attraction he felt for Olivia. If he'd thought she'd obsessed him before he'd tasted her skin and felt her explosive response to the heat of his hands, it was nothing compared to now. He could hardly think of anything beyond touching her, tasting her. Beyond the need to feel her shatter with release.

Of course, he wanted to be inside her, too. That went without saying, except . . . that wasn't everything. It wasn't even half of it.

Usually when he felt desire for a woman, it was all about sex. About finding his own release. Why then did the thought of feeling Olivia's pleasure excite him almost more than the thought of finding his own?

He wanted her beneath him, on top of him.

Beside him.

On some oddball level he didn't understand, he wanted her company, her frosty gaze, her sharp heels and tongue. He loved trading barbs with her, loved watching her try to hide the attraction she felt for him.

Damn, he just loved being with her.

Which was completely fucked up. He was perfectly happy with his own company and always had been.

The scent of dog had him detouring across the street. Not that he couldn't hold his own against any creature, even as Mini Jag. But the less attention he drew to himself, the better, all the way around.

With a conscious effort, he pulled his mind from

Olivia and concentrated on picking up the scent he searched for. A short while later, as he traipsed through a cemetery, that unique whiff of evil and decay hit him.

Daemon.

Found it, Red.

He threw the thought out there before he bothered to find her with his mind.

Red?

Dammit, where the hell was she? Had she accidentally wandered out of range? Or had she just gotten tired of driving around with the windows down?

Neither. If there was one thing he was sure of with that woman, it was that she didn't do anything accidentally. No, if Olivia left the half-mile radius he'd requested she remain within, she'd done so deliberately and for a damn good reason.

So, what the hell was it? Had she spied the Daemon and taken off after it without telling him? No. She was too good a soldier for that. So what was Little Red up to?

A middle-aged human couple strolling through the cemetery ahead caught sight of him. The woman gasped.

"Bryan, look at him! Isn't he the strangest cat you've ever seen? Here kitty, kitty, kitty."

Damn humans. Jag ran before they could trap him. The trail of Daemon scent led him into the woods on the other side, growing stronger as he ran. Little by little, the scent became mixed with another. Blood. Human blood.

Red, where are you? I'm on the trail of the Daemon, and he's killing. Or killed.

The trail ended suddenly in a blaze of scent that nearly fried the insides of his cat's nose. His keen animal senses told him he was alone, so he upshifted to his full-sized jaguar. If he came upon the thing, there'd be a fight, and since his knives didn't stay with him any better than his clothes when he shifted, fangs and claws were his only weapons.

Where are you, you bastard?

Jag leaped for the nearest tree and began to climb, hoping to catch sight of the creature, but as he rose, the scent grew fainter. Not significantly so, but enough that he noticed. He stretched out on a thick branch about ten feet from the ground and looked around, sending his cat's heightened senses out in every direction.

And that's when he saw it. Not the Daemon, but a mound of dead leaves that looked out of place below. As if they'd been piled there intentionally. To hide something.

He leaped out of the tree, shifting back to his human form midleap, and landed on two feet. Kneeling beside the mound, he shoved the leaves away to reveal a dark blue tarp. The smell of blood and carnage nearly obliterated the stench of Daemon, and he knew there would be no rescuing this victim.

He pulled the tarp back . . . and wished he hadn't.

Well, hell. Victims, plural. Body parts from at least half a dozen humans lay in the shallow grave. Heads, arms, parts of torsos, all of which had most of the flesh stripped from the bones.

Jesus.

He pulled the tarp back farther , and froze, his stomach cramping.

Not Cordelia.

But, *goddess.* As he stared at the half-destroyed face of a thirtyish woman, memory of another overlaid it— half a face where the flesh had tried one last time to regenerate over the charred remains of bone and blood, before her Therian body had finally given up.

Cordelia.

His head began to pound, cold sweat rolling down his temples as old horror shot through his gut. He stumbled back and fell to his knees, retching into the dirt, the memories stabbing him like red-hot steel.

When his stomach had emptied, he rose on shaky legs, arching his back, hands in his hair, until he forced the memories down. Then he returned to the mass grave.

Ten bucks said he'd found the humans who'd gone missing in this town the past few days.

That goddamn pain-feeding Daemon was history.

But as he lifted the tarp back over the bodies, he stilled, a thought slamming into him.

Everything they understood of wraith Daemons told them they were nonthinking creatures. Animals. Monsters. They literally fed on the pain and fear of others as a human or Therian might feed on marinated pork or ham steaks. They did not plot or plan. Or bury their victims in tarps and hide them in the woods beneath a pile of leaves.

But someone had done just that. Someone who didn't want the public . . . or the Ferals . . . to know the Daemon was here.

A thousand bucks said he knew who was behind this.

The Mage.

Olivia drove out of Harpers Ferry, out of the reach of Jag's extraordinary senses, and headed west on the highway, hoping to find a diner or bar—anyplace where more than a few humans gathered. She had to be careful with humans. Early on, she'd learned trying to feed off fewer than four or five at once, even at low levels, could drain them fast.

She'd never actually killed one—at least not accidentally—that she knew of, but she'd dropped a few unconscious when she was young.

Large crowds were definitely best.

When she found the Wal-Mart, she smiled, then parked the Hummer and strolled into the store, opening herself to a free, careful feeding at last. The store was most crowded in the electronics department, so she headed there, wandering among the rows of DVDs and video games, skimming a fine layer of life force from every human she passed. A layer they'd never miss, not with so many to feed from. A layer they'd soon replenish.

Strong energy radiated off a small gathering of humans in the iPod aisle, two human males past their prime, their bellies swollen with excess, and two teenage girls who seemed none too pleased with the attention of the males.

"She's a pretty little thing, isn't she?" the male with the Redskins cap said, eyeing the darker-haired girl.

The girls glanced over their shoulders at the pair, but continued what they were doing, looking over several items on the racks. Though uncomfortable with the boorish attention, they didn't appear to be genuinely worried.

Olivia wondered if they should be. She continued to feed lightly as she watched with an eye toward stepping in.

But the second boor noticed her, his eyes lighting.

"I'm partial to redheads," he said, hitching his pants up under his protruding belly.

Olivia said nothing, just held his gaze as she slid one of her knives out of the sheath hidden beneath her jacket, twirled it around her finger in a quick arc, then made it disappear again.

The man's eyes widened, and he blanched, taking a step backward.

"Let's go, Earl."

"What? Why?"

But the other one grabbed his arm and took off around the end of the aisle.

"Jerks," one of the girls said under her breath when they'd gone.

Olivia had to agree. As she moved away, the girls' voices carried to her, excited talk of iPods and birthdays and prom.

She found herself smiling, their pleasure infectious, but her smile quickly faded. Humans knew so little of what really went on in their world.

She prayed to the goddess the Ferals and other immortals could keep it that way. If Satanan and his Daemon hordes ever managed to get free, life as the humans knew it would be over. As they'd done five thousand years ago, the higher, thinking, Daemons would once more begin to round up humans by the thousands, mostly children, torturing and terrorizing as they fed on their pain and fear. Panic and misery would quickly rule the world.

Olivia continued to walk and feed for a few minutes more, until she felt full and strong, then headed for the doors. As she strolled into the sunshine, she wondered how long before she turned hungry again. She'd gone almost twenty-four hours without feeding this time. Would she be able to go longer next time? Or less? Almost certainly, she'd have to escape Jag again sometime tomorrow. When the time came, she'd have to come up with another excuse.

She headed for the Hummer, anxious to get back to Harpers Ferry before Jag realized she was gone. Ahead, she saw the two boorish males hitting on yet another female in the parking lot.

One adjusted his hat while the other tugged up his pants. Then suddenly, as one, they went perfectly still, their arms dropping limp at their sides.

Olivia's eyes narrowed, her instincts ringing a warning alarm. As she passed the trio, she glanced at the attractive auburn-haired woman, then looked quickly away, her heart beginning to race. The woman's green eyes had been ringed in copper.

Mage eyes.

Which meant the enthrallment of those men was real.

Why? What would a Mage possibly want with humans, and two such poor examples of the species, at that?

Keeping her stride casual and even, she continued to the Hummer, watching out of the corner of her eye as the three climbed into the red pickup truck they'd been standing in front of. The men moved like automatons.

Olivia climbed into the Hummer, then pretended to study herself in the rearview mirror as she watched the truck drive off at a calm, sedate pace.

She started the bright yellow vehicle and followed, wishing like hell she was in something a little less eye-catching. Clearly Jag's work rarely called for clandestine pursuit. If only she could contact him to tell him she was following a Mage and her victims.

But she was out of range, and on her own. For the time being, they both were.

She followed the truck back toward Harpers Ferry, but lost it as it turned left between too small a gap in oncoming traffic for her to follow. And by the time another gap presented itself, her quarry was nowhere to be seen.

Olivia?

The sound of Jag's voice in her head sent her pulse into a small, odd skitter.

I'm here.

Where in the hell have you been?

Thank goodness she had a decent excuse. *I saw something suspicious and followed. A Mage witch enthralled two human males. I tried to follow their truck, but I lost them.*

Shit.

What would a Mage want with humans, Jag?

I'm afraid I know. Get back here and pick me up, and I'll fill you in. We've stumbled onto more than a wraith Daemon on the loose, Red. This is going to get ugly.

When the Mage were involved, it always did.

* * *

"Where do you put all that? It's bigger than you are."

Olivia took another bite of the footlong sub piled high with everything she could fit on the sandwich as she met Jag's disbelieving look with a shrug.

"I have a healthy appetite." And she had no way to know when she'd get another chance to feed her way.

Jag had bought three footlongs for himself and she'd have liked to have bought herself a second, but he really would have gotten suspicious.

They sat across from one another in the back booth of a deli down the road from Harpers Ferry, in Charles Town. Jag had been afraid to eat in town, not knowing how many Mage were about or whether any might recognize him as a Feral. He'd taken to wearing the green military-style canvas jacket he apparently kept in the back of the Hummer to cover his armband. They needed to figure out what the Mage were doing before the Mage realized they were here.

After she'd let him in the car, and he'd shifted back to human and dressed, they'd driven up and down every road in that town, hunting for the red truck while they filled one another in. But they'd found no sign of it.

"How do we know the Mage don't have the Daemon caged again, as they did in the caverns?" she asked. "I thought you believed the wraith Daemons weren't controllable."

"I don't know what the Mage are doing, or what their

involvement is. All I know is I'm catching Daemon scent all over the place. That thing is definitely loose."

"Would the Mage have a reason to follow along behind it, cleaning up the mess he leaves? And if the Daemon is feeding on its own, why did they enthrall those two men this afternoon?"

"All good questions, and I can't answer a one. The scent's old. Better part of a day. As if it hasn't been through here since last night."

"You think it's nocturnal."

"Yep. That's what we've suspected all along, and that scent trail supports it."

Olivia finished her sandwich and wadded up her trash, watching with envy as Jag took a big bite of his third.

"What's our next move?" she asked.

"As soon as it's dark, I'm going hunting."

She caught the singular. "I'm going with you."

"That would be a *no way in hell*, Red. You heard what Lyon said about Kougar and Hawke running across a draden swarm in the mountains. There were nearly forty of them. I'm good, but even I can't take out forty at once. Unless you want to get your pretty little ass killed, you'll be hanging out in the Hummer until daybreak."

"You must be kidding." What she wouldn't give to be able to tell him the truth, that she couldn't be harmed by the draden. Even so . . . "What do you think the Therian Guard are, Feral? Not all of us have the advantage of being able to shift, but you're not the only ones who can fight draden."

He leaned forward, anger flashing in his eyes. "How many do you fight at a time in Scotland? Not forty. Not even half that."

She bit off her argument, because he was right. And while she could handle more draden than any other guard, she did it through weakening them by feeding on them.

And she wouldn't be able to here. Not if Jag were anywhere around. She'd have to fight them with nothing but knives. And forty would be way too many.

Still, the thought of being consigned to the Hummer all night seriously rankled. Except she wouldn't be, would she? All she had to do was get far enough away from Jag, and she could hunt and feed all she wanted.

"I'm good at what I do, Jag." She was keeping up appearances, now. Arguing, as he expected her to.

"I didn't say you weren't."

She shook her head, releasing a disgusted huff. "So, what? My role is to play chauffeur to a cat?" Appearances or not, she was annoyed. Honestly, what use were any of the Therian Guard going to be if the Ferals insisted on keeping them locked behind warding every night?

His eyes took on a devilish gleam as his gaze slid leisurely down to her breasts. "I can think of another role you could audition for."

"Not amused. Why am I here, Jag? And for once, can you forget the sexual?"

His mouth pursed, the carnal light leaving his eyes as he nodded. "If I find the Daemon trail, we'll follow it during daylight. With the Mage in the picture, I'm absolutely going to need backup, Olivia. Goddess only knows what we've stumbled onto."

Their gazes met, for once without the light of sexual awareness blinding everything else. In his gaze, she saw the steel-hearted warrior, the man determined to find and bring down this enemy no matter what it took. For once, he allowed her a glimpse behind the mask, and something inside her lifted, responding. Recognizing a kindred soul.

"All right?" he asked.

She nodded slowly. "Yes." She knew he thought she was agreeing to bide her time in the Hummer tonight in exchange for the promise of a purpose tomorrow.

But he'd be getting that backup sooner than he expected. And not exactly in the way he planned. Because he wasn't the only one going draden- and Daemon-hunting tonight.

And if she was very, very careful, he would never know.

Kougar drove Hawke's Yukon north along Skyline Drive while Hawke scanned police reports on his laptop beside him.

"No reports of any murders in the area," Hawke said. "Which probably only means no one's found the victims yet."

Kougar had to agree. They'd been so close last night to catching one of the Daemons. They'd had the bastard. He'd been right there, hovering over the pond, clearly drawn to the trap. But the magic that should have snared him hadn't.

His hands tightened on the steering wheel as he replayed the moment in his head when he'd first seen the thing, seen a Daemon again for the first time in five thousand years. Though Kougar no longer felt much in the way of emotions, his mind had been more than capable of taking in the chilling magnitude of the moment. Never in his worst nightmares had he thought he'd see the day when Daemons once more terrorized the world.

The one last night had been drawn to the trap, as they'd planned. But he'd hovered over it for several seconds, then flown off again instead of being pulled in. The magic hadn't worked.

The two Ferals had given chase, Kougar on the ground, Hawke in the sky, but the thing had eluded them and eventually lost them. Because they could fly, Daemons were brutally hard to hunt.

"Any idea why the trap didn't work?" Hawke asked.

"We need Ilina blood. And Ilina magic. I was hoping we could get by without them, but apparently we can't."

"The two things we can't possibly get," Hawke said in a tone that warned that his mind had latched onto a subject that intrigued him. He looked up to stare out the window. "I've studied the Ilinas extensively, though there's little enough written about them. They were artists and philosophers, dancers and musicians, at one time. A peaceful race who suddenly turned violent. Like the sirens of lore, they began to lure men, human and immortal, with their beauty and song, into the Crystal Realm, where they tortured or enslaved them for the remainder of the captives' short lives. That's the legend."

Hawke turned to glance at him. "You know the truth."

"No one knows what happened to their victims once they entered the Crystal Realm. It's all speculation."

"Because none returned to tell the tale."

"Because none survived. No corporeal being, mortal or immortal, can live long in that place. But the rest of what you've described is as I remember."

Hawke nodded. "Most believe they were infected by dark spirit. That Queen Ariana destroyed her race herself when she saw what they'd become."

Kougar didn't comment. He didn't know the answer himself. All he knew was the beauties they'd all once adored had turned into evil bitches, perpetrating untold atrocities before faking their extinction and disappearing. He'd been duped like all the rest. It was only in very recent years that he'd learned the truth—that they weren't gone at all and never had been.

Hawke made a sound of frustration. "So traps are out."

It wasn't a question, and Kougar didn't answer. Because he wasn't giving up on the traps just yet. They were by far their best chance of catching the Daemons without Feral casualties. He just had to get the right ingredients.

Come nightfall, he was going hunting.

For Ilina.

Jag climbed out of the Hummer and stripped out of his clothes, tossing them in the back. It was an hour after full dark. The draden should be out anytime now, and with any luck, so would the Daemon.

Olivia sat in the front, arms crossed over her chest. She'd really expected him to take her with him? He knew what it was like to hunt draden as a mere Therian. He'd done it hundreds of times. And it was damned dangerous. And that was in places where the draden traveled in packs of no more than a dozen. Goddess only knew what they'd find out here.

"If I'd sent Niall with you, would you have allowed him to hunt?"

"Can he shift?"

"That wasn't my question."

"It's the only one I'm asking. If you can shift, you can come."

"You're obnoxious."

"Yeah, don't I know it. So sue me for trying to keep you alive. Stay put until I call for you, Red. That's an order." He slammed the door shut against her further arguments.

He had to hand it to her—she had courage to spare. But she wasn't dying out here tonight, that was all there was to it.

He pulled on the power within him, the power of the jaguar. In a rush of pure pleasure, he shifted into his animal form and took off at a run. He'd remain in his full-sized jaguar tonight. Not only would he cover more ground that way, but in the dark, no one would be able to get a good look at him.

Ferals' eyesight in the dark was almost as good as in daylight. Not so, humans.

He roamed the woods and streets of Harpers Ferry, finding nothing but old scent. If this kept up, it was going to be a damned long night. He'd been at it an hour or two when his thoughts turned back to Olivia.

Thinking about me, Sugar?

He expected some sharp retort concerning voodoo dolls and pins in his groin. Instead, he got no reply, just a dark sense of fear. His pulse began to thrum with a mix of dread and concern.

You see him, don't you, Red? You see the Daemon.
Yes.
Shit. Stay in the Hummer. I'll be right there.

Goddess, what if the thing was strong enough to tear

open the doors? He was already running full bore back the way he'd come when she answered.

I'm not in the Hummer, Jag. I'm about a mile upriver on the Shenandoah side.

He turned midstride and headed west, his brain scrambling to keep up. She wasn't in the damned Hummer.

Your listening skills suck, Red, you know that? Has the Daemon seen you?

He's hovering about six yards away, staring at me. Jag heard the tremor she tried to hide, a tremor of the mind and spirit. She was fucking terrified. And she wasn't the only one.

Dammit. Dammit! He ran as fast as his four legs would travel, but he was all too afraid he wasn't going to make it in time. Something raw and painful ripped through his chest.

Stay calm, Red. I'm not far from there. I'm on my way.

Hurry, Jag.

She wasn't going to die. Dammit, Olivia was not going to die.

But he knew what Daemons could do.

And he feared he was going to be too late.

Cold sweat ran down Olivia's temples as she covered her nose against the awful stench and stared at the gruesome sight, at the monster a dozen times more terrifying than anything her imagination had been able to dredge up. A Daemon. An honest-to-God Daemon.

Her breath trembled in her lungs, her damp hands gripping her knives until her fingers ached as her gaze raked the creature's hideous and contorted face. Its features were as indistinct as a draden's, as if the face had been made from wax left too long in the sun. Sharp, uneven fangs hung from a sloping mouth while small, wicked daggers protruded from his fingertips in the form of claws. Thick ropes of black hair hung from his head, each shimmering with frightening iridescence as it embraced the long, black cloak that encased his hovering body.

After Jag left her in the Hummer, she'd given him a small head start, then tried to follow on foot, but she'd already lost him. She might be fast, but the jaguar was faster. So she'd opened her senses, the ones tuned to draden, to see if she might be able to pick up an energy trail. Sure enough, as she'd neared the Shenandoah, she'd felt a prickle of current run over her skin. She'd followed it as it grew hotter and more urgent, right to the Daemon.

As he floated closer, she spread her feet fighting distance apart, gripping her knives as her heartbeat thudded in her ears. Opening herself, she pulled at that swirl of Daemon energy, pulling it into her. Feeding. If Jag were close enough to feel something, she'd blame it on the Daemon.

But she nearly vomited. The energy wasn't true life force, but something else. Something rancid. Foul.

The Daemon hissed, an ugly, inhuman sound of anger as if he'd felt her. He moved closer, his wicked claws extended, a huge creature, easily as big as Jag. Sweat rolled between her shoulder blades as she braced herself for the fight of her life.

As the Daemon flew at her, she struck, slicing one knife across his outstretched hand, spinning and stabbing her second knife into his shoulder before leaping away again.

The Daemon screamed, a terrible, high-pitched sound.

Olivia marveled at the speed and ease with which she'd just moved—faster than she'd ever moved before. Was it adrenaline? Or the Daemon's energy? The latter. She could feel it inside her, swirling, strengthening. The stuff might taste foul, but it was powerful. Opening herself, she took more.

The Daemon hissed and struck, raking one of his claws down her left arm, shredding her jacket and her flesh. Pain screamed through her body, the pain of the wound, and more. As if he'd not only cut her open, but poured acid inside. She clamped down on the scream that roared up her throat and spun away, feeding harder, faster.

But the acid raced through her blood, counteracting the strength of the Daemon energy itself. Slowing her down.

The Daemon struck a second time. She spun and ducked beneath the wicked claws aiming for her face. And felt the sharp piercing of the flesh of her back.

The scream ripped from her throat, even as she rose, stabbing the Daemon through what should have been his gut. But her knife met only air. What in the hell was beneath that robe? She stabbed high into his chest, and this time her blade found purchase close to where his right shoulder blade met his clavicle. Something wet and sticky splattered over her hand.

The Daemon made a horrible, furious sound, like nails on a chalkboard, and flew back. As he rose into the sky, the acid burned through her body until she could barely breathe through the pain.

She sank to her knees, no longer able to stand. Would he be back to finish her off?

Or, goddess help her, was she already as good as dead?

The first scream tore through the night, raking his jaguar's eardrums—an unearthly screech of pain that sent razors flaying his nervous system and terror clawing at his heart even as he cheered at the sound. A sound that had to be the Daemon's.

Go, Red!

But the second scream tore at his insides in an entirely different way. Because this one hadn't come from the creature. It was Olivia's.

On four legs, Jag tore through the woods, racing through the trees until he came upon a sight that chilled him to the depths of his soul—the Daemon hovering over Olivia. But even as he watched, the thing flew up into the air as Olivia sank to her knees.

The warrior inside him demanded he go after the escaping Daemon and kill it, but the man in him had other priorities. He ran to Olivia, shifting into his human form, and fell to his knees beside her. As she listed forward, her eyes glassy, he grabbed her.

"Red." He gripped her tight. "*Olivia.*"

"Catch him." Her voice was breathless, tight with pain.

"He's gone."

"Follow . . . him." Her back had been opened, a thin strip of flesh hanging loose, her ribs shining in the moonlight through a river of blood.

"Goddess, what did he do to you? You're not healing."

"Poison. Feels like . . . poison."

"From what?"

"His claws."

"Venom. They must have venom in their claws." His fingers spasmed on her upper arms. "Dammit, Olivia. Why didn't you wait in the Hummer like I told you to?"

"I'm a warrior. Not a . . . thumb-twiddler. Would you have waited?"

"Hell no, but I rarely do what I'm supposed to."

"Catch him, Jag."

"Later." Shit, she looked like hell. Her clothes were half-torn from her. Her creamy skin looked pale as sand, and he feared if he let her go, she'd fall over onto the ground and never get up again. "You need help, Red. We've got to get you back to Feral House."

Her small hand tried to lift, but fell to her side. "I'll heal. Catch him before he kills again."

"And leave you out here for the draden to finish off? Not. Bloody. Likely." He pulled her against him, then lifted her, one arm under her hips, the other across her shoulders as he avoided the destruction of her back. She continued to bleed fiercely. Her body would continue to make new blood for hours, but eventually, even a Therian body would shut down. And goddess knew what the Daemon venom was doing to her.

She wrapped her good arm around his neck, hanging on, clinging to him with quaking muscles, her body taut as a bowstring. Her other arm hung loose and ragged.

Dammit, he should have been the one to take on that thing. He'd have killed it.

She pressed her face against the curve of his shoulder, her body trembling, but she made no sound. Her silent suffering only bolstered his admiration for her.

He should have known she wouldn't stay behind. Everything about her cried *warrior*. Both the way she stood and the way she carried herself spoke of a strength and self-confidence of the body as well as the spirit. The confidence of someone used to fighting. Used to winning.

That confidence had a lot to do with why he was attracted to her, if he were honest.

"What did you do to it to make it fly away, Red? I need to know."

"Knifed him." Her voice sounded a little stronger, her trembling felt less violent than a moment ago.

He prayed that meant she was beginning to heal. The knot of fear he hadn't even realized he'd been feeling began to ease.

"I stabbed it where its gut should have been, but I hit air."

Jag grunted, frowning. "Just like a draden. Next time go for the heart."

"I tried. It wasn't where I thought it would be."

Next time? Was he out of his mind? Was he really going to let her hunt that thing with him?

Hell.

He carried her awkwardly through the woods, trying not to hurt her more than the Daemon already had even as he kept his senses open. He was stark naked, carrying a wounded woman in his arms. Company of any kind—human, Mage, draden, Daemon—would prove awkward at this point, if not downright deadly. All he could do was try to get her back to the Hummer without another incident.

What were the chances?

He'd barely posed the question when he saw the shadow pass overhead, blotting out the moon's glow. An unnatural shadow he knew all too well.

Shit. "Draden."

Olivia's fingers dug into his bare shoulder. "How many?"

He swallowed. This was going to be close. "I'm guessing about a dozen. I need your knives, Red."

"I thought Ferals fought draden in your animals."

"They're only drawn to Therian energy, not the animals. If I shift now, you'll be the only one they attack." In her weakened state, they'd kill her before he could destroy them. No way in hell he was letting that happen.

Above him, he felt the small cloud of draden pressing down, descending through the treetops, and he set Olivia on the ground at his feet. She managed to sit up, barely, pulling one knife after another out of her inner jacket pockets.

She handed two to him and palmed the third. He suspected she'd have gone for a fourth, except her injured arm still hung useless at her side.

Their gazes met, her eyes looking pained and dazed. "You okay, Red?" If only the Hummer were nearby. If only he could lock her safely behind its warded windows. She was too weak for this.

She nodded, giving him a pained smile. "Let's kill some draden." Injured and dazed, about to face a second mortal enemy in a matter of minutes, she should be terrified. Beaten.

Instead, the light of battle shone in eyes bright with courage.

He met that smile slowly, a fierce determination to protect her, and something more, some emotion he couldn't even name, blooming warm and thick inside him. "You got it, Red. Let's kill us some draden." He winked at her and turned, spreading his feet shoulder-width apart as he prepared for the assault.

As the first draden descended, he attacked, digging his knives into their bodies and popping their hearts, one after the other. Four kills. Five. The key was to kill them before they latched onto him. Once they were on his back or scalp, he'd play heck getting them off him again and be forced to shift into his animal before they drained him dry. But the moment he shifted, they'd go after Olivia.

Instead, he moved cleanly and quickly, turning to keep them off him, circling Olivia to keep them off her.

One of the suckers got through and latched onto his shoulder, its sharp teeth burying deep into his flesh. Fortunately, it was where he could reach it, and he quickly killed it.

Two came in low and tried to attack Olivia directly, but she dispatched them with quick, practiced ease. The last five flew at him from opposite sides, dive-bombing him at once. He killed three, but one caught in his hair and latched onto the back of his skull. Another dug sharp teeth into his right flank.

The pain seared hot and sharp. He popped the one on his flank, but as he lifted his knife to go at the one on his head, he caught sight of a second shadow moving high above.

He looked up, and froze.

Holy shit.

"We've got trouble, Olivia. Looks like this was just the scouting party." High above them, another swarm descended, three times the size of the first. Maybe four.

As he killed the thing on his scalp, cold sweat broke out on his flesh. His head began to pound as the truth crashed over him. He couldn't take on a swarm that size in his human form. They'd kill him long before he destroyed half of them. But if he shifted back into his jaguar and saved himself, Olivia was as good as dead.

Dammit. His hands clenched and unclenched around the knife handles as the hopelessness of the situation rained over him like sharp pellets of ice. *Dammit.* She was going to die. Fury boiled inside him, spilling over in a hot rush, finding an outlet.

He whirled on Olivia. *"Why didn't you stay in the fucking car?"*

She gaped at him. "It's a little late to be worrying about that now!" Her voice had steadied, turning strong again. She struggled to her feet and slowly pulled yet another knife out of her jacket with her injured arm. But the knife slid through her fingers and dropped to the ground.

Jag growled, his mind searching desperately for an answer. If he thought he could outrun the swarm, he'd toss her over his shoulder and take off, but draden on the scent could fly twice as fast as even his cat could run. On human feet, he and Olivia would be nothing but sitting ducks.

Running wasn't an option. And Olivia sure as hell wasn't up for defending herself. How could anyone defend himself against more than forty draden? *She was going to die.*

Unless he shifted, they were both going to die.

The cold truth washed down his spine in an icy sweat. *No!*

"Back on the ground, Red. Now!"

Pulling on the power of his animal, he shifted into his jaguar, not for the first time wishing he possessed the ability to make his animal larger instead of just smaller. Still, at more than six feet long, not including his tail, he could protect most of her. Her back. He had to protect her back.

When he looked up at her through his jaguar's eyes, she was still standing, still determined to fight.

Your listening skills need some work, Red. Get on the ground, now! Fast!

"Why?" She sank to her knees.

On your back and keep your knife at the ready, though I'd consider it a favor it you'd try not to stab me.

She looked at him like he'd lost his mind, but after only a small hesitation, she finally did as he ordered. As the first of the draden descended, Jag dove on top of her, blanketing her with his animal's body.

Get under me. And tell me if they bite you anywhere.

"Jag, this isn't going to work. We have to kill them."

I'll bite the ones I can reach.

"And the rest will wait here, trying to get at me for the rest of the night. We won't find that Daemon."

Screw the Daemon. I'm trying to keep you alive. If I get up, they'll swarm you. You'll be dead in minutes.

The draden cloud descended over them, fighting their way in, pressing into every opening. And they were reaching her, dammit. He snapped at them, eating the tasteless things, draden after draden, but he didn't seem to make a dent in the numbers.

They're getting you.

"I'm okay." But her voice said otherwise. He heard pain. A thread of fear.

His mind spiraled back to that other place, that other time. He felt those blows to his far younger body, the fists attacking him as the enclave leader's furious voice roared in his head across three and a half centuries.

"You let her die. You let her die! You selfish, cold-hearted bastard."

Yes, yes he was all those things. But not this night. Not *this* night. Olivia was not going to die while he lay here, protected and safe. *Useless.*

In a flash of colorful light, he shifted back into a man. In one corner of his mind he reveled in the feel of her soft curves beneath him. Then the draden attacked, and any thoughts of lust disappeared as if they'd never been.

"What are you doing?" Olivia cried.

He leaped off her. "Curl up, Red!"

The draden swarmed them both, but he grabbed the knives off the ground and fought them with everything he had, keeping them off himself as best he could, but his focus was on her. He had to kill the ones who came near her.

She is not going to die.

Those gray eyes would not turn cold and sightless, that fiery spirit would not be doused. Goddess knew what she'd done to him, but she'd touched him, connected with him in a way no woman had, perhaps ever. They might do nothing but battle one another, but he was beginning to care about her, dammit. He *cared.* He wasn't going to let her die.

Olivia ignored him and sat up, stabbing draden nearly as quickly as he did. Still, they kept coming. There must be fifty of them. With two hands, he couldn't get them all. They latched onto his shoulders, his scalp, his back and flanks and legs.

"Jag, shift back!"

"No."

"You idiotic, stubborn, Feral!" she shouted.

He ignored her, his concentration on one thing and one thing only. Killing the draden. He fought until the sweat ran in rivulets down his temples, until his body became a mass of searing pain. Until his legs began to weaken.

The damn draden were winning. He didn't know what else to do. What he'd done wasn't enough.

It wasn't enough.

Ah, goddess, what do I do?

The question tore through Olivia's quaking mind as she fought the draden with a desperation beyond anything she'd faced in over five and a half centuries. Because she couldn't fight them her way, by stealing their energy for herself. Jag would know.

But if she didn't, if they didn't dispatch the draden soon, they were both going to die.

Jag loomed over her, killing most of the draden that tried to attack her. She looked up and gasped at the sight of him. They were covering him. *Covering him.* Even as she watched, his movements began to slow, and he lurched drunkenly.

They were killing him.

"Jag, shift!"

"No." His voice was low and flat, as if he'd already accepted his own death.

But he wouldn't die if he shifted, dammit. They couldn't hurt him in his animal.

My God, he was sacrificing his life in a hopeless attempt to save hers when all she had to do to live was steal the energy from the draden around her.

Which would give her secret away.

Which would destroy her life.

But what choice did she have?

If she did nothing, if she let the draden kill him, then saved herself, no one would ever know, and her secret would be safe. And the man who was sacrificing his life to save her would be dead.

"Jag, listen to me. You must shift. They can't hurt me."

He didn't look at her.

"Jag, I'm draden-kissed!"

But he didn't respond, focused only on staying alive. On keeping them both alive.

She crawled out from under the slash of his knives and pushed herself to her feet, her body still weak from the Daemon venom.

He swung to her, his gaze unfocused. "Olivia, no. They'll kill you."

"They can't kill me unless I let them." Meeting his gaze, forcing herself to watch the knowledge leap into his eyes, she spread her arms and let them bite her, then sucked them dry, not fighting them. Not needing to.

As his eyes went wide with understanding, she felt as if a knife had been plunged into her chest.

"They can't hurt me, Jag. Shift!"

Staring at her, he did. Once more, that magic swept over him, racing over her skin like a sparkling spray. With an angry squawk, the draden who'd been attached to him shot into the air, then dove for her. As they covered her like a many-mouthed blanket, she saw the jaguar sink to the ground, the last of his energy expended in the shift.

She had to feed fast, or the draden would kill her before she could save herself, but if she caught Jag in the feeding . . . Could she hurt him in his animal form? She didn't know and wasn't about to risk it. He had nothing left to give.

Olivia stumbled away, covered with draden and still suffering the weakening effects of the venom. But as she moved, she fed. Slowly at first, then harder as she put distance between her and Jag. And harder still. Finally, she opened herself fully, drinking of the draden energy, growing stronger and steadier as the draden grew weaker until, one by one, they fell away from her, disappearing in tiny puffs of smoke.

Her skin was torn and stinging from the dozens of draden bites, her body still slow and lethargic from the Daemon venom, but she felt strong again, her life force fully replenished.

If only she didn't feel the hard fist in her stomach, the terrifying certainty that her life itself had shattered.

She turned and returned to Jag, walking over the leaf-strewn ground on leaden feet. He remained on the ground, on his stomach, now, his chin resting on his paws, watching her approach through laser-sharp jaguar eyes.

He knows what I am.

Her limbs turned weak, her skin cold, as the ramifications of what she'd done slammed into her.

Jag knew. Her life was over. Her work. The Therian Guard would never let her near them again. No Therian would come near again. She'd be outcast. Ostracized.

Olivia pressed a fist to her stomach as if she could hold back the waves of shock.

Sooner or later, someone would end the threat she posed by snapping off her head or plucking out her heart.

Would that person be Jag? Would that time be now? Tonight?

Goddess help her, she had to get away from him.

She turned, shock squeezing her rib cage until she could hardly breathe, until she thought her body would cave in on itself, her heart imploding, turning her to dust.

Where would she go? She had nothing but the clothes on her back. Nothing.

She moved as if walking through ice water, each step a struggle as her body slowly went numb. With painful stiffness, she moved through the trees, traveling in no particular direction, with no destination. Only away. Away from the truth.

She never heard Jag approach. Whether he caught up to her on two feet or four, she didn't know, but suddenly fingers closed hard around her arm, jerking her fully around to face the man and the thunderous expression on his healing face.

"You nearly let me die!"

She blinked, not expecting those to be his first words after what he'd learned of her, but perhaps she should have. "It would have been so easy." The words escaped her lips, low and pained. "No one would have known. But I couldn't. I couldn't let you die to save myself."

"You damned, life-sucking bitch. I was ready to give my life for you!" He shoved her away from him, and she stumbled backward, barely staying on her feet.

"I know. I couldn't let you do that. Let me go, Jag. Let me walk away. You'll never hear from me again. I'll go someplace far from the Therians." Of course, far from the Therians there would be few to no draden. Her purpose would be lost. Her reason for living gone. Pain closed around her throat as she tried to speak. "No one will ever hear from me again."

Jag came at her slowly, every line in his body menacing. Part of her shouted at her to run, the part that wanted to live regardless of how hollow her life was destined to be.

But she didn't move. Jag wanted his pound of flesh, and she couldn't force herself to run from that. From him. With the Daemon venom still thick in her blood, she doubted she could run if she tried.

The dangerous anger in Jag's eyes had her pulse thundering in her ears, and she felt as if she were finally facing the fate that had hovered at the edges of her life since the night her mother died.

Jag stalked her, forcing her to back up or be pushed to the ground. Not until a tree slammed into her back did he halt his forward drive, his powerful male body towering over her, gleaming in the moonlight. Heat poured off him even as his expression turned to granite.

His hand shot out, pressing against the tree directly over her head. A little while ago she might have thought he needed to brace himself, but she sensed that the energy racing through his body was strong and whole. He'd fully recovered from the draden attack, except for the bites themselves.

His mouth twisted nastily. "No wonder you're faster and stronger than you should be. You steal the power from your opponents."

"I don't kill them. I never even hurt them." Tendrils of cold snaked and curled around her internal organs, freezing everything they touched. "I control it, Jag." Her voice sounded wooden. Flat, in direct counterpoint to the chaos tearing through her brain. "I've always controlled it." Almost always.

Deep inside her, a small desperate voice cried out. *Beg him not to tell. Beg him to keep your secret.* But no one did she trust less than this Feral. He would toy with her before he struck. Torment her. But strike he would, of that she had no doubt.

His other hand shot to her jaw and gripped it hard, forcing her face up to his. "You're the one I felt in the war room yesterday." He growled, a low, deadly sound. *"You were feeding off us."*

Olivia swallowed convulsively. "Yes. I often feed at low levels. It doesn't hurt anyone. No one's ever felt it before."

The hand gripping her jaw dropped to her throat, clamping hard as he lifted her onto her toes. Her heart began to thud. If he decided to end her life, he would. Her training and advantages were nothing compared to his raw strength and the power of his animal.

Draining him of his life force would take time. Ripping her head off her shoulders, not so much.

"Feed off me, now," he growled.

"No." The word croaked past the constriction of his hand.

He squeezed her neck until tears sprang to her eyes. "Do it!"

Her stomach twisted and knotted until she feared she was going to be sick. But she opened her senses and fed. Hard.

His hand spasmed. "Stop," he growled.

She stopped. His hold loosened, and she sucked air in too fast and went into a coughing spasm.

"Now feed at the level you did in the war room."

She looked up into cold, cold eyes. Swallowing hard against tears that tried to spring, she forced herself to feed at her normal, low-level grazing speed.

"It's different," he murmured, as if to himself. "Looks

like I'm the lucky one. You can't suck me dry without me knowing, can you?"

"No one has ever felt it before."

Slowly, he released her and took a step back, his arms crossing over his broad chest, his legs spread shoulder width, his sex lying thick and heavy against his thigh.

He cocked his head, his brows hard and angry as he watched her.

Olivia waited, sweat popping out on her brow, the tree at her back the only thing that kept her from collapsing beneath the weight of the disaster that threatened to destroy her.

"Looks like we have us a little situation here, doesn't it, Sugar?" Jag drawled. The sharp edge of deadly anger was gone from his voice, but the wickedness that replaced it raked cold fingers of dread down her spine. "What do you think will happen when everyone learns what you are?"

She stared at him, light-headed with shock and fear. "We both know what's going to happen."

"Damned straight, we do." Jag clucked his tongue, watching her with a look that turned increasingly cunning, heightening her dread. "Lyon might order you killed on the spot. He'll certainly have no more need of your services, and I guarantee he'll never let you near Feral House or the Radiant again. The Guard will kick you out. Can't have you sucking the boys dry, now can they?"

"I don't kill." She swallowed, the lie sticking in her throat. She hadn't killed in a long, long time.

"But you could. Hell, you could destroy them in their sleep, and they'd never know. If the Mage had gotten their hands on you, turned you, you could have been their greatest weapon. Except for one thing. I can feel when you're feeding."

Sweat began to dampen her tank top. He was too close, the anger pouring off him as he toyed with her.

"I'm not dangerous, Jag. I've been draden-kissed since I was seven."

That seemed to stun him, but not for long. He gave her a nasty smile. "You want me to keep your secret, Sugar?"

A small hope leaped inside her, then died. This was Jag. She could never trust him. Never.

"Maybe we'll have to come to a little understanding," he drawled.

Olivia raked her hand through her hair, resisting the urge to squeeze her eyes closed. *Goddess, I can't take this!* What did he want from her? How far would his torment go before he finally brought the guillotine down on her neck? "What kind of . . . understanding?"

A slow, predatory smile lifted his lips. "You do exactly what I say, Little Red."

"And . . . ?" What? He'd let her live or he wouldn't tell? There was a hell of a difference.

"And you'll do exactly what I say." His finger reached

out to trace a line from her throat down her chest to the edge of her tank. "Take off your clothes, Sugar. Every last scrap. Then get down on your hands and knees."

Her scalp crawled, anger and desperation twining within her. "I won't be your slave, Jag."

He closed the distance between them, his eyes daring her to do anything about it. His hand closed around her breast, and he squeezed hard, just short of hurting her. "You will be whatever I want you to be. You're mine now, Red. *Mine.*"

The word struck at her pride, infuriating her. Damn him. *Damn him.* As she stared into his cruel eyes, her pride railed. But hope flared red-hot and stayed her hand when all she wanted to do was strike him.

If she did what he wanted, would he keep her secret?

She could only guess. Jag did what Jag wanted and nothing more.

But what if he did? What if her capitulation, her whoring herself, kept him quiet?

No, she'd seen him in action. Capitulation wasn't what he wanted. He wanted conflict. Fight. He didn't want a placid whore. He would only be happy as long as he knew she hated every minute of everything he did to her.

Which would be no problem. None. Because it would only be the truth.

But would it be enough? And how long could she keep it up, keep him too interested in her to give her away?

As long as she had to.

She was playing with fire. Yet what choice did she have? Ostracism, maybe even death. Or Jag.

Her pride or her life.

There was no contest. No question. None.

As her gaze dropped to his thickening, lengthening sex, her fingers unbuttoned her pants.

Chapter Eight

Jag watched Olivia unfasten her pants, all too aware of the shaking of her fingers. Dammit.

Deep inside him, something balked. Even he had lines he refused to cross. He might be an ass, but he got no pleasure in another's pain. He stayed far away from the weak and the vulnerable.

And while there was nothing weak about this woman—hell, no—she'd just landed ass first in the vulnerable. Because he held her life in his hands now, and they both knew it. He didn't want her vulnerable. Mad as hell, yeah. He liked watching her eyes glitter with fury.

There were traces of anger in her eyes now, but that was it. Mostly she just looked shell-shocked.

Hell.

He opened his mouth to tell her to forget it, when she shrugged off her jacket and began to lift the hem of her tank. His mouth snapped shut as that creamy skin revealed itself, and the thoughts in his head dissipated, all but one.

He had to touch her.

His body grew hotter, longer, heavier moment by moment. Goddess, he couldn't have taken his gaze off her if his life depended on it. She was small, her movements stiff from the Daemon venom as well as her own reluctance, he was certain. Still, there was a sureness about her movements, an innate grace that drew him, pleasing his senses beyond anything reasonable.

She lifted her tank up and over her head, revealing ripe curves caught within the confines of a black sports bra. Her pale skin shone like alabaster in the moonlight, making his fingers curl into his fists as the need to touch her nearly overwhelmed him.

"What if the Daemon returns?" she asked him, her voice tight.

"I'll smell him long before he gets here." He tore his gaze from her creamy skin long enough to glance up at her face. Her eyes were focused on him, eyes aglow with wariness and razor-sharp resentment.

Draden-kissed. A pariah.

The knowledge rocketed through him all over again. Only in recent decades had the Therian council urged pity on those afflicted. It wasn't like they'd had any choice in the matter. You couldn't choose to be draden-kissed. You were simply one of the lucky few who hadn't died after being attacked. Though, in truth, few considered it lucky.

"How in the hell did you keep your secret when you were seven?"

He almost forgot to listen for her answer when her arms crossed in front of her, and she pulled her bra up and over her head, revealing the most perfect pair of breasts he'd ever seen.

Pure desire shot through his body as he stared at those full mounds, their nipples large and pink, begging to be sucked. And, goddess, he wanted to give them that.

"My father knew. The draden had killed my mother and my entire enclave, but he wasn't there that night. He kept me away from others and taught me to control my feeding."

"It's phenomenal you didn't kill him."

Her mouth compressed. "I did. Not right away, but eventually I made a mistake, and I did."

Shit. The guilt she must be living with. "When were you draden-kissed?"

"Fifteenth century."

Now he stared. "Six hundred years . . . and no one knows?"

"No one but you has ever been able to feel me feed.

My control is excellent. I'm no danger, Jag. I haven't been a danger to anyone in a very long time."

He was in no mood for empathizing.

"No danger, Sugar? You damned near let me die!" Dammit, he'd been terrified. Not for himself. He honestly didn't give a rat's ass about himself. But thinking he was going to watch her die had sent him tumbling into his nightmares, into those dreams he'd had every fucking night after Cordelia died. Into a place he never wanted to go back to again.

He'd thought the draden were going to kill Olivia, and hard as he'd tried, he couldn't do anything to stop it. Yet she hadn't needed saving. And she hadn't said a word.

Damn her.

She lifted one foot after the other, untying and removing boots and socks, then slowly unzipped her pants, pushing them down over slender hips to reveal a small scrap of black lace. She pushed the pants down her legs and stepped out of them. But as her fingers went to that tantalizing black lace, he stopped her.

"Leave the panties on."

She just stared at him. "Won't they be in your way?"

"Eventually. I'll get rid of them when they are."

She lifted her chin, the warrior beaten, but not broken. Never broken. "Are you into rape, Jag?"

"It won't be rape, Sugar. You're going to be begging me to fuck you before I'm done with you."

"That does not mean I'm ever going to want you."

"You'll want my body. You'll beg for the release I can bring you." He stepped toward her, closing the distance between them. Even before he touched her, the lush, warm scent of her filled his senses, turning his limbs weak, his cock hard. His fingers curved around one firm, perfect breast, and another breath of fire shot between his legs. "I told you I'd have you on your knees before me, didn't I? Now, Red. On your hands and knees like an obedient little slave."

Anger sparked in her eyes, but it was a fury banked by resignation. He had her up against the wall, and she knew it. Her life now sat firmly in his hands.

Slowly, her eyes blazing into his the entire way, she knelt on the ground, then bent over onto all fours as he'd ordered.

Jag sank to his knees beside her, unable to keep his hands off her a moment longer. As his fingers slid over the creamy skin of her back, then curved around, cupping one round breast, his own hands began to shake.

Never had he needed to touch a woman this badly. Olivia might be on her knees before him. But he was beginning to wonder which of them was truly the one enslaved.

The ground was rough beneath Olivia's palms and knees—pine needles and dead leaves scratching at her skin. The night air breezed coolly over her bare flesh, but the shiver that tore over her had nothing to do with cold.

Inside, she quaked.

Everything she'd built, everything she'd fought for now lay in the hands of a man she couldn't trust.

Her pride railed, hating him for forcing her to her knees. The sex itself was of little import. She was Therian. For goddess's sake, they had sex all the time. All the time. She'd taken every man in her ranks into her body at least once and most dozens, even hundreds of times. But never because she'd had to. Never because she'd had no choice. Never because her life hung in the balance.

Jag said he wouldn't rape her, and she believed him. She'd felt that hand of his and knew all he had to do was touch her, and she'd be wet and open and ready for him.

No, it wasn't the fact that he intended to have sex with her that she couldn't forgive. It was the fact that she had no choice.

She tried to ignore the large, warm hand covering her breast, but she was far from immune to him, no matter how badly she wanted to be. An attraction existed between them more explosive than anything she'd known for as far back as she could remember.

He stroked her back with one hand, his fingers warm and surprisingly gentle as if he enjoyed the feel of her skin. With his other hand, he kneaded her breast, his touch firm and hot.

She glanced over her shoulder at him and found him watching her with a rapt intensity that sent fire racing through her blood. His hand moved down her spine and back up again, then back down and lower, sliding over her panties and down her thigh, avoiding her moist center. Over and over, he touched her with gentle strokes as if he were a blind man memorizing every inch of her body. His fingers curled around her shoulders, stroked the back of her neck, then slowly slid back down her spine while his other hand played with her breast, gripping, rolling her nipple between his finger and thumb, tugging gently.

Though he touched her, he never once pressed his palm against her, shooting that unnatural pleasure into her. No, the pleasure he gave her was all too real.

High on her shoulder blade, she felt the brush of whiskers and the soft press of his mouth. A shiver went through her as she realized he was tracing the Daemon's claw marks. He was kissing her healed wounds, creating a sweet ache inside her that was not of the flesh but the spirit.

Inexplicably, tears sprang to her eyes. She found herself beginning to relax beneath his caresses, her body moving sensuously with each stroke of his hand.

Dammit, she didn't want to be moved by his gentleness. She didn't want to enjoy his domination.

"Jag . . ."

"Getting impatient, Sugar?" His finger slid between her legs, a single soft stroke that touched her sensitive flesh, eliciting a moan she couldn't bite back. His fingers slid beneath the back elastic of her panties and down, cupping one cheek.

She tensed for the onslaught of pleasure she was sure he'd attack her with, but he did nothing but rub her bare flesh. Even so, the pleasure came, hot and real. He released her breast and with both hands, pushed her panties down her hips to her thighs. Both hands caressed her buttocks, kneading her, parting her. With a single finger, he traced the line between, from the base of her spine down over her anus, sliding to where she was hot and wet and open, then back up, trailing the moisture.

"Do you want me to take you, Red?"

"No. Never." Her words were breathless, her body at once delighting in the feel of his hands, and tense.

His finger stroked the swollen, weeping opening of her vagina. "Wrong answer, Sugar."

"Go to hell."

But he continued to play with her, sliding his finger around the edges until her body ached with a white-hot need, and she had to clamp her jaw shut to keep from moaning.

"Your body tells a different story," he said huskily. And then he was behind her, and she prepared for him to mount her with a combination of dread and rich, hot anticipation.

She felt his thick, hard cock between her legs, but instead of pushing inside her, he ran it along the same path his finger had taken moments before, touching her but not penetrating. Then he shoved the length of it between her legs and rubbed it against her hot, swollen, aching flesh.

She struggled to keep from pressing against him to increase the delicious pressure.

"You want me." Jag's voice sounded as tight and strained as her body felt.

"No."

"Liar. Beg me to fuck you, Red, and take us both out of our misery."

"No. I'll never beg you. Never want you."

"A challenge, eh?" His voice turned hard and rough. But his touch remained gentle as his hands framed her bare hips. His palms pressed against her, and, suddenly, heat rushed into her hips, into her rear and thighs and deep within the hot center of her, making her swell with a need that turned almost painful.

"Jag," she gasped. His cock remained pressed between her legs, but not inside her, and she tried to rock against it, but the thick length moved with her. "Oh, God."

"Beg, Red."

"No." But the word had become nothing but habit, now, and pride. Her body begged. She needed him inside her. Deep, deep inside.

The pleasure kept rushing into her, turning her nearly mindless from the need for release from the building, swirling tempest. Her hips rocked violently, out of control, needing. Wanting.

"Jag."

"Say the words, Red."

"No." But the knowledge she would eventually lose this battle was all that kept her sane. She didn't know how much longer she could hold out, and the thought of her defeat brought nothing but a fierce, carnal joy.

His hands left her hips to cup her breasts, at first simply playing with them, tugging at her nipples, but then he pressed warmth into her there, too. The pleasure made her cry out, the fire of need flaming higher.

Again, he shifted his hands. As she gasped from the onslaught, he slid one hand between her thighs and pressed hard against her swoller. center. Her breath caught and held, her body tensing for the rush of cataclysmic pleasure she knew would come.

But nothing happened. He simply cupped her, his hand unmoving.

"What do you want, Red?" he asked softly, his voice as full and aching as her body felt.

"You . . . to go to hell." She could hardly breathe through the exquisite anticipation.

He chuckled low. "You want me to stand up and walk away?"

"Yes." Oh, God, no. "Could you? Could you get up and walk away right now?"

"Get up, maybe. Walk? Not on your life. I'm not a liar, Red. I'm in pain. Your sweet little ass, your soft as-silk skin. I can smell your need as rich as the sweetest cream. I want you, Olivia. And I know you want me, too. But I'm not taking you until you beg me."

"I'm not going to beg you."

"Yeah. You will." With that, he drove the pleasure straight up into her core. She screamed, and he pulled away, the orgasm shooting up, then crumbling, leaving her rocking with desperate need.

"Jag."

"Want me to do that again?"

"No!" She wouldn't survive any more of this.

"What do you want me to do, then?"

"Fuck me, dammit. Fuck me!"

"I thought so." He grabbed her hips and drove himself deep inside her, and she came, the release exploding with contraction after glorious contraction. Over and over, he thrust inside her, then out, then in again while he held her hips. Through his palms, he pressed that warm, lush pleasure into her, the unnatural heat melding with the natural pleasure his body gave her until she was gasping, coming and coming and coming while he released. Then again. And again.

Never had she known anything like it, and when he finally pulled out of her, she collapsed onto her side on the ground, utterly spent.

She pressed her arm to her forehead and looked up at Jag kneeling beside her, framed by the moonlit canopy of trees. His expression lay hidden in shadow, but she heard his own erratic breathing and sensed a disquiet in him that rivaled her own. What in the hell had just happened? He'd demanded her capitulation, yet seduced her with hot, gentle touches as he stubbornly waited for her acquiescence. Then he'd given her more pleasure than any man ever had.

The minutes stretched silently between them as their breathing slowly recovered.

Jag broke the fragile connection, rising and turning away with a scowl. "Get up and get dressed, Olivia." His voice was clipped, humorless, the gentleness gone as if it had never been. "We have a Daemon to catch." The voice of a warrior.

She stared at him, uncertain whether he'd given her a gift, in an unspoken promise to keep her secret. Or just latched a choke chain around her throat. She struggled to her feet, her body still throbbing, still slow from the effects of the Daemon venom.

Emotions battered her as she pulled on her ripped clothing. The ever-present fear that Jag only played with her, that the moment he had the chance, he'd out her. And the strange elation that came from a powerful sexual experience with a man determined to bring her pleasure. Incredible pleasure. A man she couldn't trust on any level and didn't even like most of the time, though, heaven help her, she liked his hands. She'd be lying if she said she didn't.

Dressed, she sat on the ground and pulled on her socks and boots, then rose and faced him.

He watched her from the shadows with an intensity she could feel but couldn't read. An intensity that, even now, had her pulse elevating and quickening. Not with fear, though certainly she should be feeling that, too. But with desire.

All her life, she'd fought for control, yet that was the very thing he'd stolen from her. She wondered now if she'd ever get it back or if her life were doomed to be forever cast into chaos.

Fate had closed in on her at long last.

Chapter Nine

On four legs, Kougar ran up the steep hillside, deep in the woods, until certain he was completely alone. He could have no audience for what he meant to do.

In the thickest part of the forest, he shifted back into a man and prepared himself for an encounter he'd long been dreading. With a deep breath, he closed his eyes and looked inward, deep inside to the very core of the ice that had long ago stolen his ability to feel anything intensely. In that cold, cold center, he searched for, and found, the brittle filaments of a connection long severed. Focusing on those bright, icy tendrils, he sent out the call, a silent demand for an audience.

Queen Ariana! While no true telepathy took place

in his man form, this call wasn't a communication as much as a demand. *Heed me!*

But he felt no change in the breeze, saw no shimmer and sparkle of refracted crystals in the air.

Ariana! Over and over, he made the demand, pounding at that invisible door until his mind felt beaten with exhaustion. But just as it became clear his attempt to contact the Ilinas would be in vain, a strong, telltale scent of pine teased his nose, telling him his call had been answered.

But when he turned, he found not the queen standing before him but two of her minions. His mind flickered annoyance, but his emotions remained unengaged, as always. The pair of petite warriors stood side by side, two of the queen's elite private guard, each dressed in the usual uniform—a brown tunic and flesh-colored breeches, soft leather boots, and a knife strapped at her waist.

"Melisande. Brielle. I sought Ariana, but you'll do."

"What do you want, Kougar?" Melisande asked, her thick blond braid draped across one slender shoulder. Though her features had a delicate cast, her bright blue eyes were hard as flint.

Kougar lifted a cold eyebrow. "You forbid me entrance to the Crystal Realm?"

"You are not welcome. Queen Ariana grants you no audience. You're lucky she lets you live at all, Feral, knowing what you know."

A fact of which he was all too aware. He'd often pondered why she hadn't made an attempt on his life.

His gaze focused on Melisande. "Are you aware the Mage have freed three wraith Daemons from the blade?"

The woman's only reaction was a tiny jerk backward, but the move told him enough. She hadn't known.

"The traps won't work without Ilina blood and magic. I've tried. I need your help. Join with me to catch them."

Melisande's face hardened. "The Daemons are not our concern. We're no longer of your world."

"That's a lie, and we both know it." Kougar took a step forward, but the pair held their ground. "If Satanan's freed, it's only a matter of time before he discovers your secret. You're fooling yourselves to believe otherwise."

"Involving ourselves in your battle could compromise our safety. I'll not allow it, Feral." Melisande's eyes flashed with threat. "The safety of my race is a responsibility I take very, very seriously."

"Thousands, perhaps millions will die if Satanan rises again."

"That's not my concern."

"Your queen would have cared once."

"Many things that once were are no more."

Kougar's hand flexed with the need to grab her, to steal her blood and force her compliance, but the act would be useless. The moment he reached for her, she would simply turn to mist.

As if reading his mind, or his wish, the pair lost form, turning transparent, floating before him like spirits. "Go, Kougar. And don't come back. The next time, your summons will not be answered." As one they disappeared.

Kougar went feral, clawing the air where the women had stood moments before in a move that reeked of emotion.

Seeking the help of the Ilinas had been a waste of time. The Daemons were going to remain on the rampage, the traps useless.

They were going to have to find another way.

From beneath the trees, Jag watched Olivia finish dressing, the moonlight glinting in her hair. When she was done, he pulled on the power of his animal and shifted into his jaguar, the exquisite pleasure of the magic that raced through him a pale shadow of the rich enjoyment he'd experienced inside Olivia's hot little body.

The pleasure that had continued to pulse through his man's body dissipated with the shift but continued to resonate through his mind. Touching her, entering her, feeling her release break over him again and again had been an extraordinary experience, as different from his usual sexual encounters as fine whiskey to flat beer. Being inside her had felt . . . right. That was the only word he could think of. As if all this time he'd been looking for the lock that fit his key, and he'd finally found her.

Never had he been this hot for a woman. Never had his release been so complete. He loved the feel of her skin beneath his fingertips and against his lips, almost as much as he loved the way she fought him. She'd refused to give them what they'd both wanted right up until she couldn't fight it a second more. Then he'd buried himself inside her and released again and again and again. Never had it been like that for him, his body so fucking wound up he couldn't stop coming.

And all he could think of was doing it all again. Which was precisely the reason he'd pulled out and ordered her to get a move on.

As he watched her dress, her soft hair swinging against her cheek, drawing his gaze to her mouth, he felt a weakness inside his man's mind, a wish to take her into his arms. To kiss her.

But, although he loved sex, there was something about kissing he'd never embraced. Something too . . . intimate . . . about it. Mouth to mouth, eye to eye. Kissing took a level of closeness, of tenderness, he gave no woman.

So it disturbed him that he wanted to give it to Olivia.

He pushed the uncomfortable thoughts away as he watched her pull on the leather jacket with the Daemon-claw-size holes in the back and arm.

Just what had that thing done to her? Daemon venom. Who knew that Daemons had venom in their claws? It had been so long since any had terrorized the Earth, they had nothing to go on but legend and superstition, which left them in total guessing territory when it came to what Daemons could really do.

As soon as he got back to the Hummer and his phone, he'd have to find some cell service and let the others know what they'd learned.

Ready? he asked her. When she nodded, he took off through the woods at a human-friendly pace. She quickly caught up to him, then walked at a quick clip at his side.

He swung his cat's gaze toward her. *Have you recovered from that Daemon attack?*

"Mostly."

Describe it to me. What did he do to you?

"I think he partially paralyzed me. I could move my arm, but it felt heavy. Numb. I still feel slow, like I weigh three times what I did, but I can move."

No other side effects?

"Not that I'm aware of. I'm feeling better and better, so I think it's working its way out of my system. I can still fight, Jag. If we see him again, I can absolutely fight."

Strong. The word went through his head over and over when he thought of her. And he hadn't once stopped thinking about her, not since he first saw her.

Shit, she'd killed her own father yet didn't seem to be bothered about it at all. Granted, it had happened half a millennium ago, but still. You didn't get over crap like that. It became part of who you were, digging claws into you day and night for the rest of your fucking life.

Maybe the guy had been a bastard. Maybe he'd tried to hurt her. Or execute her as was once the fate of all draden-kissed.

It was none of his business, but the questions preyed on his mind until he finally asked.

Did you mean to kill your father?

"Of course not. I loved him more than anything. He was all I had."

How do you live with guilt like that? Did you finally just get over it?

She remained silent for so long, he began to think she wouldn't answer.

"You never get over it. Not a day goes by that I don't miss him, that I don't regret the lapse in control that killed him. But I eventually learned to forgive myself, to look forward instead of back."

He thought of her words on the drive out here, how she'd accused him of hating himself as she once had hated herself. He got it, now, what she must have gone through.

But it still had nothing to do with him.

They'd gone only a short distance when that god-awful scent of Daemon slammed into his nostrils again, yanking him back to the present. *Got his scent.*

"I feel something, too. A tingling of energy. It's just a shadow of what I felt when the Daemon showed up, but maybe he left a trail for me to follow."

Good. Let's get this sucker, Red.

The twin trails followed one another exactly, telling him they were on the right track, even as the paths waxed and waned. The night was quiet, the moon playing hide-and-seek with the clouds above, but his vision remained perfect either way. There were no humans around that he had to be careful of, and if the draden attacked again, it wouldn't matter.

The knowledge brought with it a strange relief. They'd each fight the suckers with their own unique gifts. Olivia could safely draw them to her while he stayed in his animal, ready to pounce. They'd make a damn good fighting team. For now.

What in the hell was he going to do with her? Lyon would be royally pissed if Jag brought her back to Feral House without warning him what she was. Hell, the Chief would be pissed if he brought her anywhere near his Ferals at all.

Olivia claimed she had complete control, but anyone draden-kissed was extremely dangerous if she ever wanted to be. Except she couldn't feed, couldn't harm anyone, without him knowing. Which meant that as long as he stayed close enough to stop her, she couldn't harm anyone at all.

And they needed her. At least for now. She was a good little fighter, a well-trained warrior with some special skills that just might come in handy against their enemies.

Eventually, he'd have no choice but to out her. As much as he enjoyed riling Lyon, keeping this kind of secret was an offense Lyon would never forgive.

In the meantime, though, Olivia was his.

Olivia hurried along beside the jaguar, jogging to keep up, which was fine with her. The night wouldn't last, and she had a score to settle with that Daemon.

If only the venom would finish working its way out of her system. The lethargy continued to tug at her limbs, though not as badly as before. Ironically, despite the heaviness in her limbs, she felt stronger, more powerful than ever thanks to the Daemon life force she'd ingested,

How often do you need to feed? Jag asked after they'd covered a good three miles.

"The energy of half a dozen draden will fill me for hours. Around Therians or humans, it depends on how many there are and how emotional the situation. I have to be particularly careful with humans. If there aren't a lot of them around, I can take very little."

How often do you kill them?

"I haven't killed anyone by accident since my father. At least not that I know of."

You've killed on purpose?

"Of course. What warrior hasn't?"

True. You use your . . . gift . . . in addition to your weapons?

"If I can drain an opponent without collateral damage to others, I'll weaken him. But I can only direct my feeding to one person if I grab him and hold on."

Too bad. A concentrated shot like that could be a powerful weapon. You ever killed someone just because they needed killing? It would be easy to do, wouldn't it?

She didn't answer right away. The question dug up old memories she'd rather leave buried. But the freedom to talk honestly for the first time in centuries proved too powerful, and she found herself telling him.

"After my father died, I was terrified of making another mistake, of killing another Therian, so I continued to live alone." She swallowed. "I became prey to humans, of course. To men."

Shit. Did you kill the bastards before they . . . ?

"No. The first time, I didn't know what they wanted. I thought they were being kind when they invited me to join their camp, and I was so lonely."

They raped you.

"Yes. I could have killed them, but I hated myself so badly for killing my father, it felt right somehow. Like the goddess had finally delivered the retribution I deserved. I let it happen again and again, putting myself in the paths of rough or drunken men, seeking that punishment."

How old were you when this started?

"Seventeen."

Olivia. I'm sorry. The pain in his tone surprised her, the honesty in his words wrapping around her like a protective cocoon. If he'd been there, back then, he'd have killed them for what they'd done to her. Somehow she knew that.

Her story had prodded those protective instincts of his into play, the same ones that had come to Pink's defense. Once more, her instincts told her that beneath the bad-boy façade lived a decent man.

She eyed the cat thoughtfully. He'd been determined to make her bend to his will when he ordered her to strip and get down on hands and knees. Then he'd been nothing but gentle. Demanding, yes. Teasing her sensually until she begged him to take her. Determined to have his way.

But he'd given her nothing but pleasure.

Her pride might be bruised, but her body felt warm and sated.

Jag pulled up. *Do you smell that, Red?*

Something scratched at her nose, a scent like garbage, only worse.

"Is that the Daemon?"

I'm sure of it. Ten bucks says it's coming from that house.

Olivia blinked and looked around. "What house?" She saw nothing but trees rising from a bed of thick underbrush.

The jaguar swung his head toward her, eyeing her with interest before returning his gaze to whatever had caught his attention. Magic rippled over her skin as he shifted back into a man, his powerful body gleaming in the moonlight.

"So now we *know* it's coming from that house. That's damn powerful warding if it's blocking even Therian senses."

Olivia looked at him with surprise, goose bumps lifting on her arms. "Where's the house? How far?"

"About twenty yards in front of you."

"No way." Trees. Nothing but trees. "Since when do the Mage possess the kind of power it takes to hide a house from a Therian?"

"Since their leader, Inir, got infected with dark spirit and has apparently tapped into some serious magic. The Mage are resurrecting all kinds of bad shit that's been lost for thousands of years. Most of it associated with dark power."

"Why can you see the house and not me?"

He gave her a smug little smile. "I'm a Feral. Fucking Superman." His hand caressed her buttocks. "Haven't you figured that out yet?"

Absently, she pushed his hand away, troubled by the fact that she could have walked right into that Mage stronghold and never realized it until it was too late.

She looked around, chills crawling up her spine. Were invisible Mage watching them even now? They could be anywhere, and she'd never know.

Her gaze flew to Jag's. "Tell me what you see."

"I can show you." The gleam in his eye told her exactly how he meant to do that. Sexual release opened the Therian mind to magic in ways nothing else could.

Goddess, her body still hadn't recovered from the last sensual onslaught. The last thing she needed right now was a repeat.

His eyes turned wicked. "I'll make it quick, but you're going to have to control those sexy little cries of yours, or we'll have them all over us."

She wanted to deny him, she really did. But she wanted to see the Mage more.

With a disgruntled sigh, she held out her hand. "Make it quick."

"Then spread your legs for me, Sugar. I'll go straight to your sweet spot."

Olivia clenched her jaw. "I don't have to pull down my pants?"

"Not unless you want to."

"I don't." Releasing a groan of disgust, she spread her legs.

Jag met her gaze, a smile pulling at his lips. Then he

moved behind her, sliding his hand over her mouth.

"Just a precaution," he said quietly, as his thumb stroked her cheek.

Leaning over her shoulder, he slid his other hand between her legs and cupped her.

"Watch straight ahead," he said against her temple.

She tensed, holding her breath for the rush of heat, and didn't have long to wait. Pleasure poured into her sensitive flesh on a river of delicious fire, her legs turning to rubber. Jag's hand held her up, pulling her tight against his body and the erection growing stiffer by the minute at her back. As the orgasm rushed up from the depths of her core, the moan exploded in her head, barely muffled by Jag's hand. It broke over her with a startling power, clenching and spasming inside her as he held her close.

"Look, Red. Look!"

She forced her eyes to focus despite the storm of pleasure ripping her body apart, and gasped in shock as a house appeared out of thin air.

As Jag had said, not twenty yards ahead of her stood a large, rickety, run-down house with dirty white siding and a wraparound porch, one section of which appeared to be rotted through. And smack-dab in front, on the dirt track that served as a drive, stood the red pickup truck.

Her body tensed, and she shook her head until Jag pulled his hand from her mouth and settled it, warm and firm, on her breast. Without thinking, she arched into his touch, her body still riding the effects of release.

"That's the truck I was following earlier," she whispered.

His hand slid out from between her legs to caress her abdomen, his hand vibrating as if he were shaking. He pressed his cheek against her temple, his voice low and pained. "You have no idea what it does to me to make you come."

Tucked tight between them, his thick erection twitched and throbbed.

"I have some idea," she said huskily.

Heat swirled around them, the fire unquenched despite her roaring release. She'd fought and fought against giving in to him the first time, but if their situation weren't so dangerous, she knew she'd be begging him to come inside her again.

Slowly, reluctantly, Jag's hands fell away and he stepped to her side. His erection stood straight out from his body, hard as oak and thick as her wrist.

"Looks painful," she murmured.

"Want to suck me off?"

Deliberate crudeness with which he intended to wedge some distance between them again. She had him figured out well enough.

But as she stared at that gorgeous thickness, desire to do just that—to take him deep in her mouth—flowed hot and rich inside her.

He lifted a lock of her hair and twisted it around his finger, tugging gently. "You keep looking at it like that, and there won't be any sucking necessary."

"Rain check?" she asked softly, lifting her gaze to his.

His brows lifted, a smile tugging at his mouth. "Every time I think I have you figured out, you surprise me."

She found herself smiling. "I'm aware of that."

His eyes lit with laughter, and he tugged on her hair. "So sure of yourself, are you?" Releasing her hair, his hand cupped her jaw, his thumb sliding across her ultrasensitive bottom lip. "We'll continue this discussion later. This is neither the time nor the place." He held out his hand to her and she hesitated only a moment before taking it. "Let's take a look around."

Jag led her through the brush and trees, keeping well back from the tree line where they wouldn't be seen if someone looked out one of the windows. There were lights on inside, but the curtains were drawn, and Olivia could see nothing.

As one, they froze as two Mage sentinels turned the corner and strode across the front of the house. Guards, no doubt.

When the Mage pair had their backs turned to them, Jag led her through the woods, circling the house slowly, then stopped so quickly she ran into him, her shoulder pressing against the warmth of his arm.

She didn't waste breath on questions. Instead, her gaze followed his to the two thick posts standing in the middle of the backyard. Attached to them appeared to be slabs of meat of some kind.

Her gaze narrowed as she pondered the why. Were they trying to attract some kind of animal?

But as her mind caught up to her gaze, she noticed the single boot hanging from the end of one bloody strip. With a hard blast of cold, she understood. Gagging, she turned her head, pressing her forehead against Jag's shoulder. A shaking bare shoulder that had turned suddenly cool and clammy.

"Motherfuckers," Jag snarled beside her. "They're using the humans as Daemon bait."

Her head began to throb as it always did in the face of stark cruelty. The humans would have been strung up alive, since Daemons fed on fear and pain. Were these the men she'd followed out of Wal-Mart? Was it their flesh hanging there, now? Dear goddess. She struggled for control, for the warrior toughness she'd learned so long ago.

Jag snatched his hand from hers, a low animalistic growl rumbling from his throat.

Olivia lifted her head, noting the fangs that had sprouted from his human mouth.

"Easy, Feral. You can't take them on alone, though goddess knows I want to help you. Especially when we don't know what they're capable of anymore." She ran her hand over his back in slow, calming strokes. "Ease down, Jag."

Slowly, his fangs retreated, and he looked at her with furious eyes. A fury not turned on her. "There could be others in there who are still alive."

"We'll call for reinforce . . ."

Jag's hand shot to her shoulder, quieting her as the door to the house opened. They watched as two people walked down the steps, a man and a woman dressed in sorcerer's robes. The same auburn-haired woman she'd seen in the parking lot of Wal-Mart.

As the woman reached the bottom step, she stumbled.

The man's hand shot out to steady her. "Mystery?"

The woman—Mystery?—waved her hand at him impatiently, her bearing cool and confident despite her near spill. "I'm fine. How long has it been gone?"

"Ten minutes. These two didn't last long."

The witch barely glanced at the corpses. Instead, her gaze went to the eaves of the house where dark orbs hung crackling with barely visible lightning.

"Long enough," she murmured.

"The power orbs are full?"

"They appear to be, yes." An expression of satisfaction settled across her face. "Raw Daemon energy. The most powerful force on Earth."

"Do you think it'll be enough?" The male sorcerer's

subservient bearing told Olivia he was the underling of the pair.

"There's no way to know. The last one to attempt this was Satanan himself. The project will be complete when it's complete."

As the male pulled down the orbs, the two guards came around the corner.

Mystery motioned to the corpses hanging from the posts. "Dispose of these." As one of the guards bowed, she continued. "Is there time before dawn for one more feeding?"

"No, Sorceress. Dawn will be upon us within a pair of hours. The Daemon will not be back this night."

"Very well." She turned and climbed the stairs back into the house.

Olivia turned to Jag at the same moment he turned to her. They're worried gazes collided. "What do you think the project is?" she asked in a whisper.

"Hell if I know. But if the last one to attempt it was Satanan, we can be sure of one thing. If they succeed, we're in deep trouble."

Chapter Ten

They walked back to the Hummer in silence, Jag in his jaguar-house-cat form since dawn had broken. The eastern sky glowed the color of fresh blood.

Olivia opened the back door of the Hummer, and the cat jumped in. She closed the door behind him as a maintenance truck rumbled by on the road below, then climbed into the front passenger seat. Behind her, magic erupted on a surge of sparkling lights. She felt it tingle along the surface of her skin, a pleasant sensation, and glanced back to find Jag a man once more, shoving one powerful leg after another into his pants. He raised his hips to pull the pants over his buttocks, his manparts lifting as if in offering. For once, it seemed to be her mind, not his, caught in an endless sexual loop. Leaving his pants unzipped, he pulled the T-shirt over his head, pulling it down like a second skin to mold his muscular torso.

Beneath one tight sleeve, his armband curled, the jaguar's eyes seeming to watch her.

Jag climbed out of the vehicle and opened the driver's door, zipping his pants before reentering.

As he started the Hummer, Olivia tipped her head back and closed her eyes, all that had happened tonight crashing over her in a massive wave that threatened to sweep her feet out from under her. Jag knew she was draden-kissed. At first, she'd been utterly certain he'd give her away, but she just didn't know anymore. The more she thought she understood him, the more of an enigma he became.

When the draden attacked, he could so easily have saved himself simply by shifting, but instead he'd nearly sacrificed his life trying to save her. Beneath the crappy attitude stood a man of rare honor and courage. A good man, though she felt certain he didn't see himself as such.

But would that honor drive him to keep her secret? Or to give her away? She couldn't know, and she feared the answer.

A soft tug on her hair had her turning her head to find Jag watching her.

"You okay?" For once, no devilment lit his eyes, only genuine concern. "Is that venom out of your system?"

As she looked into those warm, dark eyes, something happened. The solid, emotional ground beneath her feet gave way, and she felt herself falling. Tumbling.

Olivia wrenched her gaze away, staring at nothing as her heart pounded in her chest. Goddess. What was the matter with her?

Lifting an unsteady hand, she pushed the hair back from her face and took a deep, calming breath before answering him. "The venom is mostly gone. My arm still feels a little weird, a little sore, but otherwise, I'm fine."

He reached for her, his hand cupping her upper arm where the tear in her jacket exposed the bare flesh newly healed from the Daemon attack. She tensed, uncertain what he meant to do with that palm, but felt only his thumb stroking the aching echoes of claw wounds, easing the lingering pain.

"Better or worse?" he asked quietly.

She hazarded a glance at him, worried she'd tumble all over again, but he'd turned to the front. "Better. Thank you."

As he put the vehicle into gear and pulled out onto the road, she studied the strong lines of his profile. Without a doubt he was a fine-looking male.

"Where are we going?"

"The motel."

His warm fingers continued to caress her arm, and she let her eyes drift close, but her mind refused to be still. What would she do if Jag did report her as being draden-kissed? She'd have no choice but to run. Or try to run. Getting away from Jag would be no easy feat.

Dammit, she was so tired. Decade after decade, century after century, she'd held her secret tight, terrified someone would discover it. Terrified her life would be over.

And if she ran, it would be. Maybe not literally. Maybe if she took off, she wouldn't be tracked and killed. But her life would be over all the same. Her home in the Guard barracks lost to her. Her friends, her team, her purpose . . . all gone.

If she stayed and played Jag's game? Maybe she'd end up dead. But it wouldn't be at Jag's hands. If he were going to kill her, he'd have already done it. Unless, of course, she tried to hurt him or his.

If she could just get him to keep her secret a little longer. Long enough for her to help him catch that Daemon. Long enough for them to figure out what the Mage were up to and stop them.

Maybe long enough for her life to have a little more purpose. The pull of self-preservation was strong in all creatures, no less in her, but her father hadn't sacrificed everything for her to save herself. He'd given her a chance to make a difference. Whether or not that had truly been his intent didn't matter. It was the way she'd always seen it. It was the only way she could accept that he'd let her live at his own peril, the only way she could live with it.

She'd never truly been able to use her gift to any great advantage simply because she'd always had to hide it.

With Jag, she didn't.

The realization hit her, filling her with a strange and profound relief. After so many years, she was no longer alone with her secret.

Jag released her arm, pulled out his cell phone, and snapped it open. "It's me," he said a moment later.

Olivia tensed.

"Found us a Daemon," he continued. "Did you know those bastards have venom in their claws?" He was silent a moment. "Olivia took a hit. It slowed her down, but didn't seem to do anything more. We also found us a nice little Mage pit complete with sorcerers, sentinels, and some of the biggest power orbs I've ever seen."

He was silent a moment. When he spoke again, his voice had turned warrior hard. "Shit, yeah. They're definitely up to something. There's only one reason I can think of they'd want Daemon power." A pause. "You got it, Frosted Flakes. This is another attempt to free the Daemons."

Jag continued to hold the phone to his ear though he didn't say anything for a while. Olivia could hear Tighe's voice through the receiver, but not clearly enough to make out what he was saying.

"Aye, aye," Jag drawled at last. "Call when you hit town." He snapped the phone closed and tossed it onto the dash. "The gang's coming for a visit."

Olivia eyed him. "All of them?"

"Tighe's team and Kougar's. They've been tracking two different Daemons, and both trails seem to be leading this way."

"As if the Mage are calling them."

"That's what I think, Red. And what I also think is the Mage are trying to use them to free Satanan. Tighe agrees that our mission just changed. Stopping whatever the Mage are up to takes priority over the Daemons. If we can take down both at once, all the better."

He turned into the parking lot of the motel. "The plan is for everyone to meet here at two this afternoon."

"We'll attack in broad daylight?"

Jag pulled into a parking spot, turned off the ignition, and turned to study her, his mouth kicking up on one side. "Well now, Sugar, you're the only one, other than us Ferals, who doesn't have to worry about the draden. With three Therians on the team, the logical choice is daylight."

He was back in full Jag persona. The man who'd quietly and gently asked her if she was all right had slipped back beneath the mask.

Jag opened his door and climbed out, and Olivia did the same. They grabbed their duffels out of the back of the Hummer, and she followed him up the outside stairs to their second-story room—a simple, but clean one, with two double beds.

Olivia set down her duffel beside the bed closest to the door, pulled back the bedspread, then shucked her boots and crawled beneath the covers. She was spent, physically, mentally, and emotionally, but as she closed her eyes, a thought had her jerking upright.

Her gaze shot to Jag as he pulled off his boots with less haste than she had. "I don't usually feed in my sleep, but I'm so tired, I may tonight. It won't hurt you. I sleep near others all the time, and they've never even been tired come morning, but you may feel it."

He paused in what he was doing, meeting her gaze, his thoughts impossible to read. Then he pulled off his pants and T-shirt and lay down on the other bed on his side, propping his head on one hand. "When you feed hard, it's like needles. When you feed low, it's just a pleasant hum in my body. It shouldn't bother me."

She nodded. "That's good."

He continued to watch her, as if studying her. "I've been wondering about something, Olivia. Why didn't you let me die out there tonight? As you said, it would have been so easy. And a simple matter of self-preservation. Your secret would have been safe."

There were so many answers to that question, more than she had the energy to sort through at the moment, so she gave him the first one that came to mind.

"I want no more deaths on my conscience."

His mouth quirked up on one side, in a surprisingly self-deprecating smile. "Not even mine?"

"Especially not yours." She wasn't sure what made her say the last.

Jag stared at her, his gaze turning thick and intense, pulling her in. Then he scowled and flipped over onto his back and closed his eyes.

"Sleep, Red." His voice held a gruffness, not reflected in his words. "You won't hurt me without my knowing. We're both safe for now."

She watched him a moment more, then lay down and pulled the covers up to her chin.

Safe. An odd choice of words since she'd never felt less safe in her life. Yet she fell asleep without trouble, a certainty deep inside that if Jag said she was safe, he would let no harm come to her.

For now.

Jag blinked at the sight of the village square, his heart plummeting. A thousand times he'd watched Cordelia die, a million times he'd wished he could change what had happened that day. He didn't want to see it again!

A tiny, lucid part of his mind told him to turn away, that it was just a dream. But he was caught, trapped as always, forced to watch the nightmare play out yet again.

They dragged Cordelia across the village square, four big human males easily overpowering her Therian strength though she kicked and fought, demanding they free her. She'd always demanded. That had been Cordelia's way.

But the men ignored her, dragging her toward the thick, tarred pole standing black and ominous within the circle of the fire pit.

As the Jag of old watched with a conflicted blend of angry righteousness and dismay, they shoved her back against the thick wood, wrenching her arms behind her, clamping iron manacles around her wrists to hold her fast. One of the men secured a second iron shackle to her ankle, then staked it to the ground.

Sunshine glistened on Cordelia's brown hair, locks falling in rare disarray around her shoulders.

The villagers wasted no time. Before Jag comprehended what they were about, one lit the torch, then shoved it into the kindling with a single vicious thrust.

Cordelia's skirts caught almost immediately. Her gaze locked on his through the curling smoke, flaying him with sharp accusation as the flames devoured her. Fire caught at her hair, lighting the brown tips like candlewicks, racing up to engulf her face as the chant of the villagers filled the air.

"Witch! Witch! Witch!"

Cordelia threw back her head and screamed.

"No!" The strangled cry clawed at Jag's throat as he woke, bolting upright, his body drenched in sweat, burning as if he'd stood before that fire again in truth instead of only in dream.

He gripped his head with shaking hands as Cordelia's screams echoed over and over in his head, and the guilt raked at his chest like a wild animal struggling to claw its way out.

Fuck.

It had been years since he'd had the nightmare. Decades. He'd thought the memories had finally left him alone, but the events of the day had brought it all roaring back—seeing that face beneath the tarp, and the bodies tied to the posts. If only the past would leave him alone.

If only . . .

How many times had he thought those words? Those useless, fucking words.

He forced himself to lie back down even as he flung an arm across his eyes, wishing he could block out the sight. Wishing he could forget what he'd done.

Wishing, as he had a million times, that he wasn't such a bastard.

Olivia woke fully alert as she always did, despite her eyelids feeling heavy and thick. Daylight streamed in between the gap in the drapes, a gray light devoid of sun. Raindrops pattered on the roof, a steady, windless rain. If they had to attack in broad daylight, a rainy day was best. Even the Mage would be tucked inside, working their evil.

Over the patter of the rain, she heard the evenness of

Jag's breathing and remembered waking to the distraught sounds of his nightmare some hours ago. Over and over, he'd said *Cordelia*, the name filled with anguish.

Whoever Cordelia was, or had been, Olivia felt certain she was the source of Jag's pain. She remembered how he'd sat up as he'd wrenched himself from the dream, his back and shoulders bowed beneath the weight of the nightmare. If she'd known him better, if they'd been closer, she might have offered him comfort. At the very least, a warm hand to the shoulder. But instinct told her the Feral wouldn't have been pleased to know she'd seen him at his most vulnerable.

Lifting her arms high over her head, she yawned, stretching limbs that felt strong and free of Daemon venom, at last, as her mind turned to the future and the Mage battle to come. She had no qualms about taking Mage lives, for she would never forget, nor forgive, the Mage for burning the enclave of her birth to the ground, forcing them to flee into the hills that fateful, horrific night.

Especially now with the Mage losing their souls and aligning themselves with Satanan.

But the thought of going into battle filled her with equal parts excitement and trepidation. Battle posed problems for her that it didn't for her men because her unusual strength and speed came not from the deep animal nature that still lived like a shadow inside most Therians, but from the draden. From sucking the energy of her opponent, weakening him just enough that her skills overtook his.

In a large battle in close quarters, she had two options. One was to grab her opponent and hold on, sucking the life from him. Unfortunately, that was the only way she could direct her feeding, and grabbing hold of an opponent often proved difficult if not impossible.

Which left her second option—to draw her attackers away from the primary battle, away from her teammates, where she could feed openly without harming her own. And the last thing she wanted to do was harm her men. Or the Ferals.

She glanced over to find Jag on his back on top of the bedspread. He'd flung one arm wide, his hand dangling over the edge of the bed. His other lay across his eyes, his armband gleaming in the muted light. Despite the abandoned way in which he slept, she sensed the coiled tension, like a living thing inside him that never slept. Tension, yes, and a deep misery she was becoming more and more convinced poisoned his life.

But, goddess, he was a fine-looking man.

Her gaze skimmed over his body with raw feminine admiration. His thick biceps, broad chest, and flat, hard abdomen. And his legs, as solid and sculpted as any she'd ever seen.

He was a difficult, antagonistic, mercurial man. But he was more than that, better than that, though he didn't seem to know it, and she found herself drawn to him far more than she should be. She'd be smart to steer clear of him, but circumstances had stolen that option. Either she ran away from her life, or she remained at Jag's mercy until she figured out what he planned to do about her.

For now, she was staying with Jag.

Hungry in a draden-kissed way, the hunger prickling along the surface of her skin, she sat up and opened herself to a slow, gentle feed.

Almost at once, Jag bolted upright with a growl, fangs erupting in his mouth, claws sprouting from his fingertips to rake holes in the sheets at his side.

Olivia jerked, startled, and slammed down the feeding as she instinctively reached for a knife. He swung his head at her, part man, part ferocious cat, staring at her as if ready to attack.

At least she knew he wouldn't sleep through her feeding.

Slowly, his fangs and claws retracted. "What the *fuck*?"

She lifted an eyebrow, her heart pounding, but the bulk of her fear receded with his fangs and claws. "Time to get up."

He blinked, then impossibly, he began to laugh, that same wonderful rolling laugh that had pleased her senses so thoroughly when she'd found him with the puppy. A laugh that tugged and coaxed a smile of her own.

"A shit-ass way to wake up, Red. You're a woman

after my own heart." In his eyes, she saw genuine amusement and a respect that surprised her.

In that moment, as they smiled at one another, she felt something unlatch inside her, opening. Reaching.

Her breath caught, her heart swelling in a strange and awkward way.

Even as Jag's smile began to fade, his gaze held her captive. He rose with the sinuous grace of a jungle cat and climbed onto the bed with her, his knee beside her hip. For one throbbing moment, he stared at her, his gaze dropping to her mouth, and she thought he was going to kiss her lips. Instead, his head dipped and he pressed a warm, damp kiss into the curve of her shoulder.

In an instant, the hunger that had pricked at her skin was obliterated by a hunger of an entirely different kind. Need thrummed through her body, lighting a million tiny fires.

Jag's tongue stroked the sensitive skin beneath her ear, sending delicious chills rippling through her body.

"I love to taste you," he said huskily.

She reached for him, her fingers sliding into his thick, soft hair, holding on against the wave upon wave of desire that tugged at her, threatening to pull her loose from her moorings.

His hand snagged her wrists and he pulled her hands away from him, wrenching her arms above her head none too gently. As he lifted his head and looked at her, she saw the hardness sliding back into his eyes.

"You touch me only if I say you can touch me. Slave." A smile hovered at the edges of his mouth, but no kindness.

"Jag . . ." Disappointment cut her off, clamping her mouth shut. That thread of warmth that had briefly run between them had felt so real that she'd almost forgotten who he was. Or who he thought he was. And, she suspected, so had he.

Now he was determined to set them both straight.

She didn't fight him when he grabbed her ankles in one hand and pulled her legs, straightening her body and pressing her back onto the bed. He wouldn't hurt her. He might use her and pleasure her, but he wouldn't hurt her. She was sure of that now.

But that didn't mean she'd simply lie here and give in. Hell no. He wanted a fight. And she fully intended to give him one.

While one hand held her wrists above her head, his other pushed up her shirt and her sports bra, baring one breast, exposing it to the air and his heated gaze. He dipped his head and took the needy flesh into his warm, damp mouth. As his tongue slid across her nipple, she arched into his touch with a groan of pure pleasure, her body heating and ready.

Even as her body loved the feel of him, she hated what he did to her. He made her want so much more than he was capable of giving. True closeness, warmth. Caring.

Why? Why would Jag, of all people, instill this soft need in her? It wasn't just the attraction. Goddess knew she was too old to believe a little physical attraction had anything to do with affection, or even love. Attraction was a response of the body, nothing more. Yet he stirred this odd ache inside her, right in the middle of her heart.

As if reading her thoughts, he released her breast and lifted his head, meeting her gaze with a confusion that matched her own. For a second, she saw behind the mask, glimpsing a bitter turmoil, sensing pain and a loneliness as deep as those that tormented her.

He shared her need to connect on a level beyond the physical. Beyond sex. To hold and be held. To be kissed and stroked. And understood.

A moment later that glimpse of softness was gone, his smile taking on a sharp edge as if he were determined to remind them both why no one liked him.

"Scream for me, Sugar." He shoved his hand between her legs.

As heat flooded her core, and her body betrayed her, racing hard toward orgasm, she swung her leg high and fast, kicking Jag solidly in the nose with her heel as she came.

They yelled in unison.

"Bitch!"

"Damn you, Jag!"

Their gazes locked. The battle had engaged.

Chapter
Eleven

Jag's nose hurt like a son of a bitch, but he growled with pure satisfaction as he swiped at the blood on his face, then yanked off Olivia's pants as she fought him.

Goddess, he loved a woman who didn't take his shit. He had to be careful with most women. Oh, he tormented them in his own charming way, but he'd never liked tears. If they couldn't take what he dished out, he went elsewhere.

Olivia not only took it, she slammed it right back in his face. Literally.

She fought him now as he ripped her panties from her, kicking him in the chest and landing a good painful kick to his gut.

Jag stumbled back, doubled over with pain and laughter as she glared at him.

"You bastard. Why does everything have to be a fight with you?"

"I enjoy having you at my mercy, Sugar. I enjoy watching you beg me to take you."

She wrenched herself upright. "Goddess, but I hate this game."

"Which is precisely why we play it."

"Then fuck me, Jag. Please oh please," she added tonelessly. "Just do it and get it over with."

He grinned at her and grabbed her again, flipping her onto her stomach, then he straddled her bare hips, pinning her down. "I'll do that, since you ask so nicely. But not yet."

She groaned with annoyance, and he chuckled and yanked her shirt up under her arms. She fought him, trying to keep him from pulling it off her. So he drew claws and shredded the stretchy material without leaving a scratch on her skin.

"Want to keep your bra?" he asked silkily.

"Yes, damn you."

"Then take it off."

She tried to rise, and he let her. With another grumble, she sat up, her back to him. But as she moved as if to lift the bra, he prepared for an elbow to his jaw and almost got it. Grabbing her upper arms, he pushed her forward until she was off balance and unable to kick back.

"Take it off, Red, or I'm ripping it off."

"Bastard," she muttered, and yanked off the bra.

Jag pushed her face-first into the bed before she could strike back at him, then drank in the sight of her lovely, silken back.

He'd never thought himself a back man—legs, breasts, ass, oh yeah. But backs? Who in the hell was a back man? But there was something incredibly sexy about Olivia's. The way her shoulders curved, small and slender, yet somehow strong as steel. The way her back dimpled beneath her nape, the way it narrowed as it fell to the sweet swell of her hips. And that glorious, creamy expanse of lightly freckled skin.

Leaning forward, he gripped her forearms and pressed them to the bed, ensuring she didn't rear up and clock him in the nose a second time. Then he continued what he'd started the last time he had her at his mercy, what he'd been obsessed with doing since he first saw her standing in the living room of Feral House, talking to Lyon like some little flame-haired high-powered lawyer—taste every inch of her creamy skin.

His mouth dipped to her shoulder blade, his lips brushing her warm flesh as he inhaled her scent, a scent as rich and warm as her hair. *Sugar and spice and everything nice.* The ancient ditty ran through his head, and he decided it must have been written for her.

A shiver rippled through her even as she struggled against his hold. He loved that she fought him, loved that he could be rough with her and get a kick in the nose for his efforts.

His mouth trailed over the crown of her shoulder and down the top few inches of her arm, rewarded with her shiver.

"Jag, let me go." Her voice was low, husky, and filled more with anticipation than any dark emotion.

"Nope." Goddess, he enjoyed having her beneath him. The touch of her skin against his, the heat of her body between his thighs, the slender bones of her forearms safe in the cradle of his palms.

He inhaled her sweet fragrance and buried his nose in her bright hair. She was becoming an addiction, this one. After only a few days, he could barely stand not to be touching her.

But touching her wasn't enough. Not nearly enough.

He captured both wrists in one hand, then lifted off her enough to flip her onto her back.

She bucked, but he locked his thighs tight on hers and all she managed to do was brush his rock-hard balls with the sweet cream of her arousal.

He sucked in a hard breath. Her eyes tightened with need. Gray eyes locked on his. In their depths he saw no fury, and only a little anger. Frustration, yes. And heat. Goddess, but heat sparkled and danced in those eyes until the gray shone as brightly as silver.

He slid his finger between her thighs, closed against him by the tight clamp of his own. His finger brushed the hard nub of her passion, and she gasped, sucking in a ragged breath. He flicked that sensitive spot over and over, feeling the muscles in her thighs quiver and jerk even as her hips fought to rise, to give him better access.

"You want me to fuck you, Red?"

"If I say no?" she gasped.

"I'll torment you until you do."

"And if I say yes?"

He smiled, his smile deepening as she raised one imperious brow. "Then I'll torment you until I tire of the game."

"You're a bastard."

"I am indeed." He pressed his finger deeper between her thighs, encountering a slick wetness that eased his way. Finding the cave he sought, he pushed his finger deep inside her.

She arched up, her plump, perfect breasts rising as if seeking his mouth, a soft groan escaping her throat. The sound drove his own need higher, tightening his balls as his cock swelled impossibly thicker.

But he wasn't ready to end this. He wasn't nearly ready. Instead, he dipped his head and took one offered breast deep into his mouth, sucking the soft flesh until his body was so hard with need he feared he'd never be soft again. Two releases, three . . . no number would be enough.

He didn't want to feel this way, this need twisting inside him, demanding he touch her. Protect her. Possess her. She was his, dammit. His.

His slave.

A fist clenched high in his chest. A single word flickering in his mind like a spark igniting into a tiny, fragile flame.

His mate.

With a growl, he reared back.

No. *Hell no.* He did *not* think that word.

He shoved the thought aside, drawing the bitterness that lived inside him tight around him, like a rough, itchy, and all-too-familiar blanket.

Olivia met him with eyes half-closed and drenched in desire, her mouth open just enough to suck in tiny gasps of air, her lips soft and pink and infinitely lush.

His body tightened, demanding he claim that mouth as he'd claimed other parts of her. That fist high in his chest tightened, demanding he pull her into his arms and cradle her against his pounding heart.

But the thing that lived within him, that swirling, writhing mass of bitterness and bile, wanted nothing to do with either.

Driven by a need he could never fight, he flipped her onto her stomach yet again, released her wrists to grab her hips and wrench them high until she was on her knees.

With his own he spread her thighs and slid his cock between them to stroke her swollen lips. "You want this, Red. You want me inside you."

"Yes, you jerk. You know I do."

"Say it."

"Fuck me, Jag. Fuck me!"

He pulled his hips back, positioned himself at the mouth of her sheath, and drove home. Her body enveloped him, pulling him deep.

She groaned, pushing her hips back against his, forcing him deeper as he thrust into her again and again.

"More, Jag. More."

She was already starting to rise. It was so good. So damn good.

Too damn good. The darkness inside him rebelled.

Driven by a need he couldn't explain even to himself, he pressed calming cool into her body through the hands on her hips, forcing back her heat and her enjoyment.

"Jag, *what are you doing*?"

He didn't reply, for he had no answer. Only that contrary darkness urging him on as he thrust into her over and over.

"Jag, let me come. Let me come, damn you."

"No." As he continued to press the cool into her hips, her hot little sheath became tighter, less welcoming. Still, he took her hard until he reached his own blinding release. A release she didn't share.

The knowledge brought a small sting of satisfaction that quickly turned sour. Even he didn't like himself very much sometimes.

He pulled out of her and was about to slide his hand

between her legs to bring her to orgasm when she drove her heel into his thigh, missing his balls by millimeters, then twisted away from him and off the bed.

She stared at him, a small pissed off warrior with fire in her eyes. He tensed, ready for her anger. But when she spoke, her voice was low and strong as steel.

"Every time we start getting along, you ruin it. Every time. You can deny it all you want to, but you don't like yourself. And you can't stand for anyone else to like you either."

Now he was the one pissed off. "Don't presume to understand me, sister."

But she continued as if he hadn't spoken. "The sex between us could be good, Jag. Really good, and you know it. But you won't let it be, will you? If I'm not mad when it's over, you've failed."

He stood and grabbed her shoulders, his fingers flexing in anger, digging into her flesh. "You're my slave, Olivia, or have you forgotten that? The sex is for my enjoyment, not yours." But the words were a lie, every one of them. He loved pleasuring her. Loved watching the releases break over her. Why then had he denied her? Denied them both?

It had nothing to do with people liking him. That was crap and just proved she didn't know him at all.

"Let me make you come, Red. With my palm. A quick, violent release that'll melt you from the inside out."

She met his gaze with weary eyes. "Are you giving me a choice this time?"

Was he?

The bile inside him spread, nearly making him sick to his stomach. He released her and turned away, knowing what her answer would be. She didn't want him touching her.

"Go take a shower, Olivia. The others should be here in an hour."

He heard her turn and pad to the bathroom, her steps nearly as silent as his own. But her voice refused to be still in his head.

If I'm not mad when it's over, you've failed.

Bullshit. He liked what he liked, was all. Except, what he'd done had been intentionally mean-spirited. A new low, even for him.

So why had he done it?

Shit. To piss her off. Like she said.

He lay on the bed and stared at the water-stained ceiling as he waited for the shower to go off and his turn to go in. He suddenly longed for the hot, stinging spray of the shower to wash away the cold that had come upon him suddenly. A cold that he knew deep down would never be chased away by hot water.

Because this cold wasn't of the body. Olivia was stripping him raw, forcing him to feel the layer of frost that had long ago formed around his heart.

Chapter Twelve

Olivia stood beneath the spray of the hot shower, feeling emotionally battered and physically tied in sensual knots that had never been released. Because he'd fought to keep her from coming. And won.

The bastard.

He'd wanted her angry with him. Every time they began to share any kind of closeness, he turned back into a jackass. And yet she saw a loneliness in his eyes sometimes, a deep and desperate need for a closeness he fought to deny them both.

She stepped out of the shower and toweled dry, then wrapped the towel around her and returned to the bedroom, where Jag was lying on his back, still staring at the ceiling.

He rose and swung his legs over the side, rising in a sensuous, catlike movement. But he didn't move past her. He didn't move at all except to look at her, his gaze roaming her wet hair, her face, her bare shoulders.

His eyes were enigmatic, his expression pensive. "Did you make yourself come in the shower?"

"That's hardly your business."

"You didn't. I can feel the tension coiled like a knot in your body." He held out his hand to her, but didn't take a step closer. "Let me make you come, Red."

Olivia sighed. "Just leave it, Jag. I'm fine."

He stepped closer, moving silently across the carpet to stand before her, then lifted his hand to twirl a lock of her wet hair around his finger. "I'm sorry. What I did was mean."

"Why did you do it?"

His gaze dropped, then rose again as he twirled that lock of her hair around his finger. He shrugged, unhappiness etched on his face. "I don't know." His thumb stroked her cheek. "Let me make it up to you."

A better woman might have forgiven him and let him. "I'm not interested anymore, Jag."

She started to turn away, but his hand gripped her arm, holding her there.

"Your body's interested, and we both know it." The devilish gleam entered his eye. "We can do this the easy way or the hard way, Sugar. But I'm a determined man."

Mr. Nice Guy has left the room. No, not really. They were back to their battle of wills, but this was a battle she was likely to win, either way.

She met his gaze. "So I can fight you. Or I can spread my legs and let you make me come."

"That pretty much covers it."

She spread her stance, still keeping the towel tucked firmly around her. "Make it quick, please. We both need food before your friends arrive."

Devilment gleamed in his eyes, and she sighed. Goddess, when was she going to learn? Since she asked him to be quick, he'd probably do just the opposite.

But he didn't. He reached between her legs, his warm hand cupping her as she tensed for the rush of pleasure to come.

Even before he sent the warmth racing into her body, his sheer maleness overpowered her senses, his hair brushing her cheek, his sleep-warmed scent sending heat spiraling low in her body, tightening the need that coiled deep within her.

Yes, she needed this.

His cheek brushed her temple in a surprisingly gentle caress a second before the heat poured into her from his magic hand, a rush of pleasure so powerful she cried out and grabbed his shoulder to keep from going down.

Two of his fingers dove deep inside her at the same time his free arm curled around her waist, holding her against him as the orgasm roared up, crashing over her. Even as she shattered from the first one, he thrust his fingers in and out of her, pressing the pleasure into her until a second release rushed over her. And a third. Jag buried his face in her hair, his thumb caressing her bare back as he held her against him. Wave upon wave of glorious release tore through her body until she was a boneless mass kept upright only by the strong arm at her back.

Finally, he pulled his fingers out of her and she came back to herself, her gasps turning to one deep, shuddering breath.

He shifted his hold on her, the hand that had given her such pleasure was now the one at her back, holding her upright. His other was in her hair, caressing her scalp with light, gentle strokes. Her own arms had wrapped themselves tight around his waist and he held her cradled against him. As if he wanted her there. As if he cared.

Longing welled up inside her, sharp and breath-stealing. Her eyes burned as the loneliness she'd long ago buried deep ripped free of its shell, swamping her. Jag's arm tightened around her as if he felt it. As if he would slay the dragon that had long ago hollowed out her life.

For a few precious moments, she gave in to the temptation and pressed her face tighter to his chest, seeking his warmth, and shelter from that terrible emptiness.

But warmth from Jag could never be trusted. This sharp, strange connection was nothing but an illusion, no more solid than a Highland mist. She could pull away now, or wait for him to push her away.

Slowly she straightened, and he released her. She ducked her head as she struggled to regain her composure. But as she turned away, tightening the towel around her, she felt a large, warm hand cup her shoulder.

Olivia tensed as Jag turned her to face him. Their gazes met, and, for a single, brief moment, she glimpsed an ache in his eyes as deep as her own. And she felt that gossamer-thin connection between them strengthen and grow. If he'd opened his arms to her, she'd have stepped into them without hesitation.

Instead, his brows lowered, a familiar, unpleasant twist returning to his mouth, and she braced herself for the inevitable. Once more, they'd connected. Once more, he'd do something to anger her, to push her away.

But this time he only scowled, turned on his heel, and strode into the bathroom, slamming the door behind him.

Olivia raked her hair back off her face, letting her towel fall to the floor as she heard the shower turn on. Then she pressed the heels of her hands against her hot eyes. Her body throbbed with echoes of pleasure, the damp heat lingering between her thighs along with the feel of his warm hand tucked tight against her. Her chest ached from the bone-deep longing she hadn't even known she'd felt until he'd entered her life like a wild animal in attack mode.

The man was shredding her. Stealing her secrets and her will, digging up emotions and vulnerabilities she'd shut out eons ago. Worse, he kept taunting her with glimpses of something sweet and rare—a closeness, a trust, a caring—that could never exist. Not with Jag.

Not with anyone.

From the moment Jag walked into her life, he'd been systematically ripping it to shreds. She wanted it to stop. To be over. She wanted away from him, as far away as she could get.

But would he let her go? And, more importantly, would he let her go with her life intact? She just didn't know. The man she sometimes glimpsed deep inside him wasn't cruel. He wouldn't destroy her unless he thought he had to.

But that man wasn't always in control.

And the Jag she knew was a contrary beast.

For now, she was stuck with him, her fate in his hands. Unless she ran.

But running had never been her way.

Jag let the hot shower soak his hair, washing away the previous day's dust even as he wished he could somehow turn himself inside out and rid himself of the bile that ate at his insides.

What was the matter with him?

Olivia was getting to him, that was what. There were times when she looked at him that he could swear she saw all the way through him. Right down into the cesspit that acted as his heart.

There were times when she went soft on him, and all he wanted to do was hold her against him, listening to her heart beat against his. Then the bile and bitterness swirled inside him, and he couldn't get away from her fast enough.

He didn't want her soft. He wanted her strong. Tough. Angry.

The thought brought him up short. Why did he want her angry?

For half a heartbeat, he didn't know.

Her accusation came back to him. *You can't stand for anyone to like you. You need them to hate you as much as you hate yourself.*

Bullshit. Life without a little conflict bored him, plain and simple. Watching the anger spark in Olivia's eyes pleased him.

Did it? Did it really?

Hell, he didn't know. He didn't know anything anymore. He'd never been so uncomfortable in his own flesh as he had since Olivia arrived.

Grabbing the soap, he lathered his body, raking at his skin with his fingernails. Goddess, sometimes he wished he could claw his way out of himself and leave his skin behind.

Olivia meant nothing to him. Nothing but a little sex play, a little healthy conflict.

But even as he tried to convince himself of that, he ached to feel her in his arms again. His flesh warmed to the memory of the way she'd clung to him, deep in the throes of that wild release. Feelings had assailed him in those moments and the ones that followed, emotions so strong he'd found himself clinging to her as strongly as she had to him. Feelings of tenderness, and protective-ness, and a need to hold her so razor-sharp he'd feared it would puncture his heart.

He'd wanted to stay like that, his nose buried in her shampoo-fragrant hair as he cradled her against him, stroking her precious head.

Self-disgust had him slamming the soap down in the tray so hard he broke the bar. That remembered feeling of weakness made him grind his teeth together. The reason he antagonized people, the reason he pushed them away, was because he didn't like these soft-ass emotions. In fact, he hated them.

And what was wrong with that?

Nothing, dammit, that's what.

He washed his hair and shoved his head under the water to rinse it clean, turning the water temp to biting hot.

But the sudden needle pricks that dug into his skin had nothing to do with the water. He stilled as recognition slammed into him. Olivia was feeding. Hard.

Jesus. Someone had to be attacking her!

He flew out of the shower, flinging water droplets every which way, nearly skating across the slick bathroom tile as he wrenched open the door, a heartbeat away from shifting and tearing out the throat of the sucker who dared try to hurt her.

But he came to an abrupt halt as he turned the corner and found her, not in a fight for her life but sitting cross-legged on the bed, fully clothed, her laptop in front of her.

"What the fuck do you think you're doing?" She'd scared the shit out of him.

As she looked up at him in surprise, the needle pricks disappeared.

She looked confused. "I need to feed, Jag. I didn't suck hard."

He took an angry step forward. "The hell you didn't."

The look she gave him turned dismissive. "Jag, I've been doing this for centuries. I think I'd know if . . ."

A scream outside silenced her, lifting her to her feet as she flew for the window. Jag followed her, peering through the sheers over her head at the woman racing up the stairs. He glanced down at the walkway outside the room and understanding slammed into him. A young man lay sprawled across the cement. Unconscious. Or dead.

Olivia swayed, bumping him gently, and he grabbed her shoulders and turned her toward him. Her face had drained of all color, her freckles stark against the pale white of her skin.

"Easy, Red." Again, he used his gift to push a cooling calm into her instead of heat. "What happened?"

"I did this. I have to go out there. I have to help him."

"What can you do other than look guilty?" He gripped her shoulders tighter. "Can you do a reverse action on that feed of yours?"

She shook her head, her expression stricken. "It only goes one way."

"Nick!" A man's voice shouted from the parking lot.

The woman's voice answered. "He's breathing, Dave. He's alive."

"What in the hell happened?" the man's voice shouted. "Do you see any blood?"

"No. I saw him go down. He swayed like he was getting dizzy, then collapsed. He's too young to have had a heart attack!"

"Damn kid's probably been doing drugs."

"Mom?" a youthful voice asked groggily.

"Oh, thank God, son, you scared me to death."

Jag pulled Olivia away from the window. She was trembling beneath his hands. "He's fine. Now, I'm going to ask you again. What happened?"

"I don't know." Her gaze flew to his face, her eyes wide with horror. "What if he wasn't the only one? What if there were others in the rooms nearby?"

"They'll recover, just like the kid did."

"If they weren't weak to begin with."

Jag's hands moved to cup her face. "We can't go pounding on doors seeing if anyone's injured. No one can know we had anything to do with this."

"Jag . . ."

"Olivia. Liv, listen to me. There are hardly any cars in the parking lot. There's no one here. The kid's okay. They're all okay."

"If you hadn't stopped me . . ."

"Sweetheart, *what happened*?"

"I don't know. I fed like I always do, just a little. With your energy as strong as it is, no human should have been harmed by it. Jag, I've been doing this for hundreds of years. He shouldn't have been harmed!"

"What's changed?" he asked.

She stared at him, her eyes widening. And he knew.

"The Daemon," they said together.

"The venom?" he asked.

"More likely the energy I sucked from him. The venom incapacitated me, but his life force felt foul and unnatural. And incredibly strong." She would have swayed on her feet if he hadn't been holding her. As it was, her face lost what little color it had managed to recover. "What if it's changing me?"

His fingers caressed her head, her thick, soft hair alive beneath his fingertips. "Easy, Liv. Let's not jump to conclusions. You're feeding more strongly. You're just going to have to dial it down."

"What if that's not enough?" A shudder went through her. "I can't wait, Jag. I'm hungry. I need to feed."

His thumbs traced the lines of her cheekbones. "Take some from me."

She shook her head. "The only way I can be sure not to steal any more from the humans is to touch you and take it all from you. But I could hurt you. I could take too much too fast."

Despite the way he'd treated her, she was still protecting him.

"Then let's go. We'll drive into town where there are a lot of people around." But no sooner were the words out of his mouth than his cell phone went off. With a low curse, he released her and reached for the phone he'd left sitting on the nightstand beside his bed. Tighe's number flashed on the screen.

"Yo."

"We're crossing the bridge," the tiger shifter said.

Shit. They were out of time. Jag gave him directions to the motel. "We were just heading out for food. We'll meet you . . ."

"We'll bring it."

Double shit. "There's a sub shop on the way in. Bring four footlongs for us, and whatever the rest of you want."

Olivia held up five fingers.

"Make that five, and surprise us." He snapped the phone closed, shoved it in his pocket, and looked at

Olivia. "We're going to have to go for a walk, and fast. They'll be here too soon to get you into a crowd, but I'll get you away from humans, and you can feed from me at a distance."

He pulled on his pants and a tee, then held out his hand to her, pleased when she took it. Hand in hand, they left the motel together, walking down the stairs and across the parking lot to the woods beyond. When they were a good twenty yards into the woods, Jag stopped and released her.

"Feed from me, Red. As low as you can, and we'll go from there."

She nodded, turning to him, her eyes tense, her expression worried. Almost at once, he felt a strong hum thrumming over his flesh. Not uncomfortable, but not something he'd likely sleep through. "If I had to guess, you're feeding twice as hard as you did in Feral House."

Her eyes popped wide, her mouth dropping open as the feeding stopped abruptly. "That should have been a fraction of it."

"You're stronger, all right. Can you pull it any lower?"

"I don't know. I've never had to try."

He nodded at her. "Feed more, Red. You need it."

"You'll tell me if I'm taking too much?"

The fear in her voice squeezed something deep in his chest. That old urge to make her mad pricked at him, but he pushed it back, smiling at her instead.

"I'll tell you."

The buzz dimmed a little, but she continued to feed at a much higher level than she had before. Five minutes later he felt the first wave of light-headedness.

"Enough, Liv."

She stopped immediately, her eyes filled with concern. "Too much?"

"Yeah. I'm feeling it. You're not full?"

"No. It's like my metabolism has been ratcheted up half a dozen notches."

"When the gang arrives, you can try it again. Go slow, just a little at a time."

Olivia grabbed his arm. "Sit down, Jag, until it passes. If you fall, I won't be able to catch you."

"Sure about that? You're a lot stronger than you look." But he let her pull him down onto a stump.

She stood in front of him, watching him with worried eyes.

"I'm fine, Olivia. Just a little light-headed." But it was disconcerting to realize how fast she could kill him if she wanted to. Fortunately, he could tell how much that realization scared her. "You don't like to kill, do you?"

"On the field of battle, I never hesitate. But I don't kill innocents. Or friends."

Slowly, he cocked his head at her. "There must be another category, because I'm pretty sure I don't fall into either of those."

He'd been trying to ease that fear in her eyes, he realized. Hoping to draw a smile.

But the look she turned on him was far too serious. "When you're not trying to make me mad, you are my friend, Jag. For all the flaws in our relationship, you understand me better than anyone ever has. I never know what you're going to do, and I still don't know if you're going to turn me in, but for now you're the best friend I have. In a weird kind of way, maybe the best friend I've ever had. Because I can completely and totally be myself with you."

Her words hit him hard, at once a sweet, drenching rain on a parched soul, and a full-out assault on the thing that lived inside him. The bitterness. And he knew she was right. Part of him didn't want this, didn't want her to like him or call him friend. Didn't want anyone to like him.

But as that ugliness started to rise inside him, threatening this truce, Tighe's white Land Rover pulled into the parking lot. Behind it, he saw Hawke's black monster of an SUV. The GMC Yukon might be as big as Jag's Hummer, but it wasn't the gas guzzler Jag's was. The damned hawk shifter had bought a hybrid.

Jag stood, glad to find the light-headedness gone. "Let's go. Lunch has arrived. My lunch, at any rate." He glanced at her as they started back through the woods toward the motel. "What if this jump in your metabolism continues to accelerate?"

Her startled gaze met his, her eyes, for once, looking every one of her nearly six hundred years. "I won't be responsible for the deaths of innocents. I refuse. If I start harming others, you're going to have to stop me."

"I know."

And he would. He'd have no choice. But he had no illusions, either. Being forced to take Olivia's life would destroy him.

Chapter Thirteen

"How's the wanker?"

Niall asked the question beneath his breath as he and Ewan joined her in the motel parking lot, one on either side.

As Jag led Delaney and the Ferals up the stairs, Olivia held back, needing a report from her men, knowing they wanted one in return.

"Jag's a challenge," Olivia said coolly, fighting to mask the emotion she feared might creep into her voice. These two knew her far too well. And yet, in some ways, they knew her not at all. "But he's nothing I can't handle."

"If he hurts you . . ." Niall began hotly.

Ewan punched him in the shoulder. "You'll what? Attack a Feral?"

"He'll do nothing." Olivia used her command voice, the one that brooked no argument. Niall was usually a wise, levelheaded soldier, but Jag clearly brought out the worst in him. Especially when it came to her.

Niall's gaze dropped, a storm rising in his eyes as he looked at her shoulder. "He clawed you."

"No. For heaven's sake, Niall. This happened in the woods. It wasn't Jag's doing." They'd have to get into the discussion of the Daemon when they joined the others upstairs. She just prayed Jag left the draden attack out of it.

She strode forward before Niall could question her further, leading them up the stairs after the others, following the scent of warm bread and spicy meats drifting from the bags of sandwiches Tighe carried.

As they followed the others inside, the motel room quickly became dwarfed by the six huge men and two women. Tighe wore sunglasses despite the cloudy day, leaving them on in the room. She'd heard that his eyes turned to tiger eyes spontaneously sometimes, which forced him to keep them covered whenever humans were around.

He flashed dimples at his wife as she nudged him aside to place the tray of drinks on the table. As Hawke leaned his long body back against the chest of drawers, Kougar positioned himself beside the door, part of the group and yet not, as he watched them with eyes completely lacking in warmth.

Though she knew all four Ferals wore the armbands with the heads of their animals—bands through which they accessed the power of the Earth—only Jag's armband showed.

Jag sprawled across the bed farthest from the window, lying on his side and propping his head on one thickly muscled arm while Niall and Ewan sat side by side on the edge of the other bed.

Jag caught her eye and patted the bed in front of him, clearly suggesting she join him. But while a scamp's smile played around his mouth, the look in his eyes held a warning. A warning that drew her to him instead of repelling her, and not because she feared he'd give her away. Quite the opposite. The look in his eyes warned her to be careful lest she give herself away.

She found herself crossing to perch on the edge of the bed beside him instead of joining her own men as she might have done a few days ago. Everything had changed when Jag discovered her secret. He threatened everything she'd built of her life, including her life itself. But in an odd way, he'd become the only one she could truly trust.

Besides, she could no longer be sure how long she could go without feeding. She might accidentally steal energy without meaning to, possibly without even knowing she was doing it. Jag needed to be close enough to stop her if he had to. If she harmed the Ferals . . .

A shudder tore through her. She couldn't even think

about what that would mean to their battle to keep Satanan from rising again.

As long as she stayed close to Jag, he wouldn't let that happen. She'd started to believe he wouldn't turn her in if he didn't have to. She just had to make damn sure she did nothing to force him to betray her secret.

Jag sat up to catch the sandwich Tighe tossed to him. Olivia already had hers, Tighe having passed out the subs to the women first. He glanced at her bright head as she sat near his feet and unwrapped the warm sandwich. He was surprised she'd come when he'd patted the bed. The appearance of being his lapdog grated on her pride. Which was precisely why he'd done it. A dumb move since he really had wanted her close.

He wasn't sure what the others would do if she somehow gave herself away. Kougar, he worried about most. If that Feral decided she needed to die, there would be no discussion. He'd lunge, prepared to make a killing blow. And Jag would play hell protecting her if she weren't already within reach. Not that long ago being draden-kissed carried an automatic death penalty. With the power they possessed to suck life, most felt it was a matter of kill or be killed.

Olivia was different. She'd been hiding and controlling her power for centuries.

As Tighe handed out the rest of the sandwiches, Jag unwrapped his own. An Italian sub. All the Ferals were meat eaters, almost to the exclusion of everything else. After all, they were all part predatory animal. But if he had to eat a sandwich, he'd go for Italian every time. And Stripes knew it.

"Thanks, Tony man," he drawled.

Tighe cut him a tight look, clearly tensed and waiting for the rest of it—the dig or the coarse reference to what he wanted to do sexually with Tighe's mate.

When Jag left it at thanks, Tighe nodded once, his gaze wary.

Jag grunted. When had he become so predictable?

Tighe leaned back against the chest of drawers, shoulder to shoulder with Hawke, and unwrapped his own sandwich. Paper rustled as they all tore into their lunches.

Their fearless leader-in-residence gave them about a minute to take the edge off their appetites before his gaze swung to Jag. "Fill us in."

The urge to say something snide tickled his throat, but dammit, he *was* becoming predictable. And he couldn't stop thinking about what Olivia said about his doing it just to make people dislike him. He refused to believe it. And yet . . . shit. His own explanation, of simply enjoying having people mad at him, didn't make a hell of a lot of sense, did it?

It was just the way he was.

That knee-jerk need to fire off with some snide comment died, and he launched into a tight, precise explanation of what they'd seen at the Mage stronghold, the corpses strung up, the number of sorcerers and sentinels they'd spotted, the power orbs throbbing with Daemon energy, and their suspicion that the Daemons weren't necessarily under the control of the Mage but being lured back by suffering humans.

"The place is warded with magic strong enough that even Olivia couldn't see through it." His mouth lifted in a small, satisfied smile. "She can now."

Tighe frowned. "Damned dark magic. We'll assess the situation when we get there, but anyone who can't see that place is pulling back to the vehicles. I don't want anyone being ambushed."

Ewan scowled. "You'd leave us behind?"

"Only if you can't get your mind opened."

Both Ewan's and Niall's gazes swung to Olivia.

No way in hell. She's mine. Deep inside, Jag's animal leaped to his jaguar's feet, growling. A snarl rumbled from Jag's own throat, drawing the surprised gazes of everyone in the room, including Olivia's. He didn't give a shit. If either of those Therians thought they were using Olivia's body to open their minds, they were brutally mistaken.

"Use your damn fists," he growled. Olivia was his now, and he had no intention of sharing.

Tighe watched him with wary interest, then finally cleared his throat. "Anything else we need to know?"

"Yeah," Jag drawled.

Olivia jerked, just a small movement the others probably missed, but he knew what it meant. The flicker of fear echoing in the depths of her gray eyes confirmed it. She feared he meant to give her away.

Which annoyed him. Why it annoyed him, he wasn't sure. He'd pretty much threatened her with betrayal unless she did what he wanted, hadn't he? He'd forced her to her hands and knees with that not-so-subtle threat.

Still, it rankled.

He met her gaze, watching her expression as he said, "The Daemons carry venom in their claws. Venom capable of at least partially immobilizing their prey." He'd told Tighe as much. They probably already knew, but what the hell.

As he spoke, the fear in her eyes eased, the tension leaching from her body, softening her in a way that had his hands longing to pull her against him.

"Goddess, Olivia," Niall hissed. The Therian's gaze dropped to Olivia's shoulder, to the rips in her jacket, his eyes wide and horrified. "I didn't know you were the one attacked." A blanch paled his face, one far too emotional for a soldier's concern over his captain's near demise, especially when said captain sat before him, clearly fine. No, the look in Niall's eyes radiated pure fear. For a woman he felt deeply about.

The man wasn't just protective of her. He was fucking in love with her.

Something ugly and jealous slid up Jag's throat. Without making the conscious decision to do so, he reached for Olivia, cupping his hand around the nape of her neck, claiming her with a low, feral growl. Marking her in front of them all, like a mated male.

He wasn't sure who was more surprised—his brothers or himself.

Hawke's eyebrow shot up. Tighe cocked his head with warning, suspecting Jag of doing it just to annoy.

Was he?

Beneath his hand, Olivia stiffened.

The tension in the room jacked up two hundred percent, and it occurred to him they were all waiting for her to elbow him in the throat. Or the balls.

"Jag," she said instead, clearly displeased. But she didn't push him away.

He didn't release her. "Olivia had a little run-in with a Daemon last night, didn't you, Sugar?" he drawled, kneading her neck, running his thumb slowly up and down the satin length of skin. Out of the corner of his eye, he watched Niall tense like a bowstring.

Deep satisfaction warmed him from the inside out as he continued. "The venom slowed her down a little, but not so much that we couldn't have a little fun."

The look she shot him over her shoulder was sharp and frustrated. "Stop it."

Instead, he curled a lock of her hair gently around his finger, meeting Niall's furious gaze with lazy challenge.

To his surprise, the animal inside him rumbled with approval. For once, he and the annoying beast were in complete accord. Olivia belonged to *him*.

Tighe shot him a warning look but said nothing as he launched back into fearless-leader mode.

"Our original mission was to capture and destroy the Daemons before they take any more lives and before they give away the whole immortal game."

Jag played with Olivia's hair, stroking the side of her silken neck with the backs of his knuckles. A small shiver stole through her, and he smiled. *His*.

"But the game's changed now that we know the Mage are involved." Tighe threw him an annoyed flick of his gaze. "Stopping them from freeing Satanan is first priority. As soon as we eat, we'll head out to the Mage stronghold and attack. If we find any humans still alive in there, we'll do what we can for them, then when the battle's over, we'll clear their minds and send them on their way."

Hawke looked up. "What are we going to do with the captured Mage?"

"We're capturing sorcerers, only. Sentinels die."

"Mother Nature's not going to be happy," Hawke muttered. The killing of more than a couple Mage always resulted in wild weather or earthquakes, nature's fury unleashed. While the Ferals tapped into the Earth's energy through their Radiant, the Mage had always been part of nature itself. Long ago, before the defeat of the Daemons and the mortgaging of their power, the Mage had been able to affect and control many of nature's functions—the weather, the growth of plants and trees, the reproduction of many of the Earth's species. They'd thought of themselves as gods. He suspected they still did even though they'd jumped ship to the evil side.

Tighe shrugged. "Then nature's just going to have to be pissed. We'll never win this battle if we can't dispatch the enemy. Besides, the lives we take will be nothing compared to what Satanan does if he's freed. Once he and his horde rule the Earth again, no one will be safe."

Olivia started to rise, to escape his touch, he was sure. Jag's gaze met Niall's, saw the angry triumph in the other man's eyes, and Jag curled his fingers around Olivia's arm, tight enough that she'd have to make a scene to get free. And that's when he felt it.

Beneath his touch, Olivia's breathing had turned shallow and quick.

She shot him a sharp look, part warning, part fear.

Holy shit, she was rising. And he hadn't even pressed heat into her. Just the brush of his knuckles had turned her on. She was in danger of coming. In front of everyone.

"Jag," Olivia whispered through clenched teeth. "Let me go. *Please*."

Ah, crap. He might be a jerk, but he wouldn't embarrass her like that.

He kept his grip on her and pressed her with his cool, calming flow. Beneath his palm, the tension in her began to ease, her body softening. She shot him a look that at once thanked him and demanded he release her before it happened again.

He did, even though letting go of her was the last thing he wanted to do.

When he finally turned his gaze back to the front of the room, Tighe gave him a sharp look but said nothing. Stripes was no dummy. He recognized a little claim-staking when he saw it. Every man and woman in the room must know by now that he and Olivia had been intimate.

He'd made that more than clear.

What they didn't know, and were probably having a hard time figuring out, was why Olivia allowed it when she'd made it just as clear she had no use for him.

He and Olivia alone knew the real reason. That she was his because he'd forced her to be. Because he knew something about her no one else knew and had threatened to destroy her if she didn't do exactly as he said.

The truth settled in his gut like a fist-sized lump of hard clay.

She'd become his partner because he'd coerced her into it. She'd become his lover because he'd given her no choice.

But it wasn't enough. He wanted more. He wanted . . . her.

With a sudden longing that tore a strip from his soul, he wanted her to reach for him because she wanted to. He wanted to see a smile lift her pretty mouth and light her eyes and know that smile belonged to him alone. The longing hit him like a pair of fists.

And just as quickly, the bile stirred inside him, the bitterness that drove his life, decrying every thought he'd just had, rejoicing in the fact he would never see a smile in Olivia's eyes. Not for him.

He didn't want her smiles. He didn't need her reaching for him. He'd never wanted that shit from anyone. Not since . . .

Goddess.

Not since he'd watched Cordelia die and done nothing to stop it. Done nothing to help her.

His mind turned abruptly from that dark pit of nightmares, his gaze seeking Olivia's small, bright head.

His hands fisted on his thighs as he fought to keep from reaching for her.

And he ached.

The rain started on the drive out of Harpers Ferry.

Great. Olivia pressed her fingertips against the inside of the Hummer's cool window. It was as if Mother Nature knew exactly what they had in mind and was already expressing her displeasure. If they killed any Mage, the weather would only get worse.

Though midafternoon, the day was gray and colorless.

They parked the vehicles in the woods, and the Ferals shifted. Hawke took to the sky while the three house-cat look-alikes accompanied the four non-Ferals through the rain. Delaney walked beside Olivia, the hood of a raincoat covering her hair. Niall and Ewan brought up the rear.

"Did you get a good look at the Daemon?" Delaney asked, as they made their way through the underbrush. The ex–FBI agent's expression revealed little, but her eyes possessed a keen edge of dread. "Skye tried to explain it to me, but she said words failed her."

"I did see it. And Skye was right. The thing's a nightmare."

She'd had little interaction with Delaney, but after six hundred years, she'd become a good judge of character, and the woman had impressed her. Olivia's instincts told her the woman possessed both intelligence and compassion, with a fierce streak of warrior that would bode well for her ability to handle whatever they came up against.

Olivia suspected the woman had the heart. But she couldn't help but wonder if she had the strength. They claimed she'd been turned immortal, but immortal didn't mean indestructible. Would she bounce back from injury as quickly as a Therian? Tighe must think so, or he wouldn't have let her come.

"So the Daemon attacked you?" Delaney asked.

"Yes. It could have easily killed me."

"Why didn't it?"

"I struck back. I punctured something up under his shoulder with my knife, and he screamed and took off." She doubted that was the whole truth. Though she couldn't be certain, she suspected her feeding off him had had as much to do with his flying away as her knife attack.

They were nearly within sight of the house when a huge hawk swooped down through the trees and took human form in front of them. Unlike Jag's, Hawke's clothes remained when he shifted, and he stood now in all black.

"There's no one in the woods, thanks to the weather. The house up ahead—the run-down white clapboard that I assume is our Mage stronghold—appears occupied, but I couldn't get a look inside."

Tighe's voice rang in her head, as it did in all theirs, she was sure. *Any sign of Mage?*

"None. Not a sentry in sight, either outside or in. We may genuinely be able to keep the element of surprise, despite the daylight raid."

A few minutes later, the house came into view. Olivia and Hawke drew to a halt, the other nonanimals stopping more slowly.

Delaney glanced at her with surprise. "What's the matter?"

Olivia looked at her a second before she understood. "We're here. You can't see the house, can you?"

Delaney frowned. "Apparently not."

Olivia looked to her men. Each shook his head once. Ewan's eyes warmed as they slid down her body, clearly looking for an invitation. They'd been intimate from time to time when both were in the mood and had no one else to share it with. She'd always found her encounters with him adequately enjoyable.

But the thought of him holding her and entering her today, even as perfunctory as the encounter would necessarily be, left her cold. As did the thought of Niall. She couldn't even look at him now, knowing the need she'd see in his eyes—a need far more emotional than physical. A need she'd never been able to return.

The sad truth of it was, from the moment Jag had come barreling into her life, her body had lost interest in everyone else.

Tighe shimmered into his human form, his clothes also intact. Jag joined them, standing naked as a babe without swaddling and infinitely comfortable with it.

Tighe looked at Delaney, reaching for her hand as he turned to Olivia. "While I try to help Delaney, get your men's minds open or send them back to the vehicles. Blind warriors are useless. We'll be back in a few."

"I'll keep an eye out for company." Hawke shifted back into his bird and lifted into the sky. Kougar, still in his house-cat form, took off, heading toward the Mage stronghold.

As Olivia turned to her men, Jag's arm went around her shoulders and he pinned her hard against his side.

A low warning growl rumbled from his throat. "Jack off."

"Jag." She did not appreciate his undermining her authority even if she'd been about to tell them the same thing, if not quite in the same way.

Ewan shrugged and walked away, presumably to find

a little privacy to take the mind clearing into his own hand.

But Niall held his ground, his lip curling. "That decision is Olivia's, not yours."

Shit. She felt like a bone being fought over by two hungry dogs. She elbowed Jag hard in the ribs. "Quit being so damned territorial."

But his grip on her didn't loosen one whit. He was too strong to fight without stealing a bit of his strength, and the irksome man would know if she tried. He was giving her no choice.

With a huff of frustration, she met Niall's gaze. "Find release on your own, Niall. You'll not be using me for this one."

The man's mouth tightened, hurt flaring in his eyes. "I've never used you."

Oh, Niall. Now was not the time. "That was a poor choice of words on my part. But you understand my meaning. Get your mind opened and do it quickly, or you'll be waiting in the car."

His mouth tightened, his jaw hardening until she thought he might crack a tooth. "He's forcing you."

Olivia hesitated, then told him the truth, or close enough. "For the moment, we're together, Niall. And I'll not be having sex with another."

"No other?" He looked at her askance. As if she were never exclusive.

She supposed he was right. She never was, for no

man had ever caught her interest in that way. Until Jag. The Feral's effect on her body disturbed her almost as much as his hold over her life. Never had a man ensnared her so completely. Yes, he had a remarkable gift with those hands, but his touch affected her long before he intentionally pleasured her. The barest brush of his fingers made the heat rise inside her as it was doing now.

"Go Niall," she snapped when he still hadn't moved.

With a growl of frustration, Niall swiveled on his heel and stalked off, leaving her alone with Jag.

The rain continued to fall through the trees, splattering on her head and running down her cheeks, but rain had never bothered her.

Jag's grip on her loosened the barest bit, his thumb tracing circles on her shoulder. "What were you thinking about during lunch? All I did was touch your neck, yet you were rising." His mouth dipped, his warm breath teasing her temple.

"Nothing. Let me go, Jag."

He didn't. Instead, he moved to her earlobe and took it carefully between his teeth, his breath tickling the sensitive lobe and sending delicious shivers through her body.

His teeth released her ear, a soft stroke of his tongue easing the light pinch before his lips trailed down her rain-slick neck, heating her from the inside out. Deep inside, her body turned warm and soft, and damp. The restlessness began to build again, throbbing and tightening all over again.

"Jag, stop. You're doing it again," she gasped, her breath turning shallow, labored. "You can do it with your knuckles, your mouth. The heat. The pleasure."

He released her and turned her to face him, his grip on her shoulders absolute as he stared into her face. In his expression, she saw a mix of bemusement and satisfaction. In his eyes, fire.

"Goddess, you are rising again." His hands shot up under her jacket, curving around her waist.

Through the thin cotton of her shirt, she felt a sudden rush of coolness battling back the tide of heat, and shivered.

"Enough, Jag," she pleaded. "You're giving me temperature whiplash."

His mouth kicked up, a soft, amused smile. "You rise for me even when I don't try. I've never seen anything like it."

"I can't say I'm thrilled about it."

He chuckled low. "It's a good thing I can cool as well as heat."

"I suppose. That's quite a gift you have."

"It comes in handy from time to time."

"Have you always been able to do that with your hands?" She stepped closer, drawn as much to his heat as to the man himself, and slid her arms around his waist. "Or was it one of your Feral gifts?"

His hands slid to her back, pressing her closer. "I've always had the ability. When I was a boy, I used to catch forest creatures—rabbits, deer, squirrels—calming them and making pets of them if you can believe it."

She found herself smiling at the thought.

"I wasn't always an ass." A hardness entered his voice with his words, a hardness turned on himself.

Her smile died. The man he'd become, the Jag she knew, was no longer that boy. Instead, he'd grown into an angry and difficult man. Because of something that happened, something he blamed himself for, she was positive. Something that concerned Cordelia.

"Jag?"

His chin brushed over her hair. "What?"

She shouldn't ask. It was none of her business. "Who's Cordelia?"

He stiffened as if he'd been stabbed through the side. Slowly, his hands dropped away from her.

"Why?"

"You said her name in your sleep this morning."

"She's nobody. Not anymore." He stepped back and turned away. "She's dead."

Unh. "I'm sorry, Jag." She knew she was treading dangerous ground, yet something told her she needed to know. If she were ever going to help him, she needed to understand what drove him. Why she thought she could help him—or even wanted to—she wasn't sure.

"Was she your mate?"

"No." He turned his head, looking at her over one broad, muscled shoulder, meeting her gaze with eyes filled with an ancient pain. "She was my mother."

Oh, Jag.

He walked away, as if needing to distance himself from her, from the truths she'd pulled from him. She ached from the pain she'd seen in his eyes, and from the deep well of empathy she felt for him. His parent was dead, and he blamed himself. She knew that dark, bitter landscape far too well.

For long minutes she stood in the woods, alone but for the need to somehow ease Jag's torment. But how, when he wouldn't listen? When he wasn't ready to hear?

Finally, the others began to return, rescuing her from her frustratingly inadequate thoughts. Tighe and Delaney came through the trees first, hand in hand, Delaney's cheeks flushed, Tighe's eyes warm with satisfaction and love.

As Olivia watched them together, she couldn't help but wonder what it would feel like to be cared for like that. To be loved. Sometimes she caught a similar look in Niall's eyes as he watched her, but Niall's feelings lacked the depth of Tighe's for Delaney. In comparison, they felt weak and thin. Unhappy.

Unreturned. And perhaps that was the difference. Love could never be rich and full when it went only one way.

Niall and Ewan came in from opposite directions.

"Success?" Tighe asked. "Delaney's a go."

"Shit hole of a house," Ewan commented by way of an answer.

Niall nodded. But the look he gave her was nothing less than morose. Niall knew her better than anyone ever had, except, oddly, Jag. Niall had always sensed her moods surprisingly accurately and could no doubt feel that her relationship with Jag wasn't quite right.

He'd just have to deal with it.

Hawke and Kougar returned, shimmering into man shape in a concert of sparkling lights. Interestingly, while Hawke's shifting lights were multihued, as Jag's always were, Kougar's were almost colorless. White and silver and gray.

"Report?" Tighe asked.

The group had reassembled behind a thick stand of brush where no one from the house would be able to see them if they looked. Jag came up behind her. Though he didn't quite touch her, she felt his body heat at her back.

"No change," Hawke replied. "They either have no clue we're out here, or they're waiting for us inside."

Tighe nodded. "Let's hope it's the former, but we're going in either way. Hawke and Kougar, you'll take the back door with Olivia."

"No," Jag said abruptly. "Olivia stays with me."

Olivia shot him a questioning look. Was he afraid

she'd start feeding again and hurt his friends? But when she met his gaze, she saw only a fierce and startling protectiveness. Of her.

She turned back to Tighe, her heart pounding an awkward rhythm. Jag positively confused her. He was the last man in the world she needed to be involved with. And yet, wasn't that exactly what they were? Involved?

With a twist of her gut, she knew they always would be, on some level. Because as long as he alone knew her secret, he'd always hold her life in his hands.

Hell.

Tighe's gaze moved between her and Jag. Like Niall, she could tell Tighe wasn't entirely trustful of what he sensed between them. His gaze landed on her, a question in his eyes. She dipped her head in a brief nod.

Tighe shrugged. "Okay, then. Kougar, you're taking the front, with Niall and me. Ewan and D are staying outside to catch anyone who tries to escape."

As Tighe met his mate's gaze, Olivia could tell neither was thrilled with the situation. Delaney wanted to be in on the attack. Tighe didn't like the idea of being separated from her.

But she heartily concurred with Tighe's refusal to take his mate inside with him. Fighting the Mage, with their ability to enthrall, was a skill acquired over decades. A skill no human possessed. Delaney might be a fighter, but she lacked the training that would keep her alive.

"Hawke, let me know when your team's in place," Tighe said. "Let's move out."

Almost as one, the Ferals shifted into their animals, the cats downsizing. The jaguar led the way and Olivia followed close behind as they delved deeper into the woods to circle the stronghold. They kept low, ducking behind trees whenever they came within sight of the house.

The battle was bound to turn dangerous whether or not the Mage saw them coming. The Mage had magic at their disposal they hadn't had . . . perhaps ever. Magic strong enough to steal souls, free three wraith Daemons, and goddess only knew what else. Dark magic. Maybe even Daemon magic, though no one knew for sure. They needed to be prepared for anything.

The rain intensified as they approached the back of the house, and Olivia once more wondered if Mother Nature knew what they intended.

Olivia was soaked through, her hair and pants plastered against her skin, the rain having seeped beneath her jacket through the rips in the leather. But growing up in the fifteenth century and living years on her own without shelter, she'd never been bothered by physical discomfort. Besides, her Therian nature had never completely lost its basic wildness. She'd always felt more at home in the woods and the rain than in a dry, centrally heated modern house.

When we get into place, Tighe's voice said in her mind, *we'll go in fast and hard. Most of us have fought the Mage numerous times, but it bears repeating. Cut off their hands before you're enthralled. Kill the sentinels if you have to, but not the sorcerers. We need to know what they're up to. And keep your eyes open for Daemons. If we're right about them being nocturnal, they shouldn't be a problem. But we can't be sure.*

Olivia's team circled to the back of the house, easing in close as they waited for Tighe's signal to proceed. Her tense gaze traveled to the two thick wooden posts staked in the backyard, a chill slithering through her as she watched them run with watery blood.

What an awful way to die.

Hawke turned human. Olivia lifted a brow, and he explained. "Birds are of little use in battle. I'm better off with knives."

The small jaguar rubbed against her leg, then began to grow to full size in a rush of magic that tingled excitedly along her skin. The beautiful, full-sized jaguar swung his dark head to look up at her. In the cat's eyes, she saw Jag's, without hardness or devilment, but warm and rich with a demanding intensity.

Be careful in there, Red.

I will. She thought he warned her not to hurt anyone

she shouldn't, but the words that followed told her otherwise.

Be careful of the Mage, Olivia.

Now! Tighe's voice exploded in her head.

The jaguar took off at a race, Hawke and Olivia following close behind.

Jag? she thought softly. *You be careful, too.* She wasn't sure if he'd heard her. She wasn't skilled in telepathic communication.

But a low purr caressed her mind. *Will do, Liv. Will do.*

The jaguar leaped onto the porch and crashed through the front window, disappearing from sight. But as Olivia followed, she slammed into something solid and invisible, tossing her onto her buttocks in the grass, knocking the wind out of her.

"Warding," Hawke muttered beside her a second before he shifted into his bird and flew right through it. His voice rang in her head, a communication with Tighe he'd opened to her as well. *Animal forms only, Stripes. The warding . . . holy shit!*

Hawke flew through the broken window and went silent. Olivia's pulse began to race.

Jag? Jag!

But no voice answered. She looked up to find Delaney, Niall, and Ewan racing around the corner of the house.

Delaney's eyes were fierce and wild. "It's a trap! They've walked into a trap!"

"You don't know that."

"Yes, I do. Tighe and I are connected. I feel snatches of what he's feeling. And it's pain. God, it's pain."

Olivia stared at the house, her heart pounding. They couldn't lose four Ferals! Deep inside her, something ripped loose at the thought of Jag in there. Of his not coming out again.

"There has to be a way inside. We have to help them."

But even as the last words left her mouth, something flew out of the window. Something chillingly familiar.

A Daemon.

"Oh, my God," Delaney whispered beside her, pulling her gun.

"Bloody hell." Niall drew his sword, as did Ewan.

Blood dripped from the Daemon's claws and ran down his mouth and chin.

Whose blood? Whose blood?

So much for trying to help the Ferals. Their own survival would have to come first.

Olivia drew her knives. And prayed.

Chapter Fifteen

Darkness. Nothingness.

All around him Jag felt a thick, unnatural absence of light and sound. The only sense of his that seemed to work was that of scent. And he smelled Daemon.

How in the hell are we supposed to get through this soup? Jag snarled.

Hawke's voice answered in his head. *It's warding. If we can find the path, there has to be a way out.*

Jag moved forward, but couldn't tell if he moved. He couldn't feel the ground or floor or whatever in the hell was beneath his feet.

Tighe's roar of pain rang through his brain. *Shit, shit, shit. Motherfucker. That thing just tore a strip of hide off my back . . . I saw him. For an instant. Right after he attacked. He's too fast. Hawke, either find a way out of here fast, or shift. He'll rip off your bird head with a single swipe of those knifelike claws.*

I'm already shifting.

As am I, Kougar said.

Jag, I need someone to remain in animal form, or we won't be able to communicate, Tighe said. *Since you're the only one weaponless, you're my pick.*

Works for me. The putrid smell leaped at him suddenly. Understanding registered a split second before the knifelike claws tore into his shoulder, ripping flesh from his bone.

A strangled cry tore from his jaguar's throat, but no sound met his ears. *Holy fucking moly.* In the instant the claws left his flesh, he saw it up close and personal as he hadn't in the woods, its long black hair flashing like gleaming ebony around a hideous gray melted face with razor-sharp fangs.

Jag leaped at the fiend, but the venom was already doing a number on him, and the Daemon disappeared back into the darkness before he could touch him.

Fuck! Blood ran down his leg. *I'm beginning to see why they call this thing a wraith Daemon.*

You saw him? Hawke's voice.

For half a second after he attacked me. He disappeared before I could counter.

Hawke's yell tore through his head.

Hawke?

A groan of pain filled his mind, followed by Hawke's voice, tight with agony and excitement. *That thing is incredible!*

Dammit, Wings. You're the only one who would find the real goddamn bogeyman fascinating.

Jag, is everyone still with us? Tighe asked.

Kougar?

Here. Kougar's voice, though barely recognizable. *Got clawed . . . in . . . head. Mind . . . slowing.*

It's the venom, Jag said. To Tighe he said, *Everyone's still with us, but Kougar's got venom in the brain. We need to get the hell out of here, Stripes.*

For once I completely agree with you. Tell them to pull back. Dammit. I can't get out through the warding in human form. We're going to have to shift again.

Back into your animals, boys and girls, Jag said to the group. *We're leaving the way we came in.*

Tighe yelled, a cry of fury and pain. *Goddamn that hurts!*

I can't shift, Hawke said.

I can't . . . shift, either, Tighe gasped.

Kougar? Jag called. *Kougar!*

No answer.

Oh, shit. There's a second Daemon outside. Tighe's voice rang with fury and desperation. *I can feel Delaney's worry shifting to terror.*

A bolt of raw fear tore through Jag. Olivia could possibly fight the Daemon as she had before, but stealing its power at this point could kill everyone out there, and he knew her well enough to know she wouldn't risk it. She'd never endanger the others. Which would put her in grave danger herself.

They're in trouble, Tighe called. *Jag, get out there. You're the only one who can reach them!*

Hawke yelled with pain.

If he left now, he'd be leaving his brothers in the dark with that thing, with no way to communicate. No way out. Deep in his gut, he knew he was their only chance of survival.

I'm not leaving without you, he told the three. *But we've got to find a way out of here. Fast.*

Olivia wasn't going to die on him. She was not going to die.

But another slice of pain ripped down his back, and he wondered if they hadn't all reached the end of their lives.

Olivia's flesh literally rippled as she watched a Daemon approach for the second time in as many days, the experience no less horrifying . . . no less terrifying . . . than the first time. Because, although she'd discovered a defense against the Daemon, she couldn't use it without harming her friends.

Did this son of a bitch hurt Jag? Kill him?

The thought stole her breath like a fist in the gut. She didn't want Jag dead. *Please, not that.*

"Where do you think my shots will do the most good?" Delaney asked calmly beside her. "The head or the heart?"

"Go for the head. I'm not sure he has a heart."

The crack of gunfire shattered the stillness of the day. The humans would almost certainly come running, which would only make matters worse; but they had to stop this thing if they were going to stand any chance of reaching the Ferals.

Delaney fired several more times, hitting her target every time—twice between the eyes, once in the neck, and once in the chest where his heart ought to be, but he never slowed. He didn't seem to feel the bullets.

"Well, that sucks," Delaney muttered. She holstered her gun and pulled the hunting knife she now wore strapped to her belt.

Olivia nodded to herself as she watched the woman. Not many humans could remain calm in the face of such a monster. Tighe had chosen well.

The four stood together, shoulder to shoulder, Olivia and Delaney in the middle, Ewan and Niall on either side. The Daemon hesitated, his gaze on Olivia. Did it recognize her? She couldn't be certain, but it looked like the one that had attacked her last night.

Olivia's heart pounded, her skin crawling with sheer terror. She had to try to feed from the thing without hurting the others. Which meant she'd either have to draw it away or draw its attack.

But as she took a step forward, Niall's firm hand clamped down on her shoulder. "Olivia, no."

"Release me, Niall, and stay where you are. All of you. I've faced this thing once and survived." And it was this one, she was almost sure of it.

Niall's hand fell away. But as she moved forward, the Daemon floated back. Interesting. Did it sense her plan? Did it remember her, too? Maybe it would just keep moving back, away from them all.

Without looking back, she judged she'd put about three meters between herself and her companions. Not nearly as much space as she'd like, but the distance between her and Daemon was now less than that between her and her friends. She might be able to feed from it without endangering them.

The back door to the house opened and a woman walked out, the same woman she'd seen in the parking lot of Wal-Mart. Mystery, they'd called her. Her gaze met Olivia's and held, as if Olivia were the only one of importance, the only reason the sorceress had bothered to step outside.

"Come to me, Therian."

Olivia scoffed. "Why in the hell would I do that?"

"Rear attack!" Niall's call had her whirling in a quick arc. The sight she faced behind her chilled her as much as the one in front. While they'd faced the Daemon, four Mage sentinels had crept up from behind. *Dammit, I shouldn't have been taken off guard.*

Niall's call had alerted them all, but too late. Even as Olivia ran back the way she'd come, she watched Ewan tackled from behind by two Mage sentinels.

As the other two sentinels took on Niall and Delaney, Olivia raced to keep the first pair from overpowering and enthralling Ewan.

But even as she closed the distance between them, the big Therian went suddenly, totally still. Too late.

Goddess help us all.

Mage on one side, a Daemon on the other.

As she leaped at one of Ewan's attackers, the sentinel jumped to his feet to meet the steel of her blade with his own. All her fury, all her frustration, all her fear for Jag and the others poured into her knife arm and while her center of gravity was far lower than her opponent's, she was quick and strong and coldly driven. Within seconds, she'd cut off his hand, sending blade and appendage flying in a spray of blood.

As the Mage howled in pain, she took advantage of his distress to cut off his other hand. Without hesitation, she grabbed his arm and began stealing his life force through her fingers.

The wind kicked up in displeasure.

Her gaze strafed the battlefield. Niall, a strong, sure fighter, would have his Mage opponent down in a trice, but Delaney wasn't as adept at knife fights and appeared to be barely holding her own. Tighe had never intended her to fight. They all knew it. He'd meant for

Ewan to protect her in case they did have to take on one of the Mage.

But everything had gone to hell in a hurry.

As Olivia sucked her opponent's life force, his pain-filled eyes widened with understanding, an understanding he'd never voice. Before he could fall unconscious and give her away, she stabbed him in the chest and dug out his heart.

Just as her blade popped free of his chest, Ewan launched himself at her.

"Ewan, no!" But his eyes were dull with enthrallment, and nothing she said would make a difference. He'd fallen under the control of the Mage.

She dodged his attempt to tackle her to the ground, knowing well, after so many years, Ewan's every move, every strength and weakness. He was stronger than he was quick. And she, particularly after having taken the Mage's entire life force, was both.

As she fought Ewan, she saw Niall cut through his opponent's wrist, and watched as Ewan's second attacker went after Niall instead. Her old friend was a quick, skilled fighter. He should be okay, even against two Mage. As she watched, he ripped out the heart of his first opponent and turned to the second.

The blowing wind began to swirl.

But as she dodged a swipe of Ewan's blade that missed her hip by millimeters, her heart stopped cold. The Daemon swooped in behind Niall.

Olivia yelled, but to no avail. With one wickedly clawed hand, the Daemon dug deep into Niall's skull. With the other, he raked off a wide strip of bloody flesh from Niall's face.

The cry of pain that erupted from her old friend's throat went through her like a dull, serrated blade. Anguish and fury roared up inside her as she ducked beneath Ewan's stab and kneed him hard enough in the balls to send him falling backward.

She had to reach Niall. But as she turned to do just that, Delaney stepped directly in front of her, the two Mage at Delaney's back. The FBI agent's eyes, too, had turned dull with enchantment.

Behind them, Niall had gone still, no longer fighting, and she knew the venom must have conquered his brain. Even as she watched, the Daemon tore a second strip of flesh from Niall's skull ripping out one eye and drawing a horrible cry of pain from his nearly immobilized throat.

Olivia felt the blood drain from her face, a cold, desperate horror washing down her back. Niall would die unless she stopped the Daemon. Using her superior strength, she knocked Delaney's feet out from under her and rammed her elbow into the base of the woman's skull hard enough to knock her out cold, praying she'd remain safe like that. The Daemon fed on pain and fear and would, hopefully, ignore an unconscious woman.

As one, Ewan and the two Mage came at her as if to tackle her to the ground. She slipped by two of them, but the third cut her off, and she found herself surrounded, unable to do anything but counter the steel blows with her own blades.

Niall made another horrible cry of pain. Out of the corner of her eye, she saw that the Daemon had moved in front of him and slashed his gut wide open. With his clawed hand, the Daemon pulled Niall's intestines out of his body.

Dear goddess. She had to save him, but she was fighting for her own life, desperately trying to save herself.

Did she dare try to feed enough to scare off the Daemon? Could she possibly do so without hurting the others? The risk was terrible, for Niall already clung to life by a thread.

She had no choice. Out of options.

Olivia opened herself and fed at what had become her lowest level.

The Daemon squawked, but didn't move away. It wasn't enough. She increased her feeding strength until finally Ewan's and the Mage's attacks slowed. Ewan stumbled, and Olivia took the opportunity to escape the two remaining blades and vaulted for the Daemon.

If she could reach him, touch him . . .

Niall had fallen unconscious. Had she killed him when she fed? Had she stolen the last of his strength? Even as the horrible thought tore at her mind, the Daemon reached deep into Niall's chest cavity and ripped out his heart. And she knew whatever she'd done hadn't mattered.

Her friend was dead.

In a haze of grief and fury, Olivia ran at the Daemon, grabbing his wrist with her left hand, intending to suck the life out of him as she stabbed him with her right, but the touch of her hand against his sent a jolt of revulsion through her so strong she forgot what she was doing. His arm felt like living, writhing snakes beneath her palm. Electricity jolted through her, a cold current that chilled her to the marrow of her bones.

She shook herself out of her shock and opened herself, sucking in his essence.

The Daemon struck so quickly, she didn't see him move until it was too late. With one wicked claw, he sliced cleanly through her wrist, taking off the hand that held him.

Olivia stumbled back, pain exploding as she stared in disbelief at the stump of her wrist, watching her hand fall into the grass as the Daemon rose and flew away.

Shock vaulted through her system, and she didn't hear the men behind her until she collided with the ground. The impact cleared her mind.

Survive. She had to survive. She tried to roll onto her stomach, reaching out only to slam her bloody stump into the ground instead. A scream of pain ripped from her lungs, then cut off abruptly as Ewan landed on top of her, pinning her to the ground with his massive weight.

Ewan's fist slammed into her jaw, knocking her head back into the dirt, nearly sending her into unconsciousness.

She struggled to focus, watching as one of the Mage leaned toward her with a cold, satisfied smile. "You belong to us, now."

His hand reached for her face.

He had to reach Olivia!

But he couldn't leave his brothers behind. Never in his life could Jag remember feeling such a battle of loyalties.

Stripes, Wings! he yelled mentally. *Kougar, if you can hear me, try calling on the power of your animals.*

Good idea, Tighe said. *We've got to do something! What about Kougar?*

He's not answering.

Dammit. Alright, let's get Hawke and me back in our animals. Then I want the two of you out of here helping the Therians and D. I'll try to reach Kougar.

Hawke's shout of pain tore through Jag's head. *I got . . . a stab in . . . before he clawed me. His robe isn't . . . cloth. More like smoke. My knife went right through it.*

At least we don't have to cut ourselves, Jag drawled. *The goddamned Daemon's done that for us already.*

His mind kept going to Olivia. If only he could communicate with her, to know she was all right.

Red? Olivia!

Tighe's voice rang in his head. *I'm blooding my fist and raising it, Jag. Tell the others, then lead the chant. This may be the only chance we get. Still no word from Kougar?*

No. None.

Then let's do this.

Spirits rise and join, Jag chanted, since he was the only one still in his animal and the only one they could hear. *Empower the beast within this hell.*

He couldn't hear verbal speech, only telepathy, so couldn't hear the others repeating the words. It didn't matter. All that mattered was that they heard him.

Over and over, he repeated the chant, his body tense and ready, waiting for that moment one or all of them shouted with the joy of the shift and let him know they'd succeeded. Then he'd spring out of this shit hole and race to Olivia's side.

But no shout sounded in his mind. Nothing but dead silence. The silence of defeat.

Kougar crouched, knives at the ready, blood running down his neck from where the Daemon had ripped off a strip of his scalp. His head was healing, but the venom had seeped into his mind, screwing up his brain. Already, he'd lost speech. He couldn't even reply telepathically to Jag's calls. Though he still had complete, complex thoughts, the part of his brain that turned them into language had been disabled by the venom. He'd recover eventually.

If he survived long enough.

In his head, he heard Jag calling him, but he couldn't respond. Again, Kougar fought to move forward, but nothing happened. Was he truly making no progress, or could he simply not feel it?

The telltale movement of air warned him of another attack a split second before claws raked across his neck and shoulder, opening him wide. Kougar spun, slicing high at the creature with his knife, feeling the blade dig into flesh. His face?

The Daemon screeched and shot out of range. Kougar tried to follow, but the warding kept him trapped. It was times like this he was glad he felt little pain, or he'd be hurting like a son of a bitch. As it was, the ripped flesh was a mild discomfort, nothing more.

Jag ordered them to join him in the chant that would raise the spirit and power of the animals. Kougar tried to respond, but as before, nothing happened. He couldn't join in, which would leave him trapped in this prison, unable to move forward or back, at the mercy of the Daemon.

He fought the growing lethargy of his mind, fought

to find the power within him to shift so he could get out of this place. A glimmer of energy skated along the edges of his brain. For one brilliant moment, he thought the chant might be working, he thought he'd found the power to change back into his animal.

Then he realized what he was feeling. Not his own energy, but another. Ilina energy.

Even as the realization hit him, Melisande and Brielle materialized before him, their forms insubstantial. Mist. How they'd breached the warding, he didn't know, but he could both see and hear them.

Not in years had he been so glad to see a damned Ilina.

Melisande spoke. "You're in trouble warrior. Our psychic sees you dying here without intervention. Queen Ariana bade us let you die, but the psychic says no. You're useful still if we reconnect the link that was severed."

Reconnect the link . . . ? Kougar's mind reeled. *No.* He shook his head adamantly, unable to say the word. As much as he hated not feeling, reconnecting him would mean he'd feel everything again. Worse. A thousand times worse.

"Then you shall die. So, too, will your friends, for it's your voice they need joined with theirs to raise the power of their animals, to free them from this prison. Would you, out of stubbornness, steal four Feral lives?"

The bitch knew he wouldn't let that happen. But, goddess, he didn't want this. For a thousand years, he'd felt little emotion, and only the barest heat, cold, or pain. But the pain and the emotion lived inside him, dormant, waiting for the day they'd be free again to rise up and dig their fangs deep into his heart, making him bleed. Again.

He did not want this.

But what choice had he? Melisande might be many things, but she'd never been a liar. If she said the psychic claimed Kougar would die in this place and his brothers along with him, they would die.

A shudder tore through his mind.

Meeting Melisande's gaze, he nodded.

The Ilina floated to him, her mistlike hands curving around the golden band that circled his upper arm. At first he felt the usual nothing. Then, slowly, warmth began to seep into his flesh. Warmth that grew hotter and hotter until the band glowed like molten gold, and his flesh burned.

The heat spread up into his shoulder, flushing through his chest and up into his head, leaving a trail of searing pain. Deep inside him, the emotions that had long been encased in ice burst free—ancient grief, bitter betrayal.

Fury.

He would kill the bitch. He'd kill her!

Brielle stepped forward, the top of her head not even

reaching his chin, her small hands lifting to press against his temples. "I cannot remove the venom, Kougar, but I can pull it back and hold it until you've shifted."

Seething hatred and white-hot fury ripped across his mind, but they weren't directed at either of the Ilinas before him. No, it was another woman he had to thank for nearly destroying him.

Ariana, Queen of the Ilinas.

Ariana, his mate, his wife. The woman he'd loved beyond measure until she faked her own death, betraying everything they'd meant to one another.

She would pay. Goddess help him, he would find a way to make her pay for severing the mating bond all those centuries ago, making him believe she was dead. For a thousand years he'd suffered, his heart cold as an arctic night, his life turned to dust.

And it had all been a lie.

As Brielle worked, he began to feel the venom's lock on his brain loosen.

Jag's voice continued to chant in his head.

Jag, I'm here. Keep chanting.

He did. And this time, when Kougar tried to join him, the words came.

As Kougar joined the chant, a rumble trembled through Jag's body, a deep, rolling thunder he could feel but not hear. Even though he was already in his animal, the power jolted through him as the magic began to grow.

Hope leaped. And then he heard the sound he'd held his breath for. The triumphant shouts of the other Ferals.

It worked! Tighe shouted. *Let's get the hell out of here.*

Without a second's hesitation, Jag turned and leaped back through the warding, out of the darkness, and into a scene of rain and carnage. Four bodies littered the grass around a single, raging battle, in the middle of which lay his Red.

As he landed, his right foreleg collapsed beneath him, torn and half-paralyzed from the Daemon's venom. He rolled through the grass, righting himself and shifting back into his human form all in one move, his injured foreleg now an arm that wouldn't hamper his run.

The wind whipped violently, slashing his bare flesh with a torrent of cold, stinging rain. But he barely felt it, his focus on one thing only. Reaching Olivia.

Ewan had her pinned on the ground, slamming his fist into her jaw. One of them had to be enchanted or the male would never turn against her. He just hoped to hell it was Ewan. It had to be. Olivia wasn't feeding.

Behind Ewan, a Mage reached over his shoulder to touch Olivia. To enchant her, too. And once he did, Jag would have no choice but to kill her. To stop her before she killed them all.

He leaped, shifting in midair, and snapped his powerful jaws around the Mage's hand, millimeters from

Olivia's face. Bone crunched beneath his teeth, blood spilling warm into his mouth as he yanked the Mage off his feet, away from Olivia, then ripped the appendage from the bastard's arm.

Tighe and Hawke came running, a tiger and a man, both as bloody as he was. Behind them, Kougar stumbled and fell. Conscious, but Jag suspected, barely.

Tighe reached Ewan first and tackled him off Olivia, who continued to try to fight him but . . . Jesus. Her hand . . .

Jag's gut fisted.

Hawke attacked Ewan from behind, jamming his one good thumb into the man's neck, knocking him unconscious. The moment Ewan was down, Tighe took off to where Delaney lay, unmoving. Not far from . . . *holy shit*. Was that skeletal mass Niall?

Ah, goddess.

Hawke started for Olivia. Jag growled deep in his jaguar's throat and shifted. "Take the Mage, Hawke. I'll see to her."

Hawke looked up, his face bloody, his eyes calm. He nodded and drew his knives as Jag ran for Olivia, who was even now trying to sit up. Her bright hair flew around her face in a wind that had risen to near-hurricane force. A face far too pale and pinched with pain.

The hand would regrow, though not without a fair amount of agony. But she lived. Goddess, she still lived.

As he sank down beside her, their gazes collided.

Hers, shattered, clung to him. "The Daemon . . . ?"

"Nowhere in sight." Her gaze slid over him, pinched with misery as it returned to his. She swallowed hard, a sheen of tears bright in her eyes.

"I thought . . ."

Had she been afraid for him? A nearly overwhelming need to gather her into his arms took hold of him. But before he reached for her, she turned, her gaze flying to the corpse in the yard.

His hands fisted at his sides as tears welled in her eyes, and he knew a terrible jealousy.

"Niall?" he asked tersely.

She nodded, struggling to her feet. "The Daemon killed him." As she started for the corpse, Jag stared at her back, feeling angry, deserted. Bereft.

He turned away. The Therian bastard hadn't deserved to die, but Jag wasn't going to stand there and watch her mourn him.

Tighe strode toward him cradling Delaney's unmoving form in his arms.

Jag's gaze jerked to Tighe's face and knew at once the woman remained alive. Anger and frustration burned in the tiger shifter's eyes, but no devastation. No grief.

"She's unconscious," Tighe said, confirming Jag's observation.

"I knocked her out, Tighe," Olivia said behind him. "The Mage . . ." She gasped with pain, and he turned to find her curling around her arm. Limbs were a bitch to regrow. He'd regrown his share of them, as he was sure she had, too. No one fought for centuries without losing a few. The pain, sharp as hell, came in waves as the bone pushed through, re-forming the lost hand. The whole process didn't take long, but she would suffer.

Then she'd be fine and could fully grieve for her lost lover.

The thought burned the insides of his skull.

"The Mage enthralled her," Olivia continued when the burst of pain had apparently passed. "Be careful when she wakes. Ewan, too."

Tighe nodded, his brows pulling together in concern. "Can you walk through that? We need to get out of here. Back to Feral House for some serious radiance."

Jag stilled. No way in hell should he be taking Olivia back to Feral House. Not in her Daemon-strong condition. But he needed the radiance, needed to go back. And leaving her out here alone would raise all kinds of questions.

He wasn't leaving her out here alone. No way was he leaving her . . . at all.

Shit.

If he stayed close to her at all times, taking her back there should be safe enough. He could stop her if her feeding ever got out of control.

He prayed to the goddess it never came to that.

Hawke joined them, Ewan slung over his shoulder

like one mammoth sack of grain, Kougar silent at his side.

"What about Niall?" Olivia choked on the name. "I can't leave him here."

"I'll get him," Jag told her.

She met his gaze, a hollow look in her eyes that twisted inside him, angering him more.

There was no logic to his anger, he knew that. Niall was dead, and she'd paid him little enough attention when he lived. But logic had nothing to do with his feelings for this woman. Hell, he didn't know what he wanted, if he even wanted anything at all. All he knew was her grief made him feel like slamming his fist through something.

Because he couldn't stand seeing her in pain, even if that pain was all for another man.

Olivia curled around her left arm on the drive back to Great Falls and Feral House as pain tore through her wrist in wave after scalding wave. She felt as if someone were taking a hatchet to her, cutting off her hand over and over again.

Jag sat beside her in the Hummer, driving, his free hand gently gripping her thigh. Tighe and Delaney sat behind them and, in the far back, Ewan lay tied and unconscious.

The blood had long ago drained from her face, and her skin felt clammy, sweat mixing with the rain that had already soaked her through. Shivering with cold and the aftereffects of battle, her stomach threatened to send up the lunch her system had long ago devoured.

But it was anger that tore at her mind.

Niall shouldn't have died. She'd let herself become so focused on the damn Daemon, she hadn't seen the Mage sneaking up on them. If they hadn't lost Ewan so quickly, maybe . . . maybe . . . she wouldn't have lost Niall at all.

Pain ripped through her again, braiding with the anger. An anger she knew she had to push aside. She'd tried to save him. She'd done her best.

But she could handle the anger so much better than the alternative. On the edges of her consciousness, just beyond the fury and pain, lay another monster waiting to devour her. The grief, the horror, of watching Niall die.

She couldn't deal with that now. Wouldn't.

Another wave of agony tore through her limb, and she grabbed Jag's hand with her good one, curling her fingers around the back of his as she sucked in a hard breath and held on. His fingers curled around hers, giving her an anchor. A lifeline.

As the wave of agony passed, she began to feel her new appendage. With a shudder, she hazarded a glance down. The one thing she'd learned from prior experiences was never to watch her limbs re-form. The pain doubled when she saw the bones sticking out and growing before her eyes.

What met her gaze now relieved her. The bones were all there, the muscle knitting as she watched. One more growth spurt, maybe two, and she'd be done.

The Hummer jerked, buffeted by nature's fury over the death of four more Mage. Jag held her tight.

"You going to be able to keep this thing on the road?" Tighe asked from the backseat.

"Nature's throwing a minor tantrum," Jag muttered.

The Ferals had ultimately dispatched the Mage Olivia hadn't killed. Both Ewan and Delaney were still unconscious, but only Ewan was tied. Tighe had left his vehicle in Harpers Ferry so that he could ride in the backseat of the Hummer, his arms about Delaney, his eye on Ewan.

The fire exploded in her wrist again, bone pulsing. Lights exploded behind her eyes. Sweat ran down her temples, and she gasped for breath.

Jag squeezed her good hand, but it was Tighe who offered words of comfort.

"Hang in, Olivia. It shouldn't take too much longer. You'll be good as new in a few more minutes."

"I . . . know." Goddess, but it hurt! When she could breathe again, her gaze went to Jag, driving so stoic and silent. Had he been hurt? Had more happened than she'd realized? Or was he worrying about taking her home? To be honest, she hadn't expected him to take her back to Feral House at all now that he knew her secret.

She looked back at Tighe, Delaney unconscious on his lap. "Are the four of you Ferals all right?"

He nodded, his eyes grave. "As far as I can tell. We fell into some kind of sensory-deprivation trap with a Daemon or two waiting. We couldn't see them, but damn, we could feel their claws."

"Venom?"

"We're all still feeling the effects, which is why we're heading back to Feral House instead of rallying the forces. We need radiance. I've already called Lyon."

Olivia glanced at Jag, but he didn't look her way. He'd said virtually nothing since they set out, and she hated that she couldn't read him, that she didn't know what was going on in his head.

Another wave of pain hit her hand, shallow and weak compared to the others, and she knew from experience it would be the last. Slowly, she straightened her arm and held out her new hand, identical to the one she'd lost. As it should be. On an exhausted sigh, she tipped her head back and closed her eyes, feeling the grief pressing in. In defense, she struggled to find the anger instead and pulled it tight around her.

"What the hell?" Ewan's voice sounded groggily in the back of the vehicle.

Olivia turned, watching as Tighe pulled a wicked blade. "How are you doing, Ewan?" the tiger shifter asked calmly.

"What happened?"

"What do you remember?" Tighe's voice remained soft and even.

"Shit. Why am I tied?"

"That wasn't the question."

Ewan levered himself into a sitting position despite his bonds, his gaze finding hers and holding fast. In his eyes, she saw confusion, but no enthrallment.

"He's fine," she told Tighe.

Understanding lit Ewan's eyes. "I got tackled by the Mage, didn't I? Enthralled."

"Afraid so," Tighe replied.

"What happened to the Daemon?"

"He got away. Ewan . . ." Olivia hesitated. "Niall . . ." The words caught in her throat, and she fought to hold on to the anger. "The Daemon got to him. I couldn't stop him."

Ewan's brows drew down, his mouth tightening. "What are you saying?"

"He's dead."

Ewan stared at her. "No. No!"

He whirled to face the back, and she turned front. There was nothing more she could do. *Dammit. Dammit.* The fury turned and twisted inside her, cocooning the emotions she couldn't deal with until they were nothing but a hard mass deep in the pit of her stomach.

They continued on, the country roads quickly giving way to the congestion of heavily populated Fairfax

County. Delaney woke as they pulled into the long drive of Feral House, her mind once more clear.

Jag parked the Hummer, and Olivia climbed out, went around the vehicle, and released Ewan from the back. His gaze met hers, his eyes dark with pain, his cheeks damp as she'd feared they might be. Niall and Ewan had been as close as brothers for centuries. Seeing his devastation tore something loose inside her. She clamped her teeth together hard and climbed into the back with him as she pulled her knife and released him from his bonds.

As the big man swiped at his cheeks, hiding the telltale weakness, she crawled back out before he could touch her, or in any way try to share his grief with her. She didn't want it. Didn't need it.

Goddess, she couldn't deal with his, too. She had enough of her own.

Jag waited for her outside the vehicle, his brows low, his face hard.

Hawke and Kougar pulled up behind them in a black Yukon and got out. Each looked the worse for wear, but both were healing, their movements almost normal. Niall's corpse had been loaded into the back of Hawke's vehicle and would have to remain there until tonight, when they would perform the ancient rites, sending the body back to the earth from which it sprang.

Her mind shied from the thought of Niall consumed by that mystic fire, but Jag stole her attention when his hand gripped her arm, pulling her aside as the others passed.

His grip pinched. "Don't feed when any of the women are around, including Pink."

"All right." His words made her feel dangerous. Unclean. Like a predator he feared would turn on his friends.

And, goddess, wasn't that exactly what she was? She'd never turn on them intentionally, but she was, absolutely, dangerous.

Jag steered her after the others, and they followed them up the stairs and into the grand foyer of Feral House.

Lyon and Kara waited for them, Lyon in a gold silk shirt, his sleeves rolled up, and Kara in trim black slacks and a neat peach-colored sweater, her blond hair in a ponytail, her feet bare. Both watched them enter with eyes filled with concern.

"Wulfe and Vhyper are preparing the circle out back," Lyon said. "We're going to start with radiance and take it from there if we need to. I want my warriors healed and whole before we plan our next attack."

Two abreast, they walked through the wide hallways, into the huge dining room, and out the back door. The trees were beginning to sprout leaves, but the spring canopy was still thin, allowing rain to filter through with relative ease. Fortunately, they'd left the hurricane behind miles back, and the bulk of the natural weather front had moved through.

Lyon led them to a clearing in the back of the mansion. Even before they drew close, Olivia could feel the mystic energies. A feral circle, she'd heard it called, though as a mere Therian she'd never experienced one.

Kara stepped into the middle of the circle, and the Ferals gathered around her. Kara might be taller than Olivia, but the men still dwarfed her. Yet, to a man, they treated her with a respect and affection Olivia suspected they reserved for very few. Even Jag left his usual attitude behind when he stepped into that circle.

Lyon stood before his mate, holding out his hands. As Kara slipped hers into the cradle of his much larger ones, the others moved in close. Tighe stood directly behind her, his palm against her neck. Hawke took his place on one side, his hand on her arm, Jag on the other in the same way. Wulfe, Vhyper, and Kougar knelt at her feet, their hands on an ankle or calf.

"Ready?" Kara asked.

Lyon nodded once, his gaze gentle on his mate. "Do it, little Radiant."

In an instant, Kara lit up as if she'd swallowed the sun, her skin glowing. Radiant. And Olivia was slammed with a force of pure, perfect energy. Like an alcoholic with an open bottle thrust before her nose, she craved with a violence that scared her.

"She's beautiful, isn't she?" Delaney murmured beside her. "I never get tired of watching her do this."

Olivia nodded, desperately fighting the pull of

the energy, terrified that if she gave in and fed, she wouldn't stop. She wouldn't be able to stop. For minute after minute, the energy battered her senses, the hunger clawing to be fed.

Kara's light finally went out and that terrible hunger abated.

Goddess.

Olivia's knees nearly collapsed beneath her.

The men rose and stepped back, lifting arms and shrugging shoulders, loosening and assessing muscles like warriors preparing for battle.

Lyon crossed his arms over his chest and watched them closely, waiting. "Do we need another round?"

"I'm good," Tighe said.

Hawke nodded. "As am I."

"Kougar?" Lyon watched the cold-eyed Feral most closely.

"The fog is cleared, Roar. The radiance has completely counteracted the venom."

"Good."

Tighe walked toward the two women, his gaze all for his wife. His big hands cupped Delaney's face, his eyes filled with a depth of emotion Olivia could hardly fathom.

"Are you okay?" Tighe asked his mate softly.

"I'm fine," Delaney replied, her voice rich with love as her hands rose to cover Tighe's.

Envy twisted around Olivia's heart, squeezing that already-bruised-and-battered organ. Niall had loved her in his way. Or he thought he had. Yet he'd never truly known her.

The hard cocoon in her gut twisted, tightening every muscle in her neck and shoulders, filling her head with a tension that had her feeling like she'd explode at any moment.

Anger ate at her. Envy. Fury. She hated her life, hated what she was, hated that the only man who had ever understood her wasn't happy unless he was making her miserable. Hated that her heart wanted too much more from him. So much that he wasn't able, or willing, to give.

When Tighe dipped his head to kiss his mate tenderly, Olivia whirled and stalked off toward the house, the anger eating at the insides of her flesh until she clamored for a battle. Any kind of battle.

And suddenly Jag was at her side.

"Where are you going?"

She didn't answer. She didn't have a damned answer. This wasn't her house.

Jag's hand gripped her upper arm, pulling her to a stop.

Her anger erupted and she whirled on him, whipping out a knife. "Remove your hand or you're going to be the one regrowing a limb."

She saw her own fury mirrored in his eyes, his brows drawing down and hard. But he didn't remove his hand. "Do your worst, Sugar, but not here." He took off for the back door, dragging her along behind him.

Chapter Seventeen

Jag hauled Olivia through the house and up the first flight of stairs, pushing her through the door of his room. She was spitting mad, itching for a fight, and he was in a mood to give it to her.

She stared around the room, clearly unimpressed, and it ticked him off.

"What did you expect, the Taj Mahal?" he sneered. Though goddess knew the room was as barren as his soul.

He looked around, seeing it through her eyes. A large bed sat in the middle of the room, little more than a mattress and springs below a solid, unadorned white wall. No curtains hung at the windows, no mementoes sat on the dresser. No paintings on the wall. How many times had their previous Radiant, Beatrice, tried to put up paintings of jaguars and jungles? Exactly as many times as he'd torn them down.

Other than the fact that there were sheets on the bed—plain white—the room could have been unoccupied.

He happened to like it like this.

Olivia whirled on him so fast he took a fist to the nose before he realized what she had in mind.

He laughed, but the sound was ugly. Anger ate him alive, a mass of emotion he only knew two ways to get rid of—a good old-fashioned fight. Or sex.

He had a feeling he was about to get both.

Snagging Olivia around the waist, he lifted her and tossed her on the bed, then yanked off his shirt, intending to follow her down, but her eyes flashed with fury, and he could see she'd had enough of being his slave. The storm inside her contained not an ounce of fear. No, if he had to guess, she was transferring grief. For Niall. Which pissed the hell out of him.

"He wasn't good enough for you." He dove on top of her, careful to brace himself with his arms.

She slammed her knee between his thighs, but he clamped them together, barely keeping her from unmanning him, trapping her leg between his.

"He was a hell of a lot better man than you'll ever be."

A fist clenched inside him, driving his anger. "He was a pansy-assed wuss who let you walk all over him."

With a furious growl, she head-butted him, catching him in the damn nose again. He reared back, and she slipped out from under him and launched herself at him, stronger than any female had a right to be, especially one who barely reached his shoulder.

His male instincts told him to be careful with her. His breaking ribs told him she could handle whatever he dished out.

He tackled her down. "Did you have feelings for him?"

She punched him in the jaw. "Of course I had feelings for him! I'd known him for more than three hundred years. You wouldn't know feelings if they bit you in the ass!"

They fought, her throwing punches, him blocking most of them. The bed creaked and swayed beneath them.

"Did you love him?"

"You know the answer to that. As a friend, yes, but you know I didn't return the feelings he had for me." Her elbow slammed into his solar plexus. "But so help me, if you think I shouldn't care that he's dead . . ." Her heel drove hard into his knee. "If you think I can just forget the sight of that monster stripping his face away one strip of flesh at a time . . ." Her voice cracked. "So help me, Jag, I'm going to beat your cold ass to hell and back."

The bed collapsed beneath them with a crash. He rolled onto his feet, but Olivia followed, spinning and slamming her heel into his knee again, splintering his kneecap. With a roar, he collapsed onto his other knee just as the door burst open wide.

Tighe and Wulfe pushed inside, then halted in the doorway, staring at the wreckage of the bed, him on his knees, blood running down his face and his fire demon of a partner standing over him about to drive her elbow into his skull.

Jag grinned. Goddess, but he loved a strong woman. He wiped the blood from his mouth and gave Tighe a jaunty salute.

Olivia whirled on the pair in the doorway, her eyes blazing with unholy fire. "Unless you want to join the fight, get the hell out of here."

Tighe lifted his hands in quick surrender. "I'm gone."

Wulfe, the bastard, grinned. "Don't kill him."

The respite had given his knee a chance to heal. As Wulfe pulled the door closed behind him, Jag shot to his feet, ready for another round. He loved a good fight, and this one had gotten his blood pumping, and at the same time given him an outlet for the awful tension that had been riding him ever since that goat fuck of a battle.

But Olivia's eyes showed no such relief. Deep in those gray depths, he could see her shattering. His heart clenched in his chest as he understood. She fought the grief and her own emotions more than she fought him.

And while he'd gladly let her beat the crap out of him if it helped her, he could see it wasn't helping at all.

The emotion needed another way out. The sheen in her eyes told him that.

She launched herself at him again, but even as she did, tears began to run down her cheeks, seeming to make her madder. He let her get in a couple of good punches, then he grabbed her in a bear hug and pressed her face against his chest as she struggled.

"Let it out, Liv," he said quietly. "You're not going to get rid of it until you give in. Just let it out."

She fought him a moment more, her fists pummeling his shoulders until the storm overtook her. Sobs wracked her small body, her fists opening, her fingers clinging to him as grief swept her away.

He felt a deep and sudden need to comfort her and didn't have a clue how to do it. He'd always been great at causing anger. Soothing raging emotions was beyond him. He could always use the calming touch of his hand, but he sensed that wasn't what she needed right now. She needed to get it out.

He patted her back awkwardly.

She buried her face tighter against him, clinging to him harder, as if his attempts weren't that awkward at all.

He lifted his hand and cupped her small head, holding it tight against him. Deep inside his chest, he felt a cracking of the ice that had for so long encased his heart.

He didn't want that. Didn't need it. But even as the thought went through his head, his arms enclosed her in a vise of a protective cage through which nothing would ever harm her again.

As if she heard his thoughts, she lifted her head, meeting his gaze with eyes that swam in misery even as they clung to him. As he stared into those gray depths, he felt himself falling. Deep inside, warmth flowed from that crack in his heart, rushing through his blood and limbs, into all the cold, dark crevices. Waking his body, his mind. His soul.

And stirring the bitterness and bile into a frenzy.

Never had he felt such a pull between wanting and not wanting. Even as the darkness inside him tried to shore up the cracks in the wall of ice, draining his heart of the unwanted warmth, he found himself pulling her tighter against him.

He pressed his lips to her forehead and clung to her as she did him, conflicting emotions a tempest inside him. He was what he was. A man without love. Without family, but for the men forced to include him. Without friends.

He'd been this way for too many years to count, and would always be, even if he sometimes wished he could be someone else. How many thousands of times had he wished he were a different man? Not Jag.

Olivia lifted a single hand to press against his cheek, and he was lost. The warmth filled him, pressing back the bile and bitterness and filling him until he thought he would burst from the pressure of it.

She looked up at him, her eyes filling with tears all over again. "I thought I'd lost you," she whispered, her voice breaking.

"Lost me?"

"In that house. Delaney felt Tighe's pain, but we couldn't reach you, couldn't hear you. Then the Daemon flew out of there, drenched in blood, and I thought . . ." Her voice cracked.

He lifted his hand and stroked the bright fall of hair back from her lovely face, barely crediting her words. "You were worried about me?"

A watery smile broke over her face, sending sunshine pouring into his soul. "You drive me crazy, Jag." Her mouth tightened, her bottom lip trembling. "But I don't want anything to happen to you. I need you."

He'd been so angry, thinking her tears were all for Niall. But she'd been dealing with the remnants of fear, too, just as he had. Because, goddess, he'd been terrified when he'd realized one of the Daemons was loose in the yard.

He cupped her face in his hands. "I'm sorry about Niall. I'm sorry I let my jealousy of him get in the way of letting you know that."

Her eyes grew dark as a nightmare. "No one should die like that."

He tilted her head toward him and placed a gentle

kiss on her brow, then lifted her face to his again, meeting her gaze. "We'll get that bastard, Liv. We'll get them all. If it's the last thing I do, I'll promise you that. Because you're right. No one should ever have to die like that."

She nodded, a fierce determination lighting those gray eyes even as they remained locked on his, pulling him deeper and deeper. His gaze broke from hers, for only a second, dropping to her ripe, tear-swollen mouth. Tenderness surged through him, melding with the heat he felt every time he touched her.

His gaze returned to hers and held as he slowly lowered his face. Something shimmered in her eyes, a sweet longing that stole the last of his control, and he dipped his head and kissed her for the first time.

Her lips were soft and warm, and as sweet as he'd always known they would be. Why had he never kissed her before?

Her lips moved beneath his, a low, soft moan escaping her throat. Heat and desire swirled inside him, but tenderness won the battle, an overwhelming gentleness he hadn't felt in too long to remember.

His hand slid into her hair, cradling her head, while his other slid around her waist, holding her tight, bending her back as his mouth fused with hers.

He touched her lower lip with his tongue, fire shooting through him and eliciting another moan from her as she parted her lips, giving him access. But he felt no desire to hurry, no need to rush. He wanted to savor every taste, every touch. Goddess, he wanted this to last forever.

Soft fingers slid into his hair. Her mouth moved beneath his, her tongue darting out to stroke his own. He opened his mouth over hers and slid his tongue across the full length of hers, deep into her mouth, tasting her sweetness, falling into her warmth.

Over and over, he kissed her, memorizing the contours of her mouth, the feel of her tongue and lips, the taste of her. The kiss grew hotter with every stroke of his tongue against hers, with every stroke of hers against his until his breath was ragged, his hands tense and roaming, pulling her tighter and tighter against his growing need.

His desire for her intensified until it was a living, breathing thing inside him. And at the same time, he thought he'd be perfectly content to remain like this, just kissing this woman and holding her, for the rest of his immortal life.

His lips finally, reluctantly, left her mouth, driven by a need to taste more. To taste her everywhere. He swung her into his arms, meeting her sweet, sexy gaze.

Olivia curled her arm around his neck and stroked his cheek with her hand.

Neither spoke. No words were necessary. Besides, how many times had words gotten him into trouble? He'd become so adept at using words as weapons, he was no longer certain he knew how to use them any other way.

And now, here, he wanted no more battle between them.

Deep inside him, the jaguar purred, then let out a soft roar of possession.

Mine.

The thought rang in his head and his heart, echoing all the way to his soul.

Olivia trembled as Jag silently lowered her to the broken bed and followed her down, taking up where he'd left off, kissing her cheek, her jaw, the underside of her chin.

With infinite gentleness, he undressed her, then himself, and gathered her into his arms, laying kisses upon her breasts, her shoulders, the inner curve of her elbows.

Never had she known such gentleness. Never had she allowed it. And never in a million years would she have expected it to come from Jag.

She trembled from the uncertainty as much as from the need he lifted inside her. Every time they'd made love, it had ended badly.

But never before had they connected as they had today.

He'd held her as she cried, as the emotions tore her apart. He'd opened himself for her, giving her comfort and tenderness when she'd needed them so desperately. A tenderness that made her want to cry all over again.

His lips trailed down her body unhurriedly, pleasing her. Loving her. And when they'd finished their return path, she opened her arms to him, and her thighs, uncertain if he'd finally make love to her face-to-face or flip her onto her knees as he had before.

His gaze held hers as he lowered himself into the cradle of her body and sunk deep inside her, the move unhurried. Slow and sensual and infinitely erotic, he made love to her gently, the antithesis of the violence that had come before.

Tears burned her eyes as she cupped her hands behind his neck and held his gaze as his body melded with hers, over and over, sliding in and out, driving her up on a gentle ride of such tenderness, her heart opened like a starving flower in a warm, soft rain. Loneliness washed away after so very many years.

Deep within his eyes, she saw an understanding, a sharing of that bone-deep need for a completion of the heart. The soul. But rising with that need, she saw pain in his eyes. And dark wisps of resistance.

The sensual tension rose slowly, steadily, until they were both gasping, both driving for the release that broke over them as one. Not until they were cresting together did Jag break eye contact with her. He kissed her, the kiss only fueling that exquisite release.

Never had Olivia known such perfection in joining

with another. Never had she opened herself so completely. And when Jag pulled out of her, then rolled to his side, pulling her deep in the cradle of his arms, she ached with a fragile joy.

"I don't deserve you," he whispered sleepily against her hair. "I don't deserve this."

The depth of pain in his words brought tears to her eyes, and she wrapped her arms tight around him and held on.

"You do, Jag. You're a good man. A strong, courageous, honorable, and good man."

She felt him stiffen and stroked his back, feeling an overwhelming need to ease him, to free him from the past that had him so firmly in its claws. A past filled with a horrible guilt somehow centered around his mother.

"Tell me about Cordelia, Jag. Tell me what happened to her. Please?"

He jerked, a small flinch, but he didn't roll away from her in anger, as she half expected. Little by little, the tension drained from his limbs, and he began to talk, his words tight and emotionless.

"I discovered sex when I was fourteen. With human girls. My mother had a fit when she found out, of course, forbidding me to go to the village. And being the good son that I wasn't, I ignored her and continued to sneak out. This went on for a couple of years. When I was sixteen, she'd finally had enough. One day, she followed me, bursting into the barn where I was in the middle of a hot little tryst. She ordered me off the girl, and I ignored her, of course. I was young and crazed with lust, and I don't think I could have pulled out if I'd tried. But I didn't try.

"Cordelia was . . . demanding. Not just with me, but with everyone. And it infuriated her when I didn't do her bidding, which of course just made me ignore her more. That day, she grabbed me and tried to pull me off the girl. I was still a kid, but I was already strong. I pushed her away and she fell against the wall. I don't know what she hit—I wasn't paying attention to much except getting off. But a moment later, I heard the angry shout of a man, figured I was about to get caught by the girl's father, and pulled out. But when I stood up, I realized the situation had changed. Four men had rushed into the barn, drawn by Cordelia's yelling, no doubt. But they weren't staring at the girl or me. They were staring at Cordelia, their faces turning pale as I watched.

"It was then I realized Cordelia had blood running down her cheek, dripping from her chin. And no cut, of course. It had already healed. They'd watched it heal.

"This was 1677 and witch phobia was running rampant among the humans. One of the men ordered the others to grab her, and though she struggled, they overpowered her. My traitorous little lover yelled that I was her son, that maybe I was a witch, too. I denied it."

He went silent, a shudder tearing through his warrior's body. "I denied she was my mother." His voice came close to cracking.

Olivia brushed her cheek against his chest, holding him tighter. She doubted he was even aware that his own arms had tightened, that his hands had begun to shake.

"They dragged her out of the barn and to the square, where they bound her to the stake with iron manacles and set her on fire. I ran. I didn't return to the enclave until almost nightfall and by then it was too late for anyone to go to her. If the fire hadn't already destroyed her, the draden would. The men of the enclave retrieved her body the next morning just before sunrise."

Jag's body went rigid. In a single move, he pulled away from her and stood up as if seeking escape.

"Enough of my happy childhood." He strode into the bathroom and closed the door, and she heard him turn on the shower.

Olivia hugged his pillow to her, aching with grief over his pain, and with guilt for drawing it all to the surface again. He blamed himself, in some ways rightly. Yet he'd only been a kid, and it had all happened so long ago.

But how could she ever help him see that? He'd been living with that guilt for more than three hundred years.

As she lay there listening to the sound of the shower, she feared she was in danger of falling in love with him, with a moody, difficult, mercurial man. A man she knew deep in her heart would end up hurting them both.

Chapter Eighteen

The night was cool and clear, the breeze light as Jag stood beside Olivia deep in the woods, his arm tight around her shoulders. He felt the fine tension in her body as she tilted her face to the breeze, waiting for the draden. There was a sadness about her. A melancholy left from the pyre ritual. A short while ago, in the ritual room beneath Feral House, they'd sent Niall's spirit off in a blaze of mystic fire.

But his jealousy was gone, lost in their lovemaking and the knowledge that she'd feared for him as much as he had for her.

She'd pulled her bright hair back and secured it in a casual knot, leaving her lovely features drenched in moonlight. Gazing down at her, his chest ached.

"I feel them," she said softly, looking up to meet his gaze with warm eyes alight with hunger and excitement. "Dozens of them. Maybe more."

A tendril of fear skated down his spine at the thought of her attacked by so many draden. He'd feel better if they were hunting with the other Ferals upriver, but of course the others couldn't know what Olivia could do. What she was.

"Liv, I'm not sure about this."

"I am. I'm starving, Jag. I'll be fine."

"The Hummer's just through those trees if you need it. It's unlocked."

She lifted up on tiptoe and kissed his cheek. "Thanks for worrying about me." Her words were soft, but no less heartfelt for their quietness.

Her arms went around his waist, and she pressed her cheek against his bare chest as he pulled her close. He'd stripped down as soon as they got out here, ready to shift when the moment came.

They stood like that, locked in one another's arms, until he saw the dark blotch against the night sky that never went completely dark thanks to the light pollution of nearby D.C.

"They're here, Red." He kissed her hair. "Be careful."

"You, too. If I start draining you, move away."

"You can feed from me even in my animal?"

"I'm almost positive. I've fed off creatures before when there were no people or draden around."

•

They pulled apart and he shifted into his full-sized jaguar, watching with cat eyes as she pulled two six-inch knives from inside her ripped leather jacket.

The cloud grew closer, not as big as some he'd seen lately, but a good-sized swarm, nonetheless.

His gaze went back to Olivia, and he saw the quick trace of fear that tightened her features.

What's the matter? he asked sharply. She'd sounded so sure she could handle this.

"Nothing."

You're afraid.

She glanced at him with surprise. "No. I've done this a thousand times."

You've never done this. You've never taken on a swarm this size, have you?

"Once." A small tremor went through her. "The night my mother died. The night I was turned. I don't know how many there were, in truth, but it seemed like thousands."

He heard the pain in her voice, a pain so old, yet living inside her as sharp as if it had just happened. Some things you never forgot. He knew that all too well.

I'm sorry, Liv. Sorry you had to go through that.

She nodded, her face turned toward the approaching draden cloud. "Life is what it is, Jag. You choose to deal with it, or you don't, but it is what it is."

Her words pricked at him. He dealt with it just fine.

As Jag watched with gut-wrenching dread, the swarm

descended on her. Without hesitation, he attacked, snapping his cat's jaws around draden after draden, sucking their tasteless hearts down his throat, destroying them in puff after puff of smoke.

Olivia could have simply stood still, sucking the life from the mass around her, but she didn't. With fascination, he watched her fight them, digging out their hearts with her knives. She was magnificent, twisting and stabbing, moving with a dancer's grace as if she'd choreographed the fight, the moon glowing on her vibrant hair.

Those draden foolish enough to bite her died almost instantly. Those close by lasted only a little longer. She was a far-more-effective draden-killing machine than the Ferals.

Lyon would be ecstatic if he could see her.

If he didn't kill her first.

"Jag, I can feel them." She glanced at him with eyes as filled with excitement as her voice. "I can feel each one as a distinctive life force. This has never happened before."

A draden high above her head turned into a puff of smoke. Then another, a draden she'd touched with neither hand nor knife.

"Jag." The excitement lit her face, turning her impossibly beautiful. "I can target them!"

She pointed her knife at the group rushing toward her, filling in for those who'd already died. Like a conductor marking beats, she flicked her wrist, pointing at each, one by one.

One, two, three, four.

Puff, puff, puff, puff.

"I feel like I was blind and can suddenly see." She grinned at him, the smile illuminating her face. A fist contracted around his heart even as his chest swelled and swelled and swelled.

Strong, beautiful, precious girl.

Mine.

He sat back on his haunches, watching her with fascination, sharing her excitement. She didn't need him for this. She was a master, a virtuoso directing a symphony of massacre.

The little fiends died by the dozens, but the rest kept on coming, unthinking, drawn to her Therian energy, to their primary source of food. And they, too, died.

The cloud diminished with surprising swiftness until finally, with a last puff, the draden were gone.

Olivia did a quick turn, then stopped, facing him, hands on her hips, her feet spread, her face alight with a triumphant grin.

"I'm Superwoman."

Jag shifted back into his human form and grinned at her. "You looked like Superwoman. A one-woman draden-demolition team."

"It's never been like that. I've never been able to sense them individually. I can even . . ." She cocked her head, her expression turning thoughtful. "I can feel you. Your life force, bright and whole. I think . . ." Her brows drew together. "I think I could feed just from you. Even if there were others around, I think I could target you alone."

It occurred to him that her words should probably have him reaching for his knives, but she was no danger unless she wanted to be. He was as sure of that as he was of the sun's rising in the morning. If he hadn't been, he never would have brought her back to Feral House.

She watched him with growing intensity, as if she were studying him. "Tell me if you feel anything."

He did, that sense of her feeding. Not painfully strongly, but not lightly either.

"You're feeding."

"Yes." At once, the feeling went away. "I wonder . . ."

Again, he felt a buzz, but it was different this time. Almost like a light tingle of energy that danced along the surface of his skin, sinking inside him. The energy began to flow into him, into his blood, into his muscle. His senses sharpened, his mind felt clearer, his energy renewed.

He stared at her. "What are you doing?" But he knew.

"When I feed, I pull energy into me. Right now, I'm pushing it back at you."

"I feel it. I feel stronger. Not like I'm ready to lift buses over my head, but I feel good. Rested. Ready for anything."

Her fists dropped from her hips, and she tucked her

knives away and closed the distance between them with an air of elation that made her face absolutely glow.

"Do you know what this means, Jag?"

He grinned, caught up in her joy. "Not a clue."

"It means that if I take too much from someone, like that kid at the motel, I can give it back. I can target what I'm doing. Steal from an enemy without hurting those around me. And give back to those who need it. It's brilliant!"

He slipped his hands around her waist. "Easy, Red. It's brilliant while it lasts. But this may be temporary."

The brightness of her expression dimmed. "It may be. Then again, being draden-kissed has been quite permanent."

His hands rose to cup her face. As he stared into her shining gray eyes, he was gripped by a longing so fierce, so piercing, he had to catch his breath against the force of it.

Mine.

Deep within him, the jaguar roared his approval.

He took her into his arms and kissed her like a man too long without touch. Without tenderness. And he was that man. Goddess, he was exactly that man.

Olivia reached up and slipped her arms around his neck, her fingers caressing his flesh, his scalp. She'd walked into his life like a small flaming tornado, stirring up his existence, tossing everything he'd known, everything he'd believed, to the winds.

He wanted her with a desperation he could barely fathom. Her body, yes, but more. So much more. Her smiles, her joy of battle, her fierce pride, and her soft touches.

My mate.

But even as the words roared within his heart, that thing that lived inside him rose up with a horrific growl.

What right did he have to happiness? To love and a mate. To satisfaction. To joy?

None.

What he felt for Olivia was wrong. All wrong.

He was nothing but a selfish, coldhearted bastard who hadn't even stepped in to save his own mother. Who'd run to save himself, leaving her to die a death as awful as any Daemon could dish out.

He didn't deserve happiness, and never had. He didn't deserve Olivia.

On the edge of her consciousness, beyond the swirl of passion and hot desire, Olivia felt the kiss change from one of hungry tenderness to something sharper. Darker. The gentleness inexplicably vanishing.

The kiss turned from a sharing of passion to one far closer to a battle. For dominance and control. And Olivia never shied away from a battle.

As Jag's tongue swept into her mouth, staking a claim, her fingers tightened in his hair, pressing him closer until her lips ground against his. The kiss turned hungry and demanding, and not altogether nice.

She craved the taste of him, the touch of his mouth, his tongue, and reveled in the fierceness. She was strong, but so was he, and she exulted in his power.

His hands began to tear at her clothing and she shoved him back. With the life energy of a hundred draden pumping through her veins, she was nearly as strong as a Feral.

She pulled off her own clothing, having no desire to see any more of it ripped, and she sensed Jag was in a mood to do just that. As she tossed her bra in the grass and pulled down her panties, she met Jag's hot gaze, watching him smile wickedly.

They came together in an explosion of heat and need, nothing like the sweetness in his bedroom before. And it was war. Jag grabbed her knotted hair and yanked her head back, dipping his head to lick and suck at her throat while his other hand gripped her thigh, yanking it high on his hip, nearly lifting her off her feet as he opened her to his seeking erection and drove himself inside her.

She cried out with the exquisite pressure of him filling her, then she lifted her other leg, hooking both around his waist. He grabbed her buttocks and slammed into her, over and over, driving them both to a fast, explosive release.

But the battle had just begun. Jag pulled out of her, dropping her to her feet, then grabbed her hair and pushed her down.

"On your knees, Red."

As she dropped to one knee, he yanked her head back and shoved his cock into her mouth. She sucked hard on that damp, swollen flesh, loving the feel of it in her mouth even as she rose to the challenge of his bid for dominance.

She sucked harder and harder until he winced.

"Sugar . . ."

Olivia released her grip on his cock at the same moment she shot up, sweeping her leg and knocking his own out from under him.

Jag hit the ground hard, and she was on top of him, grabbing his cock and taking it into her mouth her way.

He groaned with intense pleasure, arching into her, and she grabbed his nuts with her free hand, yanking and pulling on them with just enough force that he quickly came in her mouth with a guttural yell of pure pleasure.

No sooner had he finished, than he clamped his legs around her and rolled, flinging her to her back in the rough grass. His body pinned hers, his mouth diving to her breast and taking it roughly. Wonderfully.

He shoved two fingers inside her, and she arched up, driving him deeper. And then he moved back between her legs, clamping his hands around her thighs and wrenching them wide. With a hard, devilish gleam, he went down on her, licking between her legs, sucking her swollen clit into his mouth.

She arched, crying out with the pleasure, then groaned as he released her and sat back. A moment later, her body began to tingle with the strange and wonderful electricity she felt every time he shifted. Her eyes flew open and she stared into Jag's as he shifted into a large, darkly spotted jungle cat.

"Jag," she breathed, transfixed. Understanding slammed into her and she made a sound that was half laughter, half disbelief. "You are not fucking me as a cat."

He didn't answer, just watched her with those hunter's eyes, his tongue flicking out between a wicked set of fangs. She knew he wouldn't hurt her, and yet on a deep, primal level lurked the illogical fear that he'd open those jaws and use those teeth to tear her asunder.

The fear thrilled through her blood, more roller-coaster fright than genuine concern, setting her heart to racing and her blood to pounding, the adrenaline ratcheting high.

The great cat rose, padding over her until he straddled her, his fanged face inches from her own. His hot breath smelled surprisingly sweet, not at all what she would have expected from a wild animal.

Then again, the wildness of this animal came from the man himself.

Without warning, with a lick of her chin, the great weight of him settled on top of her, much as it had in the woods during the draden attack. But this time she could feel his warm fur down the entire length of her bare body.

"Jag, get off me. We're not doing this."

Jag's voice sounded softly in her head. *Haven't you ever wondered what it would be like?*

"You are truly perverted."

Why? Because I like to make love to you in unusual ways?

His words caught her by surprise and rang falsely in her heart. "No. You're not making love to me out here at all. You did that only once. In your room, on the wreckage of your bed, you made love to me. Tonight, all we've done is fucked, nothing more."

She grabbed his jaguar's head in both hands. "Shift, Jag. Shift back, dammit!"

With a low growl, he began to shimmer. The magic swept over her, into her, as he shifted back into a man, the feel incredible.

And he was once more a man, his body covering hers. With a hard thrust, he entered her, shoving himself deep inside her once, twice. He pulled out, grabbed her hips, and flipped her onto her knees.

Olivia growled with frustration. "The jackass is back."

Without answering, he jerked her hips back and

mounted her hard from behind. There was no tenderness, no care in his touch. He was punishing her for her honesty. Punishing them both.

"Damn you," she hissed, and pulled her knee up, slamming her heel back into his upper thigh, knocking him back on his rear. With the speed and force gained from her feeding, she turned and launched herself at him, tackling him down. In a single move, she straddled him and took him deep inside her, face-to-face.

Jag's big hands gripped her hips, and he thrust deep, his eyes closing as he arched back.

But she locked her thighs, holding him inside her, not letting him move. "Look at me, Feral," she demanded.

His eyes opened, blinking lazily as he complied.

"We're going to have a talk, you and I."

"Now?" he asked with a laugh.

"Right now, while I have your attention."

His fingers flexed in her buttocks cheeks. "Sugar, you most certainly have my attention."

"Something happened in your bedroom."

He stroked her rear. "Damn straight it did."

"Something other than sex. You let me see the man you really are, Jag. You didn't hide behind the bad attitude. Something happened between us. I felt it. I know you did, too, because you're hell-bent on ruining it, now."

"This isn't good for you?"

"Don't play stupid, Jag. You're not. Though, goodness

knows, I think you're blind. I see what you're doing but, honestly, I don't think you do."

He rocked against her. "Let me move, Red."

"Are you so afraid to hear what I have to say?"

His brows lowered in a glare. "I'm trying to get off, in case you hadn't noticed."

"Listen to me for a few more minutes, then I'll help you get off any way you like."

"Any way?"

"Any way that doesn't involve fur." Olivia stroked his chest with her fingertips. "You blame yourself for your mother's death, Jag. You hate yourself for it. And you have for nearly three and a half centuries."

His eyes lost all trace of humor. "Careful, Sugar." The words dripped warning, but he needed to hear this whether he liked it or not.

"You've got to face that day, Jag, look it in the eye, and not from the vantage point of a sixteen-year-old kid. Look at it as an adult. Then you have to forgive the kid you were, Jag. Forgive yourself. Because, whether you see it or not, the guilt has taken over your life. It destroys every good thing that comes into your life."

His fingers bit into her hips, anger snapping in his eyes. "You don't know anything about me."

But she didn't stop. She couldn't stop. "You didn't mean for her to die, Jag. If you had, you wouldn't still be living with the guilt all these years later. You made some mistakes, but it's past time you forgave yourself.

"Bitch. Get off me."

"No." She pressed her hands hard on his abs. "You're going to hear this, Feral. You're being incredibly selfish, making everyone else miserable just to punish yourself. Stop doing it. Leave it in the past and get over it!"

His hand shot up, gripping her jaw almost painfully. Fury fired his eyes. "Why in the hell do you think it matters to me what you say? You have no right shoving your nose into my business. Into my past."

"I care about you, Jag. Goddess knows why, but you've started to matter to me."

Beneath her, he went utterly still. Then like a volcano exploding, he pushed her off him, onto the grass, and stood up, turning on her. "I don't need you to care about me." His voice rose with each word. "I don't need to matter to a draden-kissed, life-stealing bitch!"

Olivia flinched as if she'd been struck. She'd known he wouldn't want to hear the truth, but goddess, his words hurt, as he'd meant them to.

"Get away from me, Olivia." He yanked on the pants he'd shucked earlier. "Just get the hell away from me."

His every word twisted like a knife in her chest as her own insecurities rose up, threatening to choke her. He was the only one in the world who knew what she was.

She knew he'd struck out at her to hurt her as she'd hurt him, but she couldn't help but wonder if he'd told her the truth. She was damaged. Wrong. And no one who truly knew her could ever really care about her.

No one could ever love a life-stealer.

Feeling hollow and beaten, she rose and grabbed her clothes, pulling on her pants. But as she pushed her arms through the armholes of her tank, Jag suddenly moved beside her.

She looked up in surprise, and that was when she saw them. Lyon and Tighe standing in the woods, watching them.

Her pulse leaped with fear, her skin going cold. Had they heard what Jag said to her? What he'd called her?

A draden-kissed, life-stealing bitch.

The shimmers of light told her all she needed to know—five shimmers that circled the small clearing where she and Jag stood. Her heart thundered in her chest as the five Ferals—lion, tiger, wolf, cougar, and snake—shifted into their animals, into a form they must think was safe from a dangerous life-stealer.

A dangerous enemy.

Her.

Chapter Nineteen

Jag's head pounded, his body turning to ice as the Ferals surrounded them. Out of the corner of his eye, he saw Olivia sway, reeling from the shock of his inadvertent betrayal.

They knew what she was. And the five animals now circled as if to destroy her.

Are you draden-kissed, Olivia? Lyon's hard voice rang in Jag's head.

"Yes." Beside him, Olivia answered, a small quaver in her strong, sure voice, and he knew she must be as terrified as he was.

"She's safe, Roar." Jag grabbed Olivia's arm and pulled her in front of him, his hand going around her waist. Against him she stood ramrod straight. "She's been draden-kissed for centuries."

What had he done? He'd attacked her verbally, hitting her where he'd instinctively known he'd hurt her the most. But he hadn't foreseen an audience. He hadn't foreseen *this*!

Is that true, Olivia? Lyon asked.

"I've been like this for more than four hundred years, Lyon. I'm in complete control." But a note of doubt slipped into her words and he knew she was thinking of the past day and the Daemon energy that had made her too strong. "Let go of me, Jag." She pulled at his arm.

"No." No way in hell was he letting the others touch her.

"Dammit, I said let go of me!"

He released her, and at once she moved away from him. As if she couldn't stand his touch.

Ice formed in his chest.

Go, Olivia, Lyon said, the animal releasing a fierce, dangerous growl. *Before I change my mind.*

Olivia hesitated only a moment before starting for the open space between the huge Bengal tiger and the big gray wolf. As she approached, Tighe sat back on his haunches, Wulfe following his lead, as both let her pass.

Jag started to follow her, but the lion bounded into the circle, blocking his path. With a furious growl, five hundred pounds of angry cat launched at him, knocking him flat on his back on the ground.

In a spray of light, Lyon shifted, already feral. His claws clamped around Jag's neck, digging deep into his throat.

"How long have you known?" he snarled between wicked fangs.

"Long enough." His words gurgled from the blood in his throat.

"You brought her into Feral House, endangering everyone. Endangering your Radiant! *And you knew?*"

For once in his life, he felt no prick of the old desire to rile Lyon further.

"I can feel when she feeds, Roar. Every time. She can't feed without my knowing, and she would never hurt us even if she could. She isn't a danger."

"Like hell she isn't. She could kill Kara. She could kill any of us."

"If she chose to, yes. Just as Kara could kill Delaney or Skye by pulling radiance on them. Just as any of the Ferals could kill any of the women. None of us is *safe*, Roar. We're all deadly if we choose to be."

For long moments, he stared up into those furious lion eyes, the blood running down his neck and into his throat. But he didn't fight. He'd known there would be hell to pay if Lyon found out. And he was more than willing to pay it.

With a last growl, Lyon yanked his claws from Jag's throat and stood.

Jag rose to his feet, watching his chief. "I'm going

after her, Roar. I love her." The words startled him. His mind tried to recoil from the declaration and failed. Because, dammit, he'd told the truth. Deep inside, his animal growled with approval.

Lyon stared at him, his fangs receding, then scowled. "Goddess help us." But he didn't tell him not to go, and that was all the invitation Jag needed.

He took off on two legs, in the direction Olivia had gone, unwilling to lose his pants, and his free pass into human society, unless he had to.

Olivia's life was over, and it was his fault. Guilt flayed him. He might not have meant to betray her, but dammit, he *had* meant to hurt her. She'd told him things he hadn't wanted to hear, and he'd lashed out at her.

Because they'd hurt. Because deep down he knew she was right. Cordelia's death had fucked him up good. He couldn't get past it. He hated himself for what he'd done that day.

Now he had the rest of his life to hate himself for what he'd done this day, too.

Cordelia would never have won any awards for best mother, but in her own way she'd loved him.

Now Olivia claimed to care about him.

And he'd destroyed them both.

The guilt was almost more than he could bear. But he heard Olivia's words in his head again.

You're being incredibly selfish, making everyone else miserable just to punish yourself.

And that was the crux of it, wasn't it? Exactly what his leader had said all those years ago when he'd called him a selfish, coldhearted bastard. He wasn't coldhearted. But selfish? Yeah. How many lives had he darkened because of his inability to stop wallowing in his own guilt? How many had he destroyed?

But not now. Not this time. The Jag he'd been before Olivia walked into his life wanted to slink off and castigate himself for failing, for the second time, the most important woman in his life. But he wasn't that Jag anymore.

Olivia needed him. For once, it wasn't about him. It was about her. Because he loved her. And because he was goddamn tired of hating himself.

He followed her scent through the yards of one multimillion-dollar home after another. A dog barked. Jag growled, and the dog whimpered and ran the other way.

Not until he reached the cliffs high above the Potomac River did he finally spot her.

Walking now, she glanced back, as if sensing him, her expression hunted.

His hands curled into fists as he longed to carve out his own heart for doing this to her. The self-hatred swirled within him, raking him with sharp, painful claws. But he fought it. He had to deal with what he'd done. Look forward, not back. He couldn't undo what had happened, and goddess knew there was no making it right, but he could stay at her side. He could damn well protect her.

Deep inside him, his animal howled with pain.

Her pain. Because her pain had become his.

Always before, his guilt had been about him, the ultimate selfishness. This time, he could think of nothing but her.

He caught up with Olivia as she trailed across the rocks, her breaths shallow and erratic, her skin white as snow.

The guilt tried to rise inside him, and he beat it down. This wasn't about him anymore.

"Olivia. *Liv.* I'm sorry. I didn't mean for that to happen, you know that."

He might as well have been talking to the wind for all the response he got from her. He didn't deserve a response. He didn't deserve anything from her. This was his fault, his goddamn royal fucked-up . . .

It's not about me!

Maybe not. But he goddamn hated himself.

Olivia climbed out to the farthest point on the rocks and for a moment, he wondered if she would just keep going, falling into the cold, dangerous Potomac far below. Instead, she perched on a narrow ledge, pulling her knees up and wrapping her arms around them as she stared down at the raging river.

He knew she was strong, and yet at that moment she appeared tiny and delicate and so incredibly fragile.

His head pounded with cold denial that he'd betrayed her secret, inadvertently or not. Yes, she was strong, but he'd opened her to death in a thousand ways.

The fear of the draden-kissed went deep in the Therian psyche. For thousands of years, stories had been told of Therian villages wiped out in a single night, the Therians drained in their sleep without ever waking. Without ever knowing they had a life-stealer in their midst.

Logically, most understood that mass death like that almost always happened accidentally, caused by a newly turned Therian who didn't know they were a danger until it was too late. But the knowledge didn't change anything. The fear persisted.

Once word got out about Olivia, some would seek to kill her, despite the edict of tolerance. None would allow her near them or their loved ones or their enclaves. Her place in the Therian Guard would be lost

With his anger and his carelessness, he'd taken everything from her. Everything.

Jag sank to the rock behind her, burying his face in his hands.

She understood him better than anyone ever had. "You're right, Liv. As much as I've denied it, everything you said about me is true. I hate myself. I hate myself for not saving Cordelia. For getting her into that mess in the first place."

She didn't respond. He hadn't really expected her to.

His gaze drank in the sight of her vibrant head, her fragile neck bent as she stared down into the water.

"I won't let them hurt you, Liv. Any of them. I can't undo what's been done, but I can make sure you're never alone again. I'll leave the Ferals. I'll live with you, wherever you want to go. No one is ever going to hurt you."

Slowly, Olivia turned her head, meeting his gaze with eyes that even now, even after all he'd done to her, radiated with a strength greater than his own.

"Go away, Jag. I don't want you in my life anymore. I don't need you."

He met that gaze and saw no trace of the hatred that should be there. No hint that she cared anything for him at all. Only deep weariness lived in her eyes, and a sadness that tore his heart out.

"You do need me, Liv. They'll hunt you. If not the Ferals, then someone else."

She lifted a brow. "And you'd sacrifice your life and your work here to protect me?"

"I won't let anyone hurt you."

"Anyone other than you, you mean?"

The words stabbed him through the heart. "I deserved that. I didn't mean to betray you, Olivia."

"No. You didn't want to hear what I had to say, and you lashed out at me for saying it. And now it doesn't matter anymore." She turned away again. "Nothing matters anymore."

"Olivia . . . I care about you, too. I think I'm falling in love with you."

She lifted her head slowly and looked at him over her shoulder, but there was no joy in her expression.

"You don't believe me."

"I don't know, Jag," she said wearily. "Maybe you do feel something. But it doesn't matter. Your caring about me, even loving me, isn't going to do either of us any good until you love yourself. You'll just keep punishing you and hurting me. Until you learn to forgive yourself and find a way to see past your mistakes to the good person deep inside, you're not ready to love anyone else."

She pushed her hair back, propping her elbow on her knees. "It's okay to fail sometimes. We all do. The key is trusting yourself to try to do the right things. And forgiving yourself if you fall short on occasion. Until you've done that, and let go of the guilt and self-hatred, you're toxic, Jag."

Olivia turned back to face the river, turning her back on him. "Now go away and leave me alone."

Jag stared at the back of her head, at her small spine, which even now radiated strength, and he struggled with a pain almost more than he could bear. He couldn't leave her. Yet he would die before he let anyone hurt her again.

Even him.

He wasn't sure how long he'd sat there, watching the

rising sun and trying not to hate himself, when he first heard the cry. A child's cry of fear.

His head snapped around and he spied her immediately, a girl of no more than nine or ten, running through the woods toward the cliffs where they sat. She wore jeans and a Mickey Mouse sweatshirt, but the shirt was torn at the neck, and tears streamed down her terrified face.

Jag leaped to his feet and started for her.

The child saw him and ran straight for him. "Help me! He's trying to hurt me."

Jag growled in fury.

"Bastard," Olivia hissed beside him.

Jag hadn't realized she'd followed, and he met her gaze. For one fleeting moment, they were once more in perfect accord.

As one, they climbed off the rocks as the girl reached them. She held out her hands, and Jag took one as Olivia took the other. No one was hurting her.

An odd, almost sly smile broke over the child's mouth. Then she looked up at them and Jag froze. He told himself to snatch his hand from hers, but it was too late. Enthrallment descended over his mind as he stared into a pair of copper-ringed eyes.

The eyes of a young Mage.

Chapter Twenty

"Where is he?" Lyon demanded. "He's not answering his cell."

Tighe met his friend and leader's hard gaze. "Olivia didn't kill him. I don't pretend to understand that relationship, but my instincts tell me that not only is it not in her nature, but she has feelings for him. Goddess knows why. She might shatter his kneecap, but she wouldn't kill him."

"Then where the hell is he?"

"I'll find him."

Tighe called Wulfe and Hawke, and together the three set out, Wulfe in his animal form, the best tracker among them. As Wulfe set the direction, Hawke took to the skies.

I see him, Hawke said as they neared the river. *On the rocks. He's not moving.*

Hawke's words rang an ominous knell.

Dead? Tighe asked. Goddess. He'd been so sure she wouldn't hurt him. From the moment she dug her heel into Jag's instep, he'd thought the jaguar shifter had finally met his match. Everything he'd seen since had confirmed it.

Not only the way Jag looked at her, but the way she'd looked at Jag. With the eyes of a woman fighting the pull of love.

After all they'd been through together, he couldn't blame Jag for bringing her back to Feral House, especially if he thought he could control her.

But he was afraid they'd both been wrong.

We should have gone with him, Tighe said to himself as much as to Hawke and Wulfe. *We shouldn't have let him go after her alone.*

As messed up as Jag was, he wasn't all bad, not by a long shot. And he was a damn good fighter. The last thing they needed was to lose another Feral.

Well he's not alone, now. I don't see any sign of Olivia, but there are people around him. Old people. Humans.

Tighe and Wulfe caught up with Hawke. Wulfe stayed behind, away from people, stuck in the form of a huge wolf. Like Lyon and Jag, he couldn't retain his clothes when he shifted, but neither could he downsize into

something innocuous. Neither of his forms—the huge
wolf or the large, scarred, naked man—was human-
friendly. Hawke landed in the woods and shifted, then
led Tighe to the small group of elderly hikers who'd
found the Feral.

Several looked up when the two men approached.
Tighe said nothing, just eased past them and knelt
beside Jag's prone form. He touched his hand, terrified
he'd find it quickly cooling, but Jag's hand felt warm,
thank the goddess. A quick glance at his throat and he
could see the pulse pounding strongly.

He closed his eyes with the force of his relief.

"We've called 911," one of the women said.

Hell. Tighe looked up at her, a woman with shoulder-
length gray hair and wise eyes. "Was he alone when
you found him?"

"Yes. He was just like this. We tried to wake him, but
he didn't respond."

Tighe nodded, then scooped Jag up, slinging him
over one shoulder. The humans stepped back, their
eyes wide, as if he'd just performed a spectacular feat
of strength. He supposed he had, from a mortal view-
point.

"He's passed out drunk. Thank you for caring for
him." They'd seen nothing out of the ordinary except
for a little surprising strength. If there'd been time, he'd
have taken their memories, but he didn't know what
was wrong with Jag, and the sooner he got him back to

Feral House, and away from any further human contact, the better.

Wulfe, get over here. Jag's fine, but he's out cold. See if you can pick up Olivia's scent. We need to find her.

He turned back to the humans. "If you see my dog, don't panic. He looks like a big wolf, but he's harmless."

Wulfe passed them as they started into the woods and caught up to them again as they reached Hawke's Yukon.

The big wolf leaped into the vehicle, then shifted back into a man. "I followed the trail to the street and lost it. Maybe she hitchhiked out, or took a car?"

Tighe glanced back, meeting Wulfe's worried gaze. He didn't say anything. He didn't have to. They both feared that wasn't the case at all.

Tighe pulled out his phone and called Lyon. "Jag's unconscious, and there's no sign of Olivia. Wulfe followed her trail, but it disappears abruptly, as if she got into a car."

Lyon put two and two together and came up with the same number Tighe had. "He's enthralled. And the Mage have Olivia."

"That would be my guess."

"If they turn her before we can stop them, she's going to make a hell of a weapon." Lyon pulled his mouth from the phone and shouted. "Kougar, Vhyper! Load up the vehicles. Every man, every woman."

"Harpers Ferry?" Tighe asked.

"My gut's telling me that's the place."

"Mine, too."

"Get back here, ASAP. We're rolling!"

The sound of Feral voices and the rumble of an SUV engine slowly broke through the fog that encased Jag's brain.

"He's coming around," Wulfe said behind him.

"Jag?" Tighe's voice sounded close by.

His senses told him he was sitting up, the seat belt locking him tight against the seat. In Hawke's Yukon, by the sound of the engine. Jag struggled to open his eyes, blinking against the morning sun reflecting off his window as they went around a curve.

"What the fuck happened?" he asked groggily. From what he could piece together, the Ferals were road-tripping, but he'd lost the why and where. Had he fallen asleep? Goddess, he felt like he'd been hit over the head with a sledgehammer.

Or . . . enthralled.

The girl! The girl who'd run to him and Olivia.

The grogginess ripped away, leaving him reeling with shock, sending his heart into a free fall.

"Olivia."

"What happened, Jag?" Lyon asked grimly from the seat in front of him. Hawke was driving, as he'd suspected.

Tension stiffened every muscle in his body. "Where is she?"

"Gone, buddy," Tighe said. "When you didn't come back, we went looking for you. We found you on the cliffs, unconscious. We followed Olivia's scent to the road. It disappeared there."

The memory of the child taunted him. A little girl with tears on her cheeks. And copper rings around her eyes.

"The Mage have her." Jag told them about the little girl, then tipped his head back, thinking. "They must know what she is. We destroyed all the Mage we found around that house, but we couldn't get through the warding to get inside. There must have been others." His breath caught on a snag of panic. "If they take her soul . . ."

"We had the same thought," Lyon said. "We're heading back to Harpers Ferry, now."

Jag raked his hair off his face with fingers that weren't even in the same ballpark as steady. "Wings, can't this bus go any faster?"

Tighe's hand landed on his shoulder. "We'll get there as quickly as we can." He didn't remove his hand, and Jag didn't ask him to. For once, he had no desire to push anyone away. His life was crumbling around him, and all he had, all he'd ever had, were these men.

Until Olivia.

And now he'd lost her.

"You really think you've fallen for her," Tighe said quietly.

"Hook, line, and sinker." Jag laughed, but the sound was strangled. "I have a hell of a way of showing it."

"Love has a way of cutting a man off at the knees. At least until he gives in to it. It makes you weaker than you'll ever be. And stronger."

Jag met Tighe's gaze, seeing a surprising understanding in his eyes.

His own expression hardened. "Fair warning," Jag said loud enough for every man to hear loud and clear.

"Olivia's my mate." Even if she never spoke to him again. His jaw clenched, a growl rumbling from his throat. "If you try to harm her, I'll kill you."

"And if she's been turned?" Lyon asked from the front seat.

"If she's been turned, I'll kill her myself."

For several minutes, the silence in the car was absolute. Then Hawke spoke.

"I've never heard of anyone being able to feel a life-stealer feed."

Lyon turned to look at Jag over the back of his seat. "Is that what you felt in the war room, when you thought you were feeling magic?"

"Yes. She often feeds at a low graze when she's around others. It wouldn't have affected anyone, let alone hurt us, but I felt it. I always feel it."

He took a deep breath and told them everything. How she'd fed from the Daemon, and that essence had made her incredibly stronger. How she'd taken out an entire swarm single-handedly last night.

"All the more reason to keep the women out of her reach," Tighe said.

"Where are they?"

"In your Hummer with Paenther, Kougar, and Ewan. They're behind us. We weren't taking any chances until we saw whether or not you were still enthralled when you woke up."

"Paenther's back?"

"We need every hand on deck for this operation."

They rode in silence, Jag's feet tapping a Mariachi beat on the floor mat. They'd get there in time. They had to get there in time. The alternative was more than he could bear to think about. He would save her.

And then what?

He'd fucked up everything with her because of his hardheaded refusal to listen to her criticism. No, not criticism. Truth. She'd told him he had to face that day, the day Cordelia died. Face it, look it in the eye, then get over it.

A deep shudder went through him. He'd already faced that day a thousand times in his nightmares. The last thing, the very last thing he wanted to do was open it up in broad daylight. But tipping his head back against the seat, he knew he would. Because Olivia had asked him to. Demanded him to. And it might be the last thing he ever got to do for her.

The thought clutched at his chest. *No.* No, it wouldn't be the last, because he was fucking well going to save her.

He forced himself to go back to that awful day three hundred years ago. What a prick he'd been! Screwing every human girl who'd lift her skirts for him even though he'd known Therian tradition forbade him from having sex until he was twenty-five. How many times had Cordelia ordered him not to go to the village? How many times had she warned him . . . ?

Jag stilled. How many times had she warned him how dangerous the human village would be if they ever realized he healed too quickly?

The memory, long forgotten, floored him. He'd hated her dictatorial ways and had fought them every chance he got, but she'd been afraid for him, he thought with wonder. Of course she had. She'd known, as he hadn't, what would happen if they realized he was immortal. Had she told him they might try to burn him at the stake?

No. Or if she had, he'd dismissed it in his youthful arrogance. He couldn't remember now.

But she'd been afraid for him. And the day she'd tried to haul him home? The day he'd denied her?

She hadn't argued. What had she said? "He's my servant!" Goddess, she hadn't been trying to rub it in, his denial, as he'd thought at the time. She'd been trying to protect him.

He dug his hands into his hair, fighting the waves of grief as he willingly remembered that day for the first time in three and a half centuries—all of it, not just the parts his guilt kept throwing at him.

Why had he denied her? Because he was mad at her. Furious with her for treating him like a little boy when he was so clearly a man. Goddess, what an idiot he'd been. But the truth rose from the depths of his pain— he'd yelled that she wasn't his mother, but his slave master. Out of anger. He hadn't realized the danger. At sixteen, he'd had no idea what the humans had in mind. He'd thought they meant to escort her from the village and throw her out, and he'd been glad for it! Vindicated. When they'd tied her to the stake, he'd been confused. Not until he saw the torch, had he realized they meant to hurt her. That was when he'd tried to reach her, but it had been too late.

He'd forgotten that part, that he'd fought to free her. But a dozen hands had held him back. And as he'd struggled, he'd looked up and met Cordelia's pained gaze. His sixteen-year-old's mind had seen accusation in her eyes, but his memory didn't support that. Not accusation, but fear. And desperation. Run! those eyes had said. Run! Because she'd known he could so easily be turned on, too.

And they had turned on him, hadn't they? They'd

chased him for hours, for miles. Had he been injured during the fight to reach Cordelia and given himself away? He didn't remember. All he knew was they'd chased him, and he'd done one thing right that day. He hadn't led them back to the enclave, but had hidden until he could escape them.

But by the time he got safely home, it was almost dark. Too late for anyone to mount a rescue of Cordelia before the draden got her. He'd never told anyone why he'd been so late returning. He'd never gotten the chance. They'd blamed him bitterly for her death, as he'd blamed himself.

But as Olivia said to him, he hadn't meant for any of it to happen. He'd never meant for her to get hurt. His only crimes had been youthful ignorance and self-absorption.

And what was his excuse ever since?

Olivia was right. It was time to let it go. Easier said than done, but he knew where he needed to start.

He opened his eyes and glanced at Tighe. "I owe you an apology."

"Why?" Tighe asked warily.

"You, Delaney, all of you. I've been a jerk."

Tighe grunted. "That's news?"

"Smart-ass. What's news is that I'm apologizing." With those simple words, he felt a lifting of the terrible weight he'd been carrying around for so long, he'd forgotten it was even there.

"Is this Olivia's doing?" Tighe asked.

"Yeah."

"Thought so. I wasn't wrong about her, after all." Tighe thrust out his hand. "Welcome, Jag."

For once, the tiger shifter looked at him without that guarded expression he'd come to know so well. Instead, his eyes held genuine warmth.

Jag took the proffered olive branch, grabbing Tighe below the elbow, their forearms slamming in the traditional Feral greeting. Amazingly, no snide comment even formed in his mind. The bitterness and bile had slipped away.

"Don't set your hopes too high, Stripes," Jag drawled. "I was born with a bad attitude." He grew serious. "I'll apologize to Delaney."

"Do that, although she's had you figured out for a while. She told me you only targeted her because your words didn't bother her. And they did bother me. She didn't think you'd ever intentionally hurt her."

Jag's mouth twisted wryly. "Olivia told me the same thing. Damned know-it-all women."

Tighe chuckled. "Get used to it. In my experience, they're usually right."

They continued the drive in silence, yet for the first time since he came to Feral House all those years ago, Jag didn't feel like the odd man out. Surrounded by his brothers, he didn't feel alone.

Olivia had done this. She'd opened his eyes and thawed the ice around his heart. She'd saved him.

And he would do everything in his power to save her in return.

Olivia came to slowly, pain attacking her flesh and tearing through her brain. A pain that felt as if a thousand thick, red-hot needles were poking into her skin.

A pain that told her she desperately needed to feed.

She was starving, and food wouldn't do it this time, no matter how much she ate. She needed energy. The pure energy of another's life force.

Slowly, painfully, she lifted her eyelids, the burning little needles rippling along the tender flesh. Her arms had been pulled taut above her head, and she tried to lower them, but she was caught fast—chained, her wrists bound by manacles.

Blinking with confusion and disbelief, she found herself standing upright in a glasslike cylindrical enclosure about ten feet in diameter. Like she'd been inserted into some kind of giant test tube. And she was utterly alone. Beyond her cell rose the stone walls of what appeared to be an old cellar—mildewed and dusty, the corners covered in cobwebs, and lit only by a single grime-coated window high on one wall. Nothing cluttered the space—no furniture, no abandoned tools or boxes.

Where was she? Her brain struggled to remember what had happened, how she'd gotten here.

She looked up to find that the ceiling of her glass cage was lower than the ceiling of the cellar, her chain attached to the glass, or Plexiglas, itself. Her arms were bare, her leather jacket missing. A single draden-bite welt marked her forearm.

No wonder she was so weak. She must have been bitten when she was unconscious.

Where in the hell am I? Where is Jag?

Memory came at her like an iron fist.

She'd told him he mattered to her, and he'd turned on her, flaying her with his rejection. Calling her a life-stealer. And the Ferals had overheard him.

They knew what she was, now. Her stomach squeezed until she thought she'd be sick.

She'd run, Jag had followed, then a little girl . . .

A little Mage girl . . .

Realization hit her, and she gasped. The Mage had captured her. But why? It wasn't like they knew what she was. Her scalp crawled. Dear goddess, what if they did? She suddenly remembered the way the Mage witch, Mystery, had stared at her, as if she were the only one of interest on that entire field of battle.

Did they mean to steal her soul, as they had so many others, and turn her into a killing machine? A shudder tore through her at the thought of what she could do. A single feed in a movie theater would kill the entire human population. If she crept close to a Therian mansion, she could probably kill most of those inside before they realized what was happening.

Jag would stop her.

Jag. Where is he? Did they take him, too?

Did they kill him?

Goddess, please not that.

The sensation of burning needles grew stronger, harsher, and she had to clamp her jaw hard to keep from moaning with the pain. Even if there was no one to hear her, she refused to give in.

If only she could pinpoint her captors and steal their energy. At the thought, she closed her eyes, struggling to force herself past the pain, to feel beyond. But she could feel nothing, as if this test tube were the entire world. As if the Plexiglas contained her gift as well as herself.

Of course it did. The realization only confirmed her fear. If the Mage had defended themselves against her gift, they must know what she was.

A fine desperation threaded itself through her mind. Did they understand she had to feed? That if she didn't, she might die? Maybe it would be for the best if she did.

But she felt confident the Mage wanted her power for their own. And she doubted hunger could kill her. She feared she would simply linger like this, the pain growing worse until she was out of her head with it. Was that their plan?

She didn't know, and the not knowing terrified her the most.

Little by little, she managed to slip away into a different place in her mind, desperate to escape the building fire in her flesh. She thought of Jag, remembering the way he'd made love to her in his bedroom. The way he'd stroked her body. The way he'd looked into her eyes as if he were falling as deeply and completely as she was. The feel and taste of his mouth as he'd kissed her. But mostly, she remembered the gentle look in his eyes. The needs she'd recognized so well in their brown depths. A need to end the loneliness, to end the isolation. A need for the connection that had begun to form between them—a connection of the heart. The soul.

The squeak of the cellar door wrenched her out of her thoughts in a blaze of pain. In walked Mystery, her thick auburn hair hanging in waves around the shoulders of her emerald green sorcerer's robe. No expression crossed her face. No emotion flickered in her emerald eyes.

Soulless.

Was that what her own eyes would look like when they were through with her? Or would she be one of the ones excited by the prospect of another's pain?

Dear goddess, she'd rather die first.

Behind Mystery walked two middle-aged humans, their faces as blank as automatons'. A couple, she suspected, the man balding, the woman soft and round. Enthralled.

Mystery reached for the Plexiglas, opening a door Olivia hadn't seen. At once, Olivia was blasted with the rich tease of life energy rushing across her senses. The energy had no real taste, no real smell, and yet the feel of it intoxicated, driving her need. She moaned beneath the crush of hunger. A hunger she would not slake on innocents!

She struggled against the pain and the need, holding on to her control by the finest of threads. A memory broke through her struggle, a memory of her last draden feed, how she'd finally, after so many centuries, been able to target her life-stealing.

Focusing, she tried to find the Mage in her senses, tried to single her out for attack. But her hunger was so fierce, the life forces ran as one, bright and ripe.

The two humans walked into the cage and the door snapped shut behind them. Any chance of singling out Mystery was gone.

The humans stood, unmoving, as if waiting for her to take their lives. Feeling them, needing them, was torture, the need to consume them nearly more than she could stand.

Mystery stood outside the cage watching her with dead eyes. "We want you hungry, life-stealer, but not weak. Not distracted by your pain. We drained you with the draden, but he took more from you than we'd anticipated. We ordered you to feed while you were en-thralled, but you refused. So you'll feed now. From the humans."

Olivia met the witch's soulless gaze. "I'll kill them."

"Of course."

"No! Give me draden."

But Mystery simply turned and left the cellar through the door from which she'd entered, leaving Olivia alone with the offered meal.

She shook from the need to open herself and slake her terrible hunger. Sweat rolled down her temples and the back of her neck. She would not steal the lives of innocents!

Never had she killed merely to feed herself. Never! She'd killed in battle and killed those who would have attacked her. But never an innocent. Not on purpose. It was a line she'd never crossed. A line that might be blurred and murky to some but was sharp and clear to her conscience.

If she took lives, innocent lives, in order to feed, then she would be a life-stealer in truth, and all her convic-tions that the Therians were wrong, that she had never been what they feared, were lost.

Yet as she looked at the pair in front of her, she knew that refusing to feed from them wouldn't save them. Their lives had been forfeit the moment the Mage took hold of their minds. Either she killed them here, painlessly, or they would die in a nightmare of pain and blood beneath the Daemons' claws.

But even knowing that, she couldn't do it. Because crossing that line turned her into a monster, and she'd never be able to live with what she'd done. Her conscience wouldn't let her steal innocent lives any more than her pride would let her give in to her captors.

But goddess help her, she knew this wasn't the end of it. She might assert her stubbornness and refuse to fall in line with Mystery's plan.

But her control over herself and her fate were fast becoming illusions.

The two large SUVs pulled off a little-traveled stretch of highway, past the decaying remains of an old barn, and off-roaded it into the woods less than a mile from the Mage stronghold near Harpers Ferry.

"Hawke, a little recon, if you will," Lyon said, as Hawke turned off the engine.

With a nod, Hawke opened his car door, shifted into his bird, and took to the skies. The other Ferals climbed from the vehicle, the second team, including the women, joining them from the Hummer.

The air smelled of rain and spring, the forest quiet and peaceful. But there was nothing peaceful inside Jag. The moment his feet hit the ground, he yanked off his clothes and shifted into his jaguar.

Olivia? Liv!

But he got no answer. If she'd been turned, would she answer him? Would she call him into her web?

What if she wasn't out here at all? What if they'd taken her somewhere else, and he would never find her?

Dammit, he couldn't stand this not knowing.

The terrible weight of guilt tried to settle on his shoulders, and he shoved it away. He'd find her, that's all he could do. All that mattered, now.

He prowled in his animal, seeking her scent without success. But if they'd brought her in a car, he wasn't going to pick it up. Not scenting her didn't mean she wasn't nearby.

A short time later, Hawke returned, landing in the small copse and shifting back into a man.

"The house looks exactly as it did last time. The windows covered, no sign of Mage."

"We'll go in as a single force," Lyon said, his expression grim, but determined. "If we run into the same situation you did last time, we'll be separated physically and fighting Daemons, but we're prepared this time. Stay in your animals and press all the way through to the center of the house. The warding has to be finite. If we press far enough, we'll get through it. Before we head out, though, we're going to be as strong as possible."

He lifted his hand and Kara came to him, his hand

curling around her shoulders. "We'll call a Feral Circle and start with radiance, then Skye, I'd like you to call your enchantress's power as well. We're going to need every advantage we can get."

Lyon's gaze landed on Vhyper. "When the women are through, I want you and the non-Ferals back in the Hummer where you can't be surprised by either Mage or Daemon. Hawke, you'll remain outside the house this time, circling above."

Vhyper crossed his arms over his chest. "I'd rather be in on the raid. I'm not going to turn on you again, Roar."

"If I thought you would, I would never leave you to guard the Radiant. That doesn't mean I'm ready to let you anywhere near another Mage." Lyon glanced fleetingly at Skye. "Present company excepted. Vhype, you don't know any better than we do whether they still have some kind of hold on you. We can't take the risk." He clapped his hands together. "Let's get that circle up. Prepare to be blooded."

As the Ferals stripped off their shirts, Kougar chanted the words that raised a circle in the middle of the copse that no humans would be able to see through or hear the sounds within. Jag shifted back into his human form and donned his pants.

The circle was wide enough to encompass them all, but only the Ferals gathered around Kara, each touching her as she held Lyon's hands, their upper bodies bare except for the golden armbands that snaked around each man's biceps and channeled the energy she'd call.

Jag stood at Kara's side, his hand on her forearm, as she pulled the radiance, sending power tumbling through his body on a rush of warmth. For more than a minute, they drank of the energy she gave them, then she doused her radiance. They released her, and she stepped aside. The Ferals widened the circle, and Skye took her place within it.

Skye was a wisp of a woman wearing a filmy blue ritual gown, her dark hair very short, her copper-ringed Mage eyes turned to Paenther. Never in a million years would Jag have expected Paenther to take a Mage to mate. Then again, Skye was no ordinary Mage. An enchantress, she had a rare and powerful affinity to animals. Even those that turned into men.

Kougar led them in the chant as they cut their chests, one after another with one of Kougar's blades. When it was Jag's turn, he sliced his own chest, slapped his palm to the wound, then curled his hand around the blood and shoved his fist into the air.

As one, the eight Ferals tilted their heads back and yelled to the canopy of trees above, their voices roaring through the forest like a gale. "Spirits rise and join. Empower the beasts beneath this sky!"

"Dance, Beauty," Paenther urged.

As the delicate Mage began to twirl, her hands lifted

high above her head, mystic thunder rumbled, the ground beneath their feet shaking. Feral Circles were generally stronger and more effective in the power places—the goddess stone and the clearing behind Feral House. But Kara's radiance and Skye's gift had given the warriors access to the Earth's power they'd never before known.

"Empower the spirit of the lion!"

"The panther!"

"The jaguar!"

One after another, the Feral Warriors roared to the heavens, calling the power of their beasts.

This time, instead of feeling a rush of power, Jag felt pure, cool pleasure ripple through his body, inside and out. A cascade of joy as if Skye had somehow plugged them into heaven itself.

And when it was over, to a man they were grinning, Jag included for about half a second, until his fear for Olivia swamped him all over again.

"Let's go!" Lyon's roar of a command stole the last of the smiles, and the six Ferals took off, slipping through the woods on man feet, passing without a sound as Hawke took to the skies.

Lyon looked to Jag. With a nod, Jag took over lead of the group. He'd been the first to find the dilapidated Mage stronghold. And he'd be the only one to feel Olivia's feeding. He needed to be out front, and they all knew it.

As he ran through the woods, one question tormented him, raking at his mind over and over. If she'd been turned, how would he kill her? She was the air in his lungs, the heart beating in his chest. How could he destroy her knowing the chance existed that she was still in there somewhere, her soul not destroyed so much as subjugated, as Vhyper's had been?

His every instinct, even the animal spirit that shared his body, roared at him to save her. To protect her.

But his loyalty and duty to the Ferals demanded he destroy her before she destroyed them. And he had little doubt the Ferals would be her target. How would he live with the guilt if she killed one or more of his brothers because he'd failed to stop her?

He was just beginning to understand how his guilt over Cordelia's death, a death that had been far from intentional, had wrecked him for centuries. How would he live with dozens, possibly hundreds of deaths that he'd consciously, willingly, permitted?

He wouldn't, it was that simple. He couldn't let it happen. If, when he found her, he was too late, if she'd already been turned, he would destroy her.

No choice. Goddess help him. He'd take her life and likely lose his own in the process. The only bright side was he wouldn't have to live without her.

When he caught a glimpse of peeling, dirty white siding, he pulled up.

"She's not in there."

"How can you be sure?" Lyon asked him.

"I don't know." His confused gaze went to Tighe. For some reason he was certain the tiger shifter would understand. "There's a . . . brightness . . . inside me. A glow, when she's near."

Tighe nodded, his eyes telling him he did indeed understand. "The beginnings of the mating bond. And it's absent?"

"Yeah."

Tighe's expression changed, sympathy filling his eyes, and Jag knew he'd misunderstood.

"The glow isn't gone, Stripes. That's not what I meant." She wasn't dead, thank the goddess. "I still feel it. It's just not here."

Tighe's expression returned to that of the hunter. "Can you follow it?"

"No. It's not that strong." But as he turned away, determined to continue looking, Lyon stopped him.

"We're attacking the Mage stronghold, Jag."

Jag's hands fisted. "I have to find Olivia!" The need was eating him alive.

Tighe's hand landed on Jag's shoulder. "If we can catch one of the Mage and get him to talk, we might find her that much quicker."

Everything inside him rebelled. He had to find her *now*. But Tighe was right. He didn't have a clue where to look.

Lyon began issuing orders. "Spread out and circle

the house. If we get attacked and have to shift human, no other Feral should be within the arc of your blade swing or claws. Shift and get into place!"

Jag tore off his clothes, as did Lyon and Wulfe, then all shifted into their animals. While Hawke circled in the air, the others raced around the house on four legs, taking up their positions.

Jag's stomach crawled with the need to get this over with. Olivia wasn't here. And she needed him!

Now! Lyon's voice rang in his head.

Through a haze of fiery pain, Olivia heard the cellar door open. How long had she been trapped like this? It didn't matter. She wouldn't feed from the humans. Wouldn't!

Prying her eyes open, she saw Mystery, a dark ball in her hand that spit and crackled as if it encased true lightning. A power orb, identical to the ones that had hung from the eaves of the house when she and Jag first stumbled upon it. Behind Mystery, two other Mage sorcerers filed into the room, one carrying a stack of bowls, the other a small, lit torch.

Through swimming vision, she watched with growing unease as the two males laid the bowls in a circle around the outside of her cylindrical cage and lit something inside them. More than a dozen fires ringed her, fires that would no doubt be used in some kind of magic.

Not good.

Jag!

No answer. *Don't be dead, Jag. Don't be dead. Lyon? Tighe!*

But none of the Ferals seemed to be within hearing distance, or if they were, not in their animals. Or perhaps her cage, which kept her from feeding, also kept her from communicating with those outside.

She clung to the hope, however slim it might be, that the Ferals might find her before it was too late. That Jag might still be alive.

Mystery lifted her hands, and the power orb levitated to float directly over the test tube, spitting with its captured lightning.

Hunger tore at Olivia, searing her flesh, the pain a living, breathing thing inside her. Her jaw felt locked in place, clamped together hard against the scream that tore through her head.

The humans stood before her, as they had all along. Enthralled. Offering up their lives.

No, not offering.

Mystery chanted in a dialect Olivia was fairly certain was ancient Mage. As the men took up the chant, Olivia's eyelids crashed down, but she couldn't fight the sound. The voices raked at her eardrums, repeating the same string of words over and over.

The power in the room began to grow, swirling around her, knifing at her already-burning flesh. Stronger and stronger, it began to seep into her pores, snaking down into her body like hot coals, stoking the flames of the hunger. The magic crawled inside her, into her organs and into her mind, gnawing at her tightly held control.

"No!" The word broke from her lips on a cry.

"Yes, life-stealer," Mystery said tonelessly. "You'll thwart us no more."

Olivia fought to hold on, but even her formidable will proved no match for the magic. And in a single scalding rush of fire, her control was ripped free of her grasp.

And she fed.

Her eyes flew open. Fury and horror tore at her mind even as her body rejoiced. She fed of the life force that had been bombarding her senses for what felt like hours. She fed even as the humans began to sway on their feet, even as she watched them collapse. She fed until no more life force existed within her cage except her own. And still she wanted more. Needed more.

Even as the pain of hunger lifted, the horror of what she'd done flayed her heart and mind.

She'd killed them.

Not willingly. Not willingly.

But the humans were dead just the same.

"It's time." Mystery walked over to the Plexiglas door and opened it. "You're ready, life-stealer."

Olivia stared at her. "Ready for what?" But she feared she knew. She fed hard, trying to suck Mystery dry, but the sorceress was prepared for that.

The Mage witch grabbed Olivia's arm, sending her powerful will against Olivia's compromised one.

"You are ready to help us destroy the Feral Warriors."

Before Olivia could do so much as draw a breath to argue, her vision began to darken, her mind clouding over as she fell into the abyss of enthrallment.

As one, the Feral animals raced forward, leaping onto the porch or through the back, shattering what remained of the windows of the dilapidated white house.

Jag crashed through the back door and landed not in a black hole of warding like before, but in an old run-down kitchen. The smell of rotting flesh raked at his senses. Real flesh. Not Daemon.

The wolf and tiger joined him.

No warding this time, Tighe said wryly. *It stinks in here.*

Lyon padded through the interior doorway on four paws. *Bodies. Spread out. Search in pairs.*

Five long minutes later, the Ferals gathered outside, back in human form. Jag paced, every muscle twitching with his need to take off.

"Four dead humans rotting in one of the upstairs bedrooms, otherwise nothing," Paenther confirmed. "The Mage appear to have moved out."

"We have to find Olivia," Jag said through gritted teeth.

Lyon met his gaze. "Look inside you. If you've really begun to form a mating bond with her, you're the only one who can. Listen to it."

Tighe came to stand beside Lyon. "I feel the connection to Delaney in my mind. Like a bright thread. Yours may be different, but test it. See if it doesn't pull you."

Jag closed his eyes. This wasn't going to work. He might still feel that glow, because he loved her, dammit. But any connection that had been forming between them, he'd hatcheted but good.

Olivia! he shouted, knowing she wouldn't answer.

Jag?

Jag's heart leaped, his pulse racing. *Liv? Liv! Where are you.*

Don't come, Jag. Don't come.

Where are you? Tell me where you are! Liv!

But the voice in his head said no more.

Jag's eyes snapped open. "She spoke to me. She told me not to come, but wouldn't say where she is."

"She's close, then. Hawke," Lyon snapped.

"I'm on it." The bird shifter took to the skies.

Tighe grabbed Jag's shoulder. "Feel her. Don't think about where she might be, just feel."

Deep inside, that warm glow that was Olivia began to turn, slowly at first, then faster until he felt as if it were spinning in his chest like an out-of-control compass. Would it stop at some point, in the direction he needed to go?

"Tighe . . ."

"Concentrate, Jag. Feel."

Heads up. Hawke's voice shouted in his head. In all their heads. *Daemons!*

"There!" Wulfe turned feral as he stared into the trees behind the house.

"Damn," Tighe said on a hard expulsion of air. "All three of them."

Jag turned and stared at the hideous trio with a combination of frustration and bone-deep relief. Frustration that finding Olivia would have to wait. And relief that the Daemons were here and not with her.

The three Daemons appeared almost identical—the same floating, cloaklike black bodies, the same black, snakelike hair. Each with a hideous face filled with fangs, though each appeared to have a unique, if disturbing, melting pattern to his flesh. The trio moved quickly through the air between the trees, close to ten feet off the ground. And while they glanced at the Ferals, they made no move to attack, continuing along their path, as if just passing through.

Tighe made a sound of disgust. "Where are they going?"

"Do you think they're afraid of us?" Wulfe asked.

No one answered. No one had an answer to give.

"Let's go," Lyon said. "We need to destroy those things."

"If we can catch them," Tighe muttered.

As they took off running again, the spinning in Jag's chest suddenly stopped. Understanding rushed over him.

"I can feel Olivia. I know which way to go."

Lyon looked at him. "We'll split up."

Jag shook his head, his heart in his stomach. "We don't have to. The Daemons are heading right for her."

Chapter Twenty-two

Jag pulled on the power of the jaguar that lived inside him and shifted on an exhilarating rush of energy and light. Around him, the other Ferals did the same. One moment, seven men ran through the forest. The next, five large cats and a huge wolf raced across the ground as a large red-tailed hawk swooped through the trees. All could travel faster as animals than they could run on human feet.

Unfortunately, none could move as fast as the Daemons.

Jag raced through the trees, his sleek cat's body barely brushing undergrowth, barely touching the ground as he dodged and leaped. Terror pounded in his head, in his blood, that he would be too late to save Olivia. Too late.

All these years he'd waited for her without knowing he did, without dreaming a warrior angel would be the one to free him from his self-imposed prison of guilt. To steal his heart. And now he must be the one to free her.

A building in a clearing up ahead, Hawke reported. *An old brick building of some kind. Behind it, I see people tied to posts. An outer circle of five facing inward and three back-to-back in the inner circle facing out.*

Olivia? Jag demanded.

I can't be sure, but one of those in the outer circle has hair the color of hers. Two of the inner three have had their noses cut off. The way they're bleeding, they have to be humans.

The lion growled, Lyon's voice replying in Jag's head. In all their heads. *The Mage have baited the Daemons. The question is, are they baiting us?*

Doesn't matter, Jag growled. *We're going in anyway.*

It matters. But you're right, Jag. We're going in anyway.

Minutes later, the Ferals broke from the cover of the woods into a scene just as Hawke had described. The building, off to the left and facing away, had probably once housed a small factory or Civil War munitions. Directly in front of Jag, in a yard of weeds and dead grass, stood the five thick outer poles in a wide circle, perhaps ten yards in diameter.

He spotted Olivia at once. She'd been staked, her back to the post closest to the building, her arms tied at her back. Just as Cordelia had been all those years ago.

The memory slammed into him, nearly driving him to his cat's knees. He couldn't breathe.

Goddess, goddess, goddess.

For one horrible moment, the urge to run shot through his muscles, to turn tail and flee that memory in any way he could. But his animal growled inside his head, yanking him back to the present. No longer was he that angry, scared kid watching his mother die. Olivia was the one staked this time, not Cordelia.

Olivia. And she wasn't going to die. He'd move heaven and earth if he had to, but she was not going to die!

He shook his head, dislodging the memory of long ago as he forced himself to focus.

Olivia! She stood erect, her feet planted firmly on the ground, but her head dipped, her chin resting on her chest as if she catnapped.

No response. She had to be enthralled. The realization cramped his gut.

Jag, can you still feel her? Lyon demanded.

She's alive, Roar. They haven't turned her. They wouldn't need to tie her if they'd turned her.

This has the feel of a trap, Lyon said.

Jag swung his jaguar's head, his gaze meeting Lyon's.

I agree. She's enthralled, Roar. But I'm going in anyway.

Hold, Jag. We're all going in, Lyon replied. *You'll fight with us. Not only do we need you, but your best* chance of saving her is to kill those Daemons. If she starts feeding, tell us and we'll stay in our animals.

It won't be enough. She can drain the animals, too.

Silence.

If she starts feeding, I'll do what I have to, Chief. But the thought of it drove a stake through his heart.

The lion's head dipped once in acknowledgment, his gaze returning to the circle. Jag's followed.

He'd been so focused on Olivia, he hadn't even taken in the rest of the scene.

Goddess. The state of the two humans . . . females . . . in the inner circle was as bad as Hawke had described. Blood gushed down their chins, choking them as they tried to scream. They wouldn't live long like that, with or without the Daemons, who now circled them. And he could only think that was a blessing. What Hawke hadn't mentioned was that the third in the center appeared to be a Mage. A Mage sentinel by the looks of his uniform

What the hell?

Both his arms had been cut off and were slowly re-growing, his face a mask of terrible pain.

Soulless bastards weren't even loyal to their own.

All three were Daemon bait.

His gaze swung to the outer circle to the young adults, presumably human, tied to the posts. Two males and two females. This group appeared uninjured, though terrified. Conscious but for Olivia.

Look above the three in the center, Paenther said. A trio of dark orbs floated some six feet up, crackling with dark lightning. Power orbs. *This is set up like a Mage ritual, without the Mage. It has to be a trap.*

I agree, Lyon replied. *But we have no choice but to press on. We've been looking for those Daemons for nearly two weeks. This is our chance to take them.* A low growl rumbled from his lion's throat. *Spread out. We'll converge from all sides. Shifting is up to you.*

The circle may be warded, Tighe said. *We ran into that before.*

Good point. Play it by ear. Paenther and Wulfe, head left. Jag and Tighe, go right.

Jag mentally ground his teeth. Olivia was left. But he followed orders without argument. As badly as he needed to feel her in his arms and to know she was okay, freeing her when she might be enthralled was far too risky. Draden-kissed or not, the woman was a hell of a fighter.

The six Ferals took off, circling the outer perimeter and the Daemons. *Now!* At Lyon's command, they attacked. Tighe and Jag both shifted into human form, Tighe tossing Jag a knife the instant they had human hands again. The Ferals always shifted into battle in pairs—one who retained his clothes, and weapons, through a shift side by side with one who couldn't.

Jag watched the nearest Daemon rake shallow furrows in one of the human females' upper chest. As the woman screamed, Jag leaped at the fiend, Tighe right beside him.

The creature whirled, one set of his six-inch razor-sharp claws raking across Tighe's chest as the other tore through Jag's shoulder. *Dammit, dammit, dammit that hurt.* Fire licked across his shoulder and down his limb, but he stabbed at the Daemon from the front as Tighe took the back. Too quickly, Jag had to shift his blade to his left hand when his right started to go numb.

The Daemon slashed out again, but Jag ducked and drove his knife up into the bastard's chest, meeting nothing but floating cloaklike flesh. The bastard was as insubstantial as a draden.

"Where's his heart?" Tighe shouted, but Jag could barely hear him above the woman's screams.

"Hell if I know." A thick, creeping sensation crawled across Jag's flesh. Magic. "Do you feel that?"

"Yeah."

Jag's gaze shot to Olivia as her head lifted, her chest rising as if she were taking a deep, cleansing breath. Beneath his feet, the ground began to tremble.

The Daemon swung. Tighe ducked and stabbed up into his chest, but nothing seemed to slow the evil sucker. As Jag lunged for the Daemon's head, the bastard went for Jag's face. In a desperate move, Jag shifted his attack, swinging his blade down hard and fast, cutting off the Daemon's clawed hand. Yes!

The creature screamed, an earsplitting cry, and shot up into the air, out of reach.

The ground gave another hard tremble as the feel of raw magic grew stronger.

"Pull back!" Lyon yelled. "Out of the circle. Now!"

Jag followed command, realizing belatedly that Tighe wasn't with him. He turned to find him racing toward Hawke.

One of the Daemons had his claws sunk deep in Hawke's shoulder, holding him fast, even as the shifter stabbed him high with a fierce and focused determination.

"It's in his throat," Hawke shouted, his tone triumphant despite his predicament. "His heart's literally in his throat!"

Jag started forward, intending to help Tighe free Hawke, when he felt it—the telltale stabbing sensation along the surface of his skin. Olivia.

"She's feeding!" Hard. Jag turned and ran for her, his own heart suddenly in his throat. Was she still enthralled, or had she been turned? His mind shouted in denial. She had not been turned! *Please, Goddess.* At least she wasn't terribly close to them. She wouldn't drain them quickly, not with over a dozen lives to feed from. But she would drain them. And if he didn't stop her, she'd eventually kill them all.

"Out of the circle!" Lyon's voice rang out harsh and

desperate. Lyon and Kougar were on the other side, outside the circle's perimeter, but still battling one of the Daemons.

Within the circle, just ahead, Paenther struggled to help Wulfe, one of whose legs had been ripped to shreds.

The ground gave another rumbling roar.

"Out of the damned circle!"

Jag changed course and ran for the pair of Ferals, grabbing Wulfe's other arm as Paenther tried to clear him from the field. Glancing back, Jag saw Tighe and Hawke still battling. As he watched, the Daemon exploded in a blast of noxious black smoke.

"Got him!" The words were barely out of Jag's mouth when a bloodcurdling, inhuman scream tore from the Earth itself. The sky turned suddenly dark, pitch-black, as if the last angel had turned off the lights of heaven.

"Dive!" Lyon yelled.

As one, Jag and Paenther leaped clear of the circle, hauling Wulfe with them as an unearthly red-orange glow erupted behind them. Jag spun, staring as the ground wrenched open, becoming a swirling, spinning vortex that ended mere feet from the outer posts. Mere feet from where he stood.

Olivia remained, as did the other captives on the outer posts, but the three center stakes and their victims were gone, having disappeared into the hole.

His heart seized.

As had Hawke and Tighe. Only the two Daemons remained, hovering over the hell pit.

"No!"

"Wings!" Lyon shouted. "Stripes!"

Wulfe's hand landed on Jag's shoulder, hard, his voice disbelieving. "They're gone."

Jag's heart rolled, his jaw clenching against the sudden and wrenching anguish as he stood stone-still beneath the weight of shock. Until the two Daemons turned and began floating toward them.

"Roar!" Paenther shouted beside him, pointing at the old building.

Jag shifted his gaze to stare at the dozen armed Mage sentinels streaming across the yard, swords drawn.

And Jag could still feel Olivia feeding.

"Hell," Paenther growled. "They want us all in there."

"That's exactly what they want," Wulfe muttered.

"I have to get to Olivia." Jag started running.

Across the circle, Lyon shifted back into his animal. An instant later, his voice blazed in Jag's head.

We are not defeated! No more Ferals will be lost this night. Jag, it's up to you. Stop Olivia!

Jag ran, his chest filled with gravel, his mind aching. Tighe and Hawke were gone. Olivia was attacking them, almost certainly turned. He would have to destroy her.

No. He didn't know that. For this moment, *this moment*, all he had to do was reach her. But six feet from her, he hit another damned invisible wall. Warding of the thick-as-steel variety. And he knew he couldn't do even that.

"Liv!"

Olivia turned her head, finding him slowly with glazed eyes that were neither enthralled nor turned. But his heart's moment of rejoicing died as he took in the true look in those precious eyes—horror and misery.

"Jag." Her voice barely carried over the scream of the vortex. "I'm fighting it, Jag, but I can't stop feeding! The Mage have put a spell on me. You have to stop me!"

Ah, goddess. Not like this. She wasn't turned. Wasn't even doing it on purpose. It dawned on him the sharp discomfort of her hard feeding had dimmed considerably. Now that she'd shaken off the enthrallment and regained consciousness she was fighting it. But she was still strong and would eventually drain them dead, even with the addition of the sentinels to dilute what she stole from any one person.

He had no choice but to stop her.

Shifting into his jaguar, he leaped toward Olivia, half-prepared to slam into the wall again. But this time, he reached her as if there were no barrier at all. At her feet, he shifted back into a man.

Olivia's frantic gaze met his. "Rip out my heart, Jag. This won't end until you do."

"No. There's got to be another way."

"There isn't! Mystery hooked me up to those orbs, stripping me of my control, making me feed on the combined energies of the Daemons, Mage, Therians, and humans, funneling the combined energies into the orbs. There's something about the combination that's especially potent. That's what's powering the vortex. And they want all the Ferals in it. Jag! Behind you!"

He whirled just as one of the Mage leaped at him, unhampered by the barrier..

"Liv, fight it!" he shouted as he and the Mage went tumbling to the hard ground in a tangle of knives and limbs, rolling straight for the vortex. Did his attacker care nothing for his own life? No, probably not. The soulless bastard's only goal was to send Jag into that swirling hell.

Jag dug his knife deep into the ground and held on, stopping his momentum cold, then whipped his body around, kicking the Mage free of him and into the swirling mass. His own foot brushed that rushing energy, snagging him and trying to pull him in, but he held on tight.

Dragging himself free, he leaped to his feet and grabbed up his knife as two more Mage came at him, each with blank, emotionless eyes. Eyes filled with death. His death.

He shifted into his animal and leaped at the nearest man, ripping his throat out with his jaguar's ferocious jaws. As his mouth filled with blood, he felt the fiery pain of a knife stabbing deeply into his hindquarters. With a furious growl, he turned and lunged at his second attacker, biting off his hand. In an instant, he shifted back into his human form, grabbed his now one-handed attacker by his good arm, and threw him into the waiting vortex. Without hesitation, he kicked the Mage whose throat he'd just ripped out in, too, before he could recover.

Bending double, hands on his knees, he sucked in air with shallow, rapid breaths. Not only did he feel winded, but his hip was killing him, and his shoulder throbbed, numb and achy. Olivia's feeding was starting to get to him. The more lives there were for her to feed from, the less she took from any one. But he wasn't the only one dispatching Mage right and left.

And he was too close to her.

The Earth had set up an ungodly howl, melding her fury with the screaming of the vortex until he could barely hear himself think.

His gaze sought out his brothers. They were all moving with less speed, less animal grace than normal. They were all tiring. As he watched, one of the humans fell unconscious. But, dammit, the Mage weren't affected by her feeding at all. They weren't out there long enough. In twos and threes, they ran back to the brick building as reinforcements took their places.

One of the Daemons floated over the vortex where the Ferals couldn't reach him, then flew in to slice a chunk out of one of the human male's faces. His scream melded with that of the Earth's as the blood gushed from the wound.

Goddess, they had to find a way to kill these things. If only the Daemons would grow weak from Olivia's feeding instead of the humans and Ferals.

A second black cloud erupted on the far side of the vortex between Lyon and Kougar. Another Daemon down.

Jag straightened, struggling against the growing weakness just as another Mage came at him, a knife in each hand. He was so through with this shit. As the Mage dove at him, Jag ducked and rolled, using the sentinel's own momentum to send him flying into the glowing hell pit.

For the moment he was free of Mage attackers. He had to stop Olivia, though goddess, he wanted to do anything but that. He ran back to her, tried to get through the warding, and was knocked back yet again. The only way he could get through the damned wards was in animal form, but the shifting was draining him as fast as Olivia was.

No choice.

He shifted back into his cat, grabbed his knife in his mouth, and ran through the barrier, then dropped it at her feet and slowly turned back into a man.

"Jag. Quit being sentimental! You must rip out my heart."

He cupped her face in one hand, feeling a sudden, hard jolt as he took all her feeding onto himself. "Sentimental, am I? I'd as soon rip out my own heart, Liv."

"Let go! I'm feeding only from you!"

His hand dropped away, but he stared into her eyes. "I love you."

Tears sprang to her own. "Jag, just do it. Don't make this any harder than it already is."

"I know." Before she weakened him to the point he couldn't lift the knife, he had to kill her. "Goddess, Olivia, how am I supposed to live without you? You've given me back my life. My heart." And now she would rip them both from him again when she died.

At his own hand.

He was a Feral first. And if he didn't stop her, and soon, they would all die. But he wasn't giving up without one more try.

Olivia closed her eyes, bracing herself for the death that had to come. The thought of what this would do to Jag tore her heart out of her chest even before his knife touched her. He thought he loved her. Oh, Jag.

But instead of the bite of cold steel, she felt his hand once more cup her cheek.

Her eyes flew open. "What are you doing?"

His tired gaze bored into hers, a flash of devilment in their dark depths. "You turning into a quitter, Red?"

Her temper snapped. "I'm fighting it as hard as I can!" But she saw what he was doing. Making her mad. Giving her the strength to fight harder. "You want me to kick your ass, Feral?"

His mouth tightened, but his eyes crinkled at the corners. "Give me all you've got, Liv. Don't you dare give up. We're going to stop it. Together. The damned Mage are not going to win."

"Jag, I'm out of ideas."

He dropped his hands, but stared at her with eyes lit by a fierce determination. "Can you feel the lives individually like you did when you fed from the draden last night?"

"Yes, but not as well. And I can't control the feeding. I've tried!"

"What about the reverse feed? When you fed me?"

She stared at him, her mouth dropping open. "I forgot. I didn't think . . ." With a sudden, desperate hope, she found his life force, closed her eyes and willed herself to feed him. Nothing happened. She was too locked into the feeding to reverse it.

Her eyes flew open. "It's not working!"

He swayed.

"Jag, you've got to get away from me. You're too close!"

With a hand, he waved her words away, but his motion

was slow and lethargic. "Liv, concentrate." He slapped his hand awkwardly, as if he were drunk. "Inside me, I feel you. In my mind . . . I see this glow, this light, and I know it's you. It's the start of a mating bond."

His gaze bored into hers, at once achingly soft and hard as granite. "I don't know if you'll ever feel it. Goddess knows, I've never given you any reason to love me. But try, Liv. Right this moment, try to love me. Try to find that bond, then reach me through it."

"Jag, you're endangering all of your lives. I know how hard it's going to be on you, but you have to stop me. You can't feel guilty for it."

"I'm not trying to save you because I feel guilty. I'm trying to save you because I love you." His gaze snapped, as did his words. "Find that link, Olivia, now! For both of us." His eyes blazed with an emotion that burrowed deep inside her, lighting all the dark places, filling her with an incredible warmth, and igniting a matching emotion within her.

Love. It blazed within her, shoring up the crumbled mass of her heart. And deep in her mind, a light flared. A glow. A glow she knew was Jag.

Yes, she loved him. Goddess, she loved him.

With the gentlest of touches, his fingers whispered over her cheek. "I'll never survive without my heart." The anguish in his eyes tore her in two. He stumbled back, then forward again. "I'm losing it, Liv. I can't wait any longer." He bent down and rose again, slowly, a knife in his hand.

When he looked up at her, tears filled his eyes. "I'm sorry."

As her heart broke, love for him rushed up from the depths of her soul, filling her chest, her mind.

Jag lifted the knife as if it weighed half a ton, positioning the tip just beneath her rib cage.

That soft glow inside her mind burst into a flaming inferno as she poured her love into it. Into Jag. And something happened. With a shock, she realized she wasn't only pouring her love into him, but her life force as well. She was feeding him!

"Jag."

The knife dropped. His head lifted slowly, his eyes wide with wonder. "You're doing it. I'm already feeling stronger."

"Yes." Tears spilled down her cheeks.

He grabbed her face and kissed her hard, then pulled back and swiped the moisture from his own cheeks, his eyes blazing with love and triumph. "I knew you could do it." He kept hold of her, once more letting her feed only from him. "If you can still see the individual life forces, can you help the others?"

She peered past him to what little of the battle his big body didn't block. Lyon had lost an arm and was battling two Mage at once. Neither Wulfe nor Kougar looked to be in any better shape. They were fighting back to back, seven Mage surrounding them.

She focused on them and Paenther, sending energy directly to them with ease.

"It's working!" She met his gaze with a grin. "Now let go of me and let me feed from everyone. I'll weaken the Daemon and the Mage, but feed your men."

"And the humans."

She nodded. "And the humans."

Jag gave her another hard, fast kiss. "I need to untie you."

"No. I'm connected to those orbs. If you untie me, there's no telling what will happen. Leave me here. Rejoin the battle, Jag. Your men need you, now."

"How do I disengage you from the orbs?" Already, his voice sounded back to normal strength.

"Destroy them. It's the only way."

"I'm on it." With a grin that was at once fierce and breathtaking with sheer joy, he turned from her and grabbed up several knives that had slipped from now-dead hands. Standing at the edge of the glowing vortex, he threw the knives at the orbs, one after the other, but they hit and bounced off, knife after knife falling into the screaming void.

As he took off at a run toward the battle, she thought she heard him say, "Where are Delaney and her guns when we need them?"

Olivia's heart followed him, and she poured love and strength through that budding bond between them, willing him to stay safe. Helping him the only way she could as he fought to claim victory and save them all.

The other Ferals had the Mage down to a manageable seven by the time Jag reached them. The winds howled, nature's fury a living thing as lightning slashed from the sky, the bolts glowing as red as the vortex. And as if that weren't enough, the sky began to fling stinging pellets of rain.

"Get the Daemon, Jag!" Lyon called.

Jag lifted a hand in acknowledgment, his gaze zeroing in on the last of the three creatures as it floated across the pit, heading for another of the humans tied to posts ringing the swirling chasm. From what Jag was able to make out, two of the four bound humans were already dead or unconscious, though neither appeared to be badly injured. He wondered if Olivia's feeding had saved them from a worse fate.

Of the two who remained conscious, one was missing half his face and clearly danced with death. It was the other, a female with only a single, shallow slash across her cheekbone that the Daemon headed toward now. The female watched the Daemon's approach with terror in her eyes, but no screams. Humans didn't see the fiends until they'd been cut by one, and thanks to the wound on her cheek, this human had already had her eyes opened. Her expression said she saw the monster who toyed with her, a monster who promised a terrifying, painful death.

Jag skirted the vortex to intercept that pain-feeding bastard, the rain starting to come down hard. As the Daemon approached his human target, Jag eased behind the tied female, waiting for the creature to clear the vortex before he took him on. Above the Daemon, the orbs spit and glowed.

"Easy," he told the woman. "I'm going to get him."

When the Daemon didn't change directions at Jag's arrival, the Feral eased around the post, out to the edge of the abyss, ready to attack before the Daemon did.

"Jag!"

The warning, carried by the howling wind, came too late. He felt one blade bury itself into his side as a pair of hands shoved at his back, ripping his balance out from under him.

Mage. Where in the hell did they keep coming from?

With furious desperation, he tried to turn, to regain his balance, but the ground between his feet was slick with rain, and he failed. There was no going back, only forward. He was going in.

But even as the hopeless thought registered, the Daemon drew near. In a move he would later decide had been born of pure madness, he vaulted up and out, straight for the Daemon. Hooking his good arm around the fiend's neck, he swung onto its back and held on, knowing that to let go meant a one-way ticket into a swirling red death.

The Daemon cried out, anger in that hideous voice, as he shot out over the center of the vortex, bucking wildly. Right under the orbs. Hot damn.

But Jag's right arm was still half-numb from the venom. And while he held on with his left, he wasn't sure he had enough strength in his wounded arm to wield the knife still clutched in his hand. Dammit, he had to.

Squawking and bucking, the Daemon slashed at the arm Jag held on with, ripping through flesh and muscle, clipping the bone.

Jag yelled with pain and fury. If the Daemon took his left arm, it was all over. Desperation was an electric current inside him, but his nearly numb arm felt like lead as he lifted it, shoulder height, then higher. Pulling on the strength slowly pouring into him from the woman he loved, he shoved everything he had into an upward thrust, aiming for the closest orb. And missed.

Dammit, dammit, dammit.

Black ropes of wet Daemon hair slapped him in the face. Sweat began to run down his temples, mixing with the raindrops. Another claw slashed through his forearm in a different place, stripping off another chunk of flesh as the Daemon continued to thrash.

Jag bit off another yell and tried again. He. Could. Not. Fail.

Thrusting every ounce of his strength into his wounded arm, he made a hard upward stab and caught one of the orbs this time, shattering it in a flash of brilliant light.

Thank the goddess.

Deep inside his head, Olivia screamed. His heart stopped for one terrible moment, then began to pound again as he felt that glow inside him, her glow, brighten. Tearing her free might hurt her, but it was a necessary evil.

As the Daemon whirled in fury, Jag stabbed at a second orb, shattering it, too.

Again, Olivia screamed. Again, her glow grew brighter.

One more. Just one more.

The Daemon clawed at his arm, this time digging deep into the bone. Jag felt it snap and knew he was out of time. Sweat rolled down his back, his guts cramping as he held on with the last of his strength. Clutching Olivia with his mind and heart, he thrust his knife skyward one last time before he lost his grip.

The final orb shattered. The Earth rumbled as if preparing to split asunder.

His grip on the Daemon started to give, and he knew he only had seconds. Dammit, if he was going down, this sucker was going with him. Remembering Hawke's last words, he tried to dig his knife into the Daemon's throat to carve out his heart, and failed. His half-numb arm wasn't strong enough to get the angle he needed.

With a feral growl, he tossed the knife into the void, drew his claws, and sank them deep into the Daemon's throat, succeeding with brute strength where finesse had eluded him. His fingers closed around the hot, wet, pulsing mass of Daemon heart, and he yanked hard, tearing it loose, and sending the creature to hell in a puff of smoke.

As gravity took over, and Jag began to fall, he thought of Olivia, how he'd never get the chance to prove to her that he'd heard her. That he'd changed.

He'd never get the chance to show her how much he loved her.

But only a few racing heartbeats later, Jag landed on the ground with a jarring thud. As his knees absorbed the impact, his mind assimilated the astounding fact that he was standing on wet grass, that the darkness had lifted, the light changing from a red glow against darkness to rainy daylight.

With the destruction of the orbs, the vortex had closed.

The wind still whipped with hurricane fierceness, driving stinging rain against his naked flesh, but the Daemons were gone. And even as his gaze found Olivia, his brothers dispatched the last of the Mage. The battle was over.

Olivia smiled weakly, her hair lying soaked across her cheeks. She looked as beaten as he felt. As he started toward her, he found himself suddenly surrounded by the other Ferals.

Kougar clapped him on the back with a seriously un-Kougar-like enthusiasm. "Unbelievable," he shouted above the wind and rain.

Paenther thrust out his torn hand, grasping Jag's numb forearm. "I wish I'd had a camera. I'd like to see a replay of that flight."

Wulfe shook his big head, flinging raindrops. "Where the hell did you learn to drive a Daemon?"

Jag tried to laugh, but his heart was too heavy. Tighe and Hawke were gone.

Lyon clasped his arm last, meeting his gaze. "Well done. And you got Olivia to stop feeding."

Something inside Jag froze, his gaze shooting to her, watching as her bright head dropped as if she'd fallen asleep. Goddess. That soft buzz in his blood . . . It was her life force draining away.

"She's feeding us! She learned how to reverse it, but she's not stopping. It's going to kill her."

Jag took off at a run, Lyon close behind. Over his shoulder, Lyon shouted to the others. "Secure the area before we free the humans! I want no more Mage surprises."

Jag reached Olivia, no warding barring his way this time, and he pushed the wet hair off her face and cupped her cheek. "Liv, you have to shut it off! Quit feeding us." But she couldn't hear him. Couldn't comply. She was out cold.

Lyon moved behind her, drew claws and cut through her bindings. Jag caught her as she fell forward, hauling her against him with the better of his two arms and sank to the ground, pulling her into his lap until her precious head lay against his chest.

"Olivia, wake up! You have to shut if off." A wave of pain tore through his mending limb as the bone reknit, but that pain was nothing compared to that of his heart. "Olivia, please." But it was too late. She was past waking, slipping away, and he was powerless to stop her.

Jag looked into his leader's gaze, feeling more helpless than he had since he'd watched his mother burn all those years ago.

"I don't know how to save her, Roar. I have to save her, and I don't know how."

Understanding and sympathy filled Lyon's amber eyes. "She's your mate."

"How am I supposed to live without her?"

"Maybe you won't have to." The Chief of the Ferals shot to his feet, took a step back, and shifted into his lion. *Vhyper, bring Kara. ASAP!*

He shifted back to a man and knelt beside Jag and Olivia once more. "Tell me what happened. How did she strengthen us? I've never heard of such a thing."

Jag squinted against the rain as he looked into the curious face of his chief. "The Daemon energy gave her the ability to direct her feeding, or reverse it. The spell she was under wouldn't let her cut off the feeding, but she finally managed to send it back to us, to feed us. But now she's locked into that cycle. She's no longer feeding from us, but she's still giving us the last of her energy. She's giving us her life."

Lyon watched him. "She's a powerful weapon in the wrong hands."

Jag's teeth clenched. "Roar . . ."

"Or the right hands. The Mage tried to use her against us, yet through her own considerable will, she turned the tables on them. A hell of a weapon. A hell of a woman."

Jag bent over her, pressing his lips to her hair. "Don't leave me, Liv. Don't leave me."

He barely noticed when Paenther joined them.

"The place is empty," the panther shifter said. "The Mage have definitely been using it, though. There was an interesting clear cage in the basement that still echoes of energy. The other Ferals are freeing the humans and clearing their minds. One's dead. Two need medical attention, but their injuries aren't too severe. They should survive."

"Lyon!" Kara's clear voice rang out over the yard.

Jag lifted his head moments later as Kara flew into Lyon's arms and Skye rushed to Paenther. Behind them followed a pale, glassy-eyed Delaney. Goddess, she'd lost her mate. Just as he was about to lose the woman he'd have claimed as his own. Empathy for her embedded itself in his heart.

Vhyper and Ewan brought up the rear.

Kara looked at Lyon's missing arm with a mix of horror and resignation. "It'll grow back, right?"

"In an hour, it'll be good as new."

She sighed. "Good." Her expression turned instantly focused. "Why do you need me?"

"Olivia helped us. I'd like to return the favor." His hand cupped the back of her head. "Call the radiance, Kara, but only touch Jag."

Jag's gaze jerked to his chief, a flicker of hope flaring to life inside him.

"No promises," Lyon warned him. "But we're going to try."

Kara lowered herself to the ground, sitting cross-legged in front of Jag, her gaze soft but determined. "I'll pull the radiance first, then touch you for just a moment. I don't want to electrocute her."

Jag took a deep, desperate breath. "Help her, Kara."

In a flash, she called the radiance. Instantly, her skin began to glow as if she'd swallowed the sun, and it now lit the day from within her. Slowly, carefully, she touched Jag's bare foot with her fingers, then drew back.

"Anything?"

He closed his eyes, focusing, fiercely trying to sense a difference, a miracle. But try as he might, he felt nothing. Olivia continued to give up her life.

"No change," he said, his voice choked.

Kara touched him again, this time curling her glowing hand around his foot and holding on.

"Now?" she asked.

"No." He felt that glow inside him that was Olivia, sensed it wavering and sputtering, on the verge of winking out. His grip on her tightened, the desperation a storm inside him. He couldn't lose her!

She needed Kara's energy, but a direct shot would kill her as surely as a lightning bolt. Only the Ferals, through their armbands, were able to channel that kind of power.

Through their armbands . . .

Jag's back went ramrod straight, adrenaline pumping

through his blood, riding a surge of hope. He began issuing commands.

"Kara, move back. Paenther, take Olivia for me."

"What are you doing?" Lyon demanded.

"What I need to do, Roar. She needs radiance, but she's not getting enough through me. She needs a direct shot." As Paenther lifted Olivia off his lap, Jag leaped to his feet and turned to Lyon. His armband curled around the only arm he could use. He needed help.

"Get this armband off me, Roar."

Tawny eyebrows lowered over hard amber eyes. "No. Kara is not touching a life-stealer directly."

A growl rumbled out of Jag's throat. "She's not stealing. She's giving her life to us."

Beside him, Kara rose to her feet and pressed her glowing palm to her mate's chest. "I love you, Lyon, but don't keep me from doing my job."

Lyon's hand covered hers. "She's dangerous. And she's not one of yours."

"If Jag loves her, she's not only one of mine, she's one of ours."

Lyon's jaw turned to stone. For one throbbing moment, Jag heard nothing but the pounding of his own pulse in his ears, the blood turning molten in his veins.

With a harsh exhale of air, Lyon scowled. "I can't remove your armband. You're the only one who can do it."

Jag swallowed back his anger, realizing Lyon hadn't outright refused. "By the time I heal enough to be able to take it off myself, Olivia will be dead."

Lyon shook his head, as if to himself, then reached out and grabbed Jag's mending arm, lifting it in a fiery rush of pain. Curling Jag's own fingers around the silver, he pulled the band loose.

The jaguar spirit urged him on. Deep inside him, Jag could feel the animal's desperation to save Olivia, every bit as strong as his own.

As he held her, Lyon slid the jaguar-headed band around Olivia's arm, squeezing it tight so that it wouldn't fall off. In Jag's mind, he felt the jaguar nodding its head up and down, up and down.

Jag took Olivia from Paenther, cradling her against his chest, and sank to the ground.

Kara knelt beside him. "Don't move, Jag. Without the armband, I'll kill you if I touch you."

"Help her, Kara."

She met his gaze. "I'm going to start slowly again." Kara reached for Olivia's hand, touching her lightly.

Olivia jerked violently, her life glow flaring.

Kara snatched her hand back, her gaze flying to his. "Did I hurt her?"

"No." Hope began to take root. "Do it again. Hold her hand until I tell you to let go."

With a quick nod, Kara did as he requested, curling her glowing hand around Olivia's far-too-pale one.

Again Olivia jerked. But that glow inside began to grow, just a little at first, then more and more, brighter and brighter.

"It's working!" As the color slowly washed back into Olivia's cheeks, his vision blurred from the raindrops running into his eyes until he could barely see through the moisture.

Maybe it wasn't the rain. His skin rose with goose bumps that had nothing to do with the cold as his chest filled with a pressure so intense it might have driven him to his knees if he weren't already sitting.

Beneath his arm, Olivia began to stir.

Kara pulled away before he could ask her to, her glow winking out.

Jag blinked hard, clearing his vision enough to meet Kara's gaze. "Thank you."

"You're welcome. Jag?"

"Yes, Radiant?"

To his surprise, she leaned forward and placed a soft kiss on his cheek. "I'm glad you found her. Good luck."

He gave her a rueful smile. "Thanks, Kara. I may need it." He'd found the love of his existence, then made her life a living hell. How could he ever prove to her he'd changed? How could he ever convince her to stay with him? Always.

* * *

Olivia opened her eyes slowly, feeling disoriented yet surprisingly warm despite the fact she was soaking wet from the rain whipping in the wind. She knew at once Jag held her, his scent warm and safe, his heartbeat strong in his chest. As her vision cleared, she looked up to find him gazing at her with eyes filled with . . . love.

With horror, she realized she was feeding and shut it off fast. No, not feeding. At least not in her usual way. She'd been sending energy out, not pulling it in.

"What happened?" Her voice sounded groggy, her mind felt disoriented, and she tried to sit up.

To her surprise, Paenther reached for her, helping her until she could slide her arm around Jag's neck. Then he grasped her upper arm. "May I?"

She looked down and gaped at the sight of Jag's jaguar armband around her arm.

Paenther pulled the band off her and returned it to Jag's muscular arm.

Jag tightened his hold on her. "You were feeding us when you fell unconscious. We almost lost you."

"The Daemons? Are they really gone?"

"All dead."

"What about the humans?"

"Three killed by the Daemons and the Mage. Three are still alive."

"I didn't kill any of them?"

"No."

She lifted her hand and trailed her knuckles down Jag's damp cheek. "Tighe and Hawke?"

Pain darkened his eyes, and he turned his head, pressing a kiss to her palm. "We lost them."

"Oh, Jag. I'm so sorry."

"We have a problem, Roar," Wulfe said, striding up to the group. "We're having no luck clearing the minds of the humans. One appears to be blind from birth. He didn't see anything, but neither can we get into his head to clear his memories. And the two females have seen far too much."

"Are they going to live?"

"If I heal them. The male was never touched, and neither of the female's injuries is bad. I can handle them."

"Olivia was feeding them," Jag told them. "I asked her to."

"We didn't want them to die." Now it seemed that the energy she'd given them had made them too strong for mind erasing. She swallowed. "I've killed them, haven't I?" Her stomach tightened with misery, but she had no illusions. Humans could not be allowed to spread word of the immortal races.

Lyon sighed. "There's been too much death here already. Knock them out and heal them, then we'll take them back to Feral House and lock them up until the energy Olivia fed them wears off. Hopefully by then we can figure out a way to clear their minds and bring them back here."

Olivia tipped her forehead against Jag's cheek, relieved, then looked up to meet his tender gaze. He stared into her eyes, his own, fathomless pools of emotion.

"We need to talk, Liv."

"They're not dead!" Delaney's cry rang out over the battlefield. Olivia straightened as Delaney ran toward them, her eyes at once haunted and jubilant. "Tighe connected with me."

"Where are they?" Lyon demanded.

"He doesn't know. It's another void, like the warding in the Mage stronghold. He can't move, can't see, can't hear. He's in pain. Terrible pain. But he's alive, Lyon. He's alive."

"What about Hawke?"

"He doesn't know. He can't communicate with him."

Jag's hold on her tightened. "We have to dig them out."

"No." Olivia knew her voice barely carried above the howling wind and rain, but all heard. Their gazes swung to her, frowns creasing every brow. But she had to explain. They had to know. "It won't work. They're not here. The vortex was a kind of wormhole, a way to the place where they're being kept, but digging through earth won't get you there."

"How do you know?" Delaney asked, her expression turning hard.

Olivia felt horrible for dashing her hopes. "Mystery— the sorceress—told me what she was doing as she prepared me. She called the vortex a spirit trap. Its purpose is to separate the Ferals from their animals."

"The seventeen," Kougar said. "They were felled by just such a trap."

Jag growled. "So not only are Tighe and Hawke lost to us, but we're permanently down to seven?"

Kougar stroked his wet goatee. "It takes eleven days for the trap to separate man from animal. Eleven days until they die." His gaze swung to Lyon. "I'll be back in ten." Then he turned and took off, running.

Delaney lifted tormented eyes to Lyon. "Does he have a plan?"

Lyon shook his head, his expression grim. "If Kougar has a way to save them, he will."

"Dudes!" The call came from one of the humans. "We could use a little help, here."

"Let me up, Jag," Olivia said softly.

His gaze held her tight. "Do I have to?"

A smile tugged at her mouth. "Please?"

He loosened his hold and helped her up. When she was on her feet, she took his hand and pulled him up, returning the favor.

A rumble shook the ground, strong enough to have

all of them adjusting their stances to stay on their feet.

"What was that?" Jag asked.

"Look!" Delaney froze, then took off at a run. Where the middle of the vortex used to be, a pile of bodies now lay.

The others followed, but while the men searched, Olivia, Kara, and Skye stood together to one side. Olivia prayed they wouldn't find their friends.

"Are they humans?" Kara asked.

"A couple are," Olivia told her. "Or were. Most of the ones who went into that vortex were Mage."

Delaney strode around the pile of bodies, her hands clasped on top of her head as if she struggled to hold herself together.

"Dudes!" one of the humans called. "Are you going to untie us, or what?"

Wulfe growled, circling close to where the women stood. "If he calls us 'dudes' one more time, I'm ripping his throat out."

"They're not here," Lyon said finally. "Thank the goddess."

Jag returned to Olivia, his expression grave. "Liv . . ." He raked his wet hair back from his face in an agitated, almost uncertain move, then hooked his arm through hers and led her away from the others. At the edge of the woods, he led her beneath a thick oak that sheltered them from most of the rain.

He turned her to face him. In his expression, in his eyes, she saw pain, and determination. And tender, blazing love.

Her heart skipped a beat, swelling until she thought it would no longer fit inside her chest.

A flash of devilment gleamed in his eyes, but never had that gleam stroked her with such gentleness. "I just want you to know, Red, I'm giving you fair warning. If it takes a thousand years, I'm going to prove to you that I've changed. That I've dealt with my past and let go of it, and am now focused only on the future. Our future."

His fingers slid into her hair, his thumb caressing her cheek. "I'm going to be a man you could love, Olivia. Because I love you more than life."

Olivia felt the tears begin to roll down her cheeks.

"I'll never force you, Liv. At least not where it counts. You're my mate. I know it. My animal knows it. And I pray to the goddess that someday you'll know it."

In his eyes, she saw the truth of his words. And if she had any doubt, his actions today had proved that truth over and over as he'd fought desperately to save her.

That light that had flared to life in her mind, the mating light, burned brightly, filling her with an endless glow of warmth and love.

She cocked her head. "They say a leopard can't change his spots."

"Liv . . ." The word ached.

She pressed her hand to his cheek and smiled at him with all the love in her heart. "It's a good thing you're not a leopard."

He watched her, his gaze blazingly intent. "Does that mean you believe me?"

"Yes, I believe you. More than that, I love you, Jag."

The tension flowed out of his features, joy rushing in. "You are my forever, Liv. There will never be anyone but you. And I'll make you happy. I swear it."

Olivia pressed her palms to his cheeks and drew his face down, kissing him, and he pulled her fully into his arms and held her tight. Her heart sang. She had no illusions that Jag would ever be a gentleman or ever be entirely tame. But that was fine with her.

She pulled back and slid his hair back with her fingers. "I need to be able to trust you and to know that you always have my back." Her fingers trailed down his cheeks, and she leaned in and licked his nipple.

A purr rumbled in his chest, his body rising to her tease.

She pulled back and looked up at him with a devilish smile of her own. "But the last thing I want is a tame house cat."

Jag began to laugh. And then he had her pressed back against the tree, his arms pinning her as he kissed her with a fierce tenderness that brought tears to her eyes.

When he pulled back, he framed her face with his hands, both hands now, his arms all but healed. "You were meant for me, Liv. I've waited my whole life for you."

She looked into his eyes and saw no trace of the old guilt, anger, or hatred. She saw only love and devotion, and a hint of devilment that she hoped would never die.

In his eyes blazed a promise as deep as the ocean. "I'm going to spend the rest of my life proving that I was meant for you, too, Red."

Olivia wrapped her arms around his neck as she stared into the eyes of the man she loved, the man who'd been destined to be her mate.

You were meant to live. Her father's words whispered in her head from long ago. And deep in her heart she knew her entire existence had been leading her to this moment.

To Jag.

Firelight flickered over the dark-paneled walls and ceiling of the ritual room deep below Feral House two days later, the remnants of magic still charging the air. Still buzzing from an experience deeper, more intense, than anything he'd ever known, Jag lifted his precious mate down from the altar, where they'd opened themselves bodies, minds, and souls, binding themselves to one another for eternity.

Olivia's glowing, loving eyes caressed his face as he set her on the ground, her own face flushed and radiant. With her bright red hair brushing the sheer blood red of the ritual gown, she was, without a doubt, the most beautiful woman who'd ever lived.

And she was his now. His.

His mate. His love. His life.

Around them, the other four Ferals, their chests bare,

their armbands gleaming in the firelight, lifted their fists into the air, shouting their approval in a tradition as old as time. Watching from the other side of the room, their color high, their eyes bright, were the three Feral wives, Kara, Delaney, and Skye.

If not for the shitload of mess the Ferals found themselves in, with Foxx dead and Tighe and Hawke trapped where no one could reach them, this moment might just be perfect.

For the first time in centuries, Jag felt like he could breathe freely, without the terrible weight on his chest, a weight he'd never even realized he'd been carrying. Yes, he'd made mistakes, some terrible ones. But he'd never intentionally hurt anyone. And forgiving himself finally felt right. It felt . . . incredible.

Jag pulled Olivia against him, curving his arm across her strong, slender shoulders as the others gathered around to congratulate them.

Lyon clasped Jag, forearm to forearm, a smile flickering briefly over his features, for a moment lifting the grim concern that shone out of all their eyes. He turned and gave Olivia a kiss on the cheek.

"May the goddess bless this union forevermore," Lyon said formally, then held out his hand to Olivia. When she placed hers in his much larger one, he covered it with his other hand. "Jag said you were both fine with moving his bedchamber down here. I want to be certain you understand this isn't a lack of trust but strictly a safety precaution in case you ever gain unintended strength again, and Jag's not close enough to warn you."

Olivia nodded. "I not only understand, Lyon, but I prefer it this way. We'll both sleep better."

The basement extended well beyond the footprint of the house, much of it unused space. Wulfe and Vhyper had procured enough lead-lined drywall to cover the walls of a nice-sized bedchamber. Yesterday, they'd installed it, then he and Olivia had run a test to see if it worked. It had. The lead blocked nearly all of her feeding. Even if she accidentally fed hard, only someone in the room with her, or possibly standing right outside the door, would be affected. And since Jag would be the only one sharing her bed, and he always felt her feed, that wouldn't be a problem.

Jag squeezed Olivia's shoulder. "We get a brand-new room without any damned sun to keep me awake after a hard night watching my mate fight the draden."

She cut her eyes at him, pleasure dancing in their depths, making him grin. "And we can get as rough as we want without anyone beating down the door or pounding on the walls. What's not to love about this arrangement?"

Jag met his chief's gaze, turning serious. "Thanks, Lyon. You've accepted the woman I love, a woman with a gift most fear, and you've allowed us to remain under this roof when few would have the guts."

Lyon nodded, then glanced down as Kara joined him, slipping his arm around his own mate. He turned back to Jag. "Olivia's good for you. Her strength and unique skills are going to benefit all of us."

Kara slipped out of Lyon's hold and came to Jag, lifting up on tiptoe to place a soft kiss on his cheek. When she pulled away, a sweet smile wreathed her face and he felt a swelling of affection and pride for their beloved Radiant.

"I'm so happy for you, Jag." She turned to include Olivia. "For both of you."

Jag grinned at Kara even as he pulled Olivia tighter against his side. "Guess I'm going to be a good cat after all."

Kara grinned.

Olivia laughed. "Goddess, I hope not." She looked up at him, and as their eyes met, he melted inside, reborn by the depth of a love he'd never known existed. Deep in his mind, his jaguar purred.

Delaney joined them, her face pinched from worry for her mate, yet her eyes, as she looked at Olivia, were warm and welcoming. Skye joined them, a soft smile on her face.

Kara took Olivia's hand. "Jag, we need to borrow your wife. There's one more ritual we need to perform before we get out of these gowns and get comfortable."

Olivia's brow rose. "What kind of ritual?"

Kara lifted her eyebrows impishly. "No blood involved, I promise. The Feral sisterhood initiates with champagne."

"In a glass," Delaney clarified.

"The Feral sisterhood?" Olivia asked, her voice taking on a note of soft vulnerability that made Jag's chest ache. So many years she'd been alone with her secret. Years when necessity had required her to keep others at a distance, emotionally if not physically.

Delaney smiled. "You thought you were just getting a mate in this deal?" She shook her head. "You just got yourself three sisters."

"If you want," Skye added softly.

Olivia glanced at him, her eyes filled with tears and wonder. They knew what she was. They knew what she could do. Yet offered her sisterhood.

She slid out of his hold. "I want." Her words caught, a pair of tears escaping to roll down her cheeks.

As one, the other three women enveloped her in a feminine group hug. All, he saw, had tears in their eyes. And the last piece clicked into place. She'd be happy here. He knew it, now. And there was nothing he wanted more than Olivia's happiness.

As if hearing his thoughts, she turned to him as the hug ended, pressing her palm to his cheek.

"Do you know how much I love you?"

"A shitload." He grinned at her, but damn if he didn't feel water in his own eyes. "Maybe even as much as I love you." He blinked back the moisture and gave her a quick kiss, then cleared his throat. "Now, go do your sisterhood thing, just don't forget about dinner, you four! Pink's preparing a feast up there."

As the women left the room, arms linked, Lyon and Paenther joined him, one on either side, watching the women go.

"They make you weaker than you ever thought possible," Lyon murmured, slinging his arm across Jag's shoulders in a surprising move of friendship.

Paenther nodded, draping his arm over Lyon's. "And stronger."

Slowly, with a feeling of rightness, Jag lifted his hands to embrace each of their shoulders as well.

Teammates they'd always been. Fellow warriors and little more. But with the crumbling of his inner walls, friendship had taken root. And more.

"She makes my life complete," Jag said.

And the other two made sounds of agreement, understanding.

Friendship.

Brotherhood.

MORE DELECTABLE VAMPIRE ROMANCE FROM
NEW YORK TIMES BESTSELLING AUTHOR

LYNSAY SANDS

THE ROGUE HUNTER
978-0-06-147429-3

Samantha Willan is a workaholic lawyer. After a recent
breakup she wants to stay as far away from romance as
possible. Then she meets her irresistible new neighbor,
Garrett Mortimer. Is it her imagination, or are his mysterious
eyes locked on her neck?

THE IMMORTAL HUNTER
978-0-06-147430-9

Dr. Danielle McGill doesn't know if she can trust the man who
just saved her life. There are too many questions, such as what
is the secret organization he says he's part of, and why do his
wounds hardly bleed? But with her sister in the hands of some
dangerous men, she doesn't have much choice but
to trust him.

THE RENEGADE HUNTER
978-0-06-147431-6

When Nicholas Argeneau, former rogue vampire hunter, sees
a bloodthirsty sucker terrifying a woman, it's second nature
for him to come to her rescue. But he doesn't count on getting
locked up for his troubles.

LYS2 1009